Other books by Philip K. Dick

The Book of Philip K. Dick
Clans of the Alphane Moon
Confessions of a Crap Artist
The Cosmic Puppets
Counter-clock World
The Crack in Space
Do Androids Dream
of Electric Sheep
Dr. Bloodmoney;
or, How We Got Along After the Bomb
Dr. Futurity
Eye in the Sky
Flow My Tears, the
Policeman Said
Galactic Pot-healer
The Game-players of Titan
A Handful of Darkness
The Man in the High Castle
The Man Who Japed
Martian Time-slip
A Maze of Death
Now Wait for Last Year
Our Friends from Frolix 8
The Penultimate Truth
The Preserving Machine
A Scanner Darkly
The Simulacra
Solar Lottery
The Three Stigmata of
Palmer Eldritch
Time Out of Joint
Ubik
The Unteleported Man
Valis
The Variable Man
and Other Stories
Vulcan's Hammer
We Can Build You
The World Jones Made
The Zap Gun

with Ray Nelson

The Ganymede Takeover

with Roger Zelazny

Deus Irae

THE DIVINE INVASION

Philip K. Dick

TIMESCAPE BOOKS
Distributed by Simon and Schuster
NEW YORK

A Timescape Book
Published by Pocket Books
A Simon & Schuster Division of
Gulf & Western Corporation
Simon & Schuster Building
Rockefeller Center
1230 Avenue of the Americas
New York, New York 10020
Manufactured in the United States of America
10 9 8 7 6 5 4 3 2 1
Library of Congress Cataloging in Publication Data

Dick, Philip K
The divine invasion.

I. Title.
PS3554.I3D5 813'.54 80-28669

ISBN 0-671-41776-2

The time you have waited for has come. The work is complete; the final world is here. He has been transplanted and is alive.

—*Mysterious voice in the night*

1

It came time to put Manny in a school. The government had a special school. The law stipulated that Manny could not go to a regular school because of his condition; there was nothing Elias Tate could do about that. He could not get around the government ruling because this was Earth and the zone of evil lay over everything. Elias could feel it and, probably, the boy could feel it, too.

Elias understood what the zone signified but of course the boy did not. At the age of six Manny looked lovely and strong but he seemed half-asleep all the time, as if (Elias reflected) he had not yet been completely born.

"You know what today is?" Elias asked.

The boy smiled.

"OK," Elias said. "Well, a lot depends on the teacher. How much do you remember, Manny? Do you remember Rybys?" He got out a hologram of Rybys, the boy's mother, and held it to the light. "Look at Rybys," Elias said. "Just for a second."

Someday the boy's memories would come back. Something, a disinhibiting stimulus fired at the boy by his own prearrangement, would trigger anamnesis—the loss of amnesia, and all the memories would flood back: his conception on CY30-CY30B, the period in Rybys's womb as she battled her dreadful illness, the trip to Earth, perhaps even the interrogation. In his mother's womb Manny had advised the three of them: Herb Asher, Elias Tate and Rybys herself. But then had come the accident, if it really had been accidental. And because of that the damage.

And, because of the damage, forgetfulness.

The two of them took the local rail to the school. A fussy little man met them, a Mr. Plaudet; he was enthusiastic and wanted to shake hands with Manny. It was evident to Elias Tate that this was the government. First they shake hands with you, he thought, and then they murder you.

"So here we have Emmanuel," Plaudet said, beaming.

Several other small children played in the fenced yard of the school. The boy pressed against Elias Tate shyly, obviously wanting to play but afraid to.

"What a nice name," Plaudet said. "Can you say your name, Emmanuel?" he asked the boy, bending down. "Can you say 'Emmanuel'?"

"God with us," the boy said.

"I beg your pardon?" Plaudet said.

Elias Tate said, "That's what 'Emmanuel' means. That's why his mother chose it. She was killed in an air collision before Manny was born."

"I was in a synthowomb," Manny said.

"Did the dysfunction originate from the—" Plaudet began, but Elias Tate waved him into silence.

Flustered, Plaudet consulted his clipboard of typed notes. "Let's see . . . you're not the boy's father. You're his great-uncle."

"His father is in cryonic suspension."

"The same air collision?"

"Yes," Elias said. "He's waiting for a spleen."

"It's amazing that in six years they haven't been able to come up with—"

"I am not going to discuss Herb Asher's death in front of the boy," Elias said.

"But he knows his father will be returning to life?" Plaudet said.

"Of course. I am going to spend several days here at the

school watching to see how you handle the children. If I do not approve, if you use too much physical force, I am taking Manny out, law or no law. I presume you will be teaching him the usual bullshit that goes on in these schools. It's not something I'm especially pleased about, but neither is it something that worries me. Once I am satisfied with the school you will be paid for a year ahead. I object to bringing him here, but that is the law. I don't hold you personally responsible." Elias Tate smiled.

Wind blew through the canes of bamboo growing at the rim of the play area. Manny listened to the wind, cocking his head and frowning. Elias patted him on the shoulder and wondered what the wind was telling the boy. Does it say who you are? he wondered. Does it tell you your name?

The name, he thought, that no one is to say.

A child, a little girl wearing a white frock, approached Manny, her hand out. "Hi," she said. "You're new."

The wind, in the bamboo, rustled on.

Although dead and in cryonic suspension, Herb Asher was having his own problems. Very close to the Cry-Labs, Incorporated, warehouse a fifty-thousand-watt FM transmitter had been located the year before. For reasons unknown to anyone the cryonic equipment had begun picking up the powerful nearby FM signal. Thus Herb Asher, as well as everyone else in suspension at Cry-Labs, had to listen to elevator music all day and all night, the station being what it liked to call a "pleasing sounds" outfit.

Right now an all-string version of tunes from *Fiddler on the Roof* assailed the dead at Cry-Labs. This was especially distasteful to Herb Asher because he was in the part of his cycle where he was under the impression that he was still alive. In his frozen brain a limited world stretched out of an archaic nature; Herb Asher supposed himself to be back on the little planet of the CY30-CY30B system where he had maintained his dome in those crucial years . . . crucial, in that he had met Rybys Rommey, migrated back to Earth with her, after formally marrying her, and then getting himself interrogated by the Terran authorities and, as if that were not enough, getting himself perfunctorily killed in an air collision that was in no way his fault. Worse yet, his wife had been killed and in such a fashion that no organ transplant would revive her; her pretty little head, as the robot doctor had explained it to Herb, had been riven in twain—a typical robot word-choice.

However, inasmuch as Herb Asher imagined himself still back in his dome in the star system CY30-CY30B, he did not realize that Rybys was dead. In fact he did not know her yet. This was before the arrival of the supplyman who had brought him news of Rybys in her own dome.

Herb Asher lay on his bunk listening to his favorite tape of Linda Fox. He was trying to account for a background noise of soupy strings rendering songs from one or another of the well-known light operas or Broadway shows or some damn thing of the late twentieth century. Apparently his receiving and recording gear needed an overhaul. Perhaps the original signal from which he had made the Linda Fox tape had drifted. Fuck it, he thought dismally. I'll have to do some repairing. That meant getting out of his bunk, finding his tool kit, shutting down his receiving and recording equipment—it meant work.

Meanwhile, he listened with eyes shut to the Fox.

Weep you no more, sad fountains;
What need you flow so fast?
Look how the snowy mountains
Heaven's sun doth gently waste.
But my sun's heavenly eyes
View not your weeping
That now lies sleeping . . .

This was the best song the Fox had ever sung, from the Third and Last Booke of lute songs of John Dowland who had lived at the time of Shakespeare and whose music the Fox had remastered for the world of today.

Annoyed by the interference, he shut off the tape transport

with his remote programmer. But, *mirabile dictu,* the soupy string music continued, even though the Fox fell silent. So, resigned, he shut off the entire audio system.

Even so, *Fiddler on the Roof* in the form of eighty-seven strings continued. The sound of it filled his little dome, audible over the gjurk-gjurk of the air compressor. And then it came to him that he had been hearing *Fiddler on the Roof* for—good God! —it was something like three days, now.

This is awful, Herb Asher realized. Here I am billions of miles out in space listening to eighty-seven strings forever and ever. Something is wrong.

Actually a lot of things had gone wrong during the recent year. He had made a dreadful mistake in emigrating from the Sol System. He had failed to note that return to the Sol System became automatically illegal for ten full years. This was how the dual state that governed the Sol System guaranteed a flow of people out and away but no flow back in return. His alternative had been to serve in the Army, which meant certain death. SKY OR FRY was the slogan showing up on government TV commercials. You either emigrated or they burned your ass in some fruitless war. The government did not even bother to justify war, now. They just sent you out, killed you and recruited a replacement. It all came from the unification of the Communist Party and the Catholic Church into one mega-apparatus, with two chiefs-of-state, as in ancient Sparta.

Here, at least, he was safe from being murdered by the government. He could, of course, be murdered by one of the ratlike autochthons of the planet, but that was not very likely. The few remaining autochthons had never assassinated any of the human domers who had appeared with their microwave transmitters and psychotronic boosters, fake food (fake as far as Herb Asher was concerned; it tasted dreadful) and meager creature comforts of complex nature, all items that baffled the simple autochthons without arousing their curiosity.

I'll bet the mother ship is directly overhead, Herb Asher said to himself. It's beaming *Fiddler on the Roof* down at me with its psychotronic gun. As a joke.

He got up from his bunk, walked unsteadily to his board and

examined his number-three radar screen. The mother ship, according to the screen, was nowhere around. So that wasn't it.

Damndest thing, he thought. He could see with his own eyes that his audio system had correctly shut down, and still the sound oozed around the dome. And it didn't seem to emanate from one particular spot; it seemed to manifest itself equally everywhere.

Seated at his board he contacted the mother ship. "Are you transmitting *Fiddler on the Roof?*" he asked the ship's operator circuit.

A pause. Then, "Yes, we have a video tape of *Fiddler on the Roof,* with Topol, Norma Crane, Molly Picon, Paul—"

"No," he broke in. "What are you getting from Fomalhaut right now? Anything with all strings?"

"Oh, you're Station Five. The Linda Fox man."

"Is that how I'm known?" Asher said.

"We will comply. Prepare to receive at high speed two new Linda Fox aud tapes. Are you set to record?"

"I'm asking about another matter," Asher said.

"We are now transmitting at high speed. Thank you." The mother ship's operator circuit shut off; Herb Asher found himself listening to vastly speeded-up sounds as the mother ship complied with a request he had not made.

When the transmission from the mother ship ceased he contacted its operator circuit again. "I'm getting 'Matchmaker, Matchmaker' for ten hours straight," he said. "I'm sick of it. Are you bouncing a signal off someone's relay shield?"

The operator circuit of the mother ship said, "It is my job continually to bounce signals off somebody's—"

"Over and out," Herb Asher said, and cut the circuit of the mother ship off.

Through the port of his dome he made out a bent figure shuffling across the frozen wasteland. An autochthon gripping a meager bundle; it was on some errand.

Pressing the switch of the external bullhorn, Herb Asher said, "Step in here a minute, Clem." This was the name the human settlers had given to the autochthons, to all of them, since they all looked alike. "I need a second opinion."

The autochthon, scowling, shuffled to the hatch of the dome and signaled for entry. Herb Asher activated the hatch mechanism and the intermediate membrane dropped into place. The autochthon disappeared inside. A moment later the displeased autochthon stood within the dome, shaking off methane crystals and glowering at Herb Asher.

Getting out his translating computer, Asher spoke to the autochthon. "This will take just a moment." His analog voice issued from the instrument in a series of clicks and clacks. "I'm getting audio interference that I can't shut off. Is it something your people are doing? Listen."

The autochthon listened, his rootlike face twisted and dark. Finally he spoke, and his voice, in English, assumed an unusual harshness. "I hear nothing."

"You're lying," Herb Asher said.

The autochthon said, "I am not lying. Perhaps your mind has gone, due to isolation."

"I thrive on isolation. Anyhow I'm not isolated." He had, after all, the Fox to keep him company.

"I've seen it happen," the autochthon said. "Domers like you suddenly imagine voices and shapes."

Herb Asher got out his stereo microphones, turned on his tape recorder and watched the VU meters. They showed nothing. He turned the gain up to full. Still the VU meters remained idle; their needles did not move. Asher coughed and at once both needles swung wildly and the overload diodes flashed red. Well, the tape recorder simply was not picking up the soupy string music, for some reason. He was more perplexed than ever. The autochthon, seeing all this, smiled.

Into the stereo microphones Asher said distinctly, " 'O tell me all about Anna Livia! I want to hear all about Anna Livia. Well, you know Anna Livia? Yes, of course, we all know Anna Livia. Tell me all. Tell me now. You'll die when you hear. Well, you know, when the old cheb went futt and did what you know. Yes, I know, go on. Wash quit and don't be dabbling. Tuck up your sleeves and loosen your talktapes. And don't butt me—hike!—when you bend. Or whatever—' "

"What is this?" the autochthon said, listening to the translation into his own tongue.

Grinning, Herb Asher said, "A famous Terran book. 'Look, look, the dusk is growing. My branches lofty are taking root. And my cold cher's gone ashley. Fieluhr? Filou! What age is at? It saon is late. 'Tis endless now senne—' "

"The man is mad," the autochthon said, and turned toward the hatch, to leave.

"It's *Finnegans Wake,*" Herb Asher said. "I hope the translating computer got it for you. 'Can't hear with the waters of. The chittering waters of. Flittering bats, fieldmice bawk talk. Ho! Are you not gone ahome? What Thom Malone? Can't hear—' "

The autochthon had left, convinced of Herb Asher's insanity. Asher watched him through the port; the autochthon strode away from the dome in indignation.

Again pressing the switch of the external bullhorn, Herb Asher yelled after the retreating figure, "You think James Joyce was crazy, is that what you think? Okay; then explain to me how come he mentions 'talktapes' which means audio tapes in a book he wrote starting in 1922 and which he completed in 1939, before there were tape recorders! You call that crazy? He also has them sitting around a TV set—in a book started four years after World War I. I think Joyce was a—"

The autochthon had disappeared over a ridge. Asher released the switch on the external bullhorn.

It's impossible that James Joyce could have mentioned "talktapes" in his writing, Asher thought. Someday I'm going to get my article published; I'm going to prove that *Finnegans Wake* is an information pool based on computer memory systems that didn't exist until a century after James Joyce's era; that Joyce was plugged into a cosmic consciousness from which he derived the inspiration for his entire corpus of work. I'll be famous forever.

What must it have been like, he wondered, to actually hear Cathy Berberian read from *Ulysses?* If only she had recorded the whole book. But, he realized, we have Linda Fox.

His tape recorder was still on, still recording. Aloud, Herb

Asher said, "I shall say the hundred-letter thunder word." The needles of the VU meters swung obediently. "Here I go," Asher said, and took a deep breath. "This is the hundred-letter thunder word from *Finnegans Wake*. I forget how it goes." He went to the bookshelf and got down the cassette of *Finnegans Wake*. "I shall not recite it from memory," he said, inserting the cassette and rolling it to the first page of the text. "It is the longest word in the English language," he said. "It is the sound made when the primordial schism occurred in the cosmos, when part of the damaged cosmos fell into darkness and evil. Originally we had the Garden of Eden, as Joyce points out. Joyce—"

His radio sputtered on. The foodman was contacting him, telling him to prepare to receive a shipment.

". . . awake?" the radio said. Hopefully.

Contact with another human. Herb Asher shrank involuntarily. Oh Christ, he thought. He trembled. No, he thought.

Please no.

2

You can tell they're after you, Herb Asher said to himself, when they bore through the ceiling. The foodman, the most important of the several supplymen, had unscrewed the roof lock of the dome and was descending the ladder.

"Food ration comtrix," the audio transducer of his radio announced. "Start rebolting procedure."

"Rebolting underway," Asher said.

The speaker said, "Put helmet on."

"Not necessary," Asher said. He made no move to pick up his helmet; his atmosphere flow rate would compensate for the loss during the foodman's entry: he had redesigned it.

An alarm bell in the dome's autonomic wiring sounded.

"Put your helmet on!" the foodman said angrily.

The alarm bell ceased complaining; the pressure had restabilized. At that, the foodman grimaced. He popped his helmet and then began to unload cartons from his comtrix.

"We are a hardy race," Asher said, helping him.

"You have amped up everything," the foodman said; like all the rovers who serviced the domes he was sturdily built and he moved rapidly. It was not a safe job operating a comtrix shuttle between mother ships and the domes of CY30 II. He knew it and Asher knew it. Anybody could sit in a dome; few people could function outside.

"Can I sit down for a while?" the foodman said, when his work had ended.

"All I have is a cupee of Kaff," Asher said.

"That'll do. I haven't drunk real coffee since I got here. And that was long before you got here." The foodman seated himself at the dining module service area.

The two men sat facing each other across the table, both of them drinking Kaff. Outside the dome the methane messed around but here neither man felt it. The foodman perspired; he apparently found Asher's temperature level too high.

"You know, Asher," the foodman said, "you just lie around on your bunk with all your rigs on auto. Right?"

"I keep busy."

"Sometimes I think you domers—" The foodman paused. "Asher, you know the woman in the next dome?"

"Somewhat," Asher said. "My gear transfers data to her input circuitry every three or four weeks. She stores it, boosts it and transmits it. I suppose. Or for all I know—"

"She's sick," the foodman said.

Startled, Asher said, "She looked all right the last time I talked to her. We used video. She did say something about having trouble reading her terminal's displays."

"She's dying," the foodman said, and sipped his Kaff.

The word scared Asher. He felt a chill. In his mind he tried to picture the woman, but strange scenes assailed him, mixed with soupy music. Strange concoction, he thought; video and aud fragments, like old cloth remnants of the dead. Small and dark, the woman was. And what was her name? "I can't think," he said, and put the palms of his hands against the sides of his face. As if to reassure himself. Then, rising and going to his main board, he punched a couple of keys; it showed her name on its display, retrieved by the code they used. Rybys Rommey. "Dying of what?" he said. "What the hell do you mean?"

"Multiple sclerosis."

"You can't die of that. Not these days."

"Out here you can."

"How—shit." He reseated himself; his hands shook. I'll be god damned, he thought. "How far advanced is it?"

"Not far at all," the foodman said. "What's the matter?" He eyed Asher acutely.

"I don't know. Nerves. From the Kaff."

"A couple of months ago she told me that when she was in her late teens she suffered an—what is it called? Aneurysm. In her left eye, which wiped out her central vision in that eye. They suspected at the time that it might be the onset of multiple sclerosis. And then today when I talked to her she said she's been experiencing optic neuritis, which—"

Asher said, "Both symptoms were fed to M.E.D.?"

"A correlation of an aneurysm and then a period of remission and then double vision, blurring . . . You're all rattled up."

"I had the strangest, most weird sensation for just a second, there," Asher said. "It's gone now. As if this had all happened once before."

The foodman said, "You ought to call her up and talk to her. It'd be good for you as well. Get you out of your bunk."

"Don't mastermind my life," Asher said. "That's why I moved out here from the Sol System. Did I ever tell you what my second wife used to get me to do every morning? I had to fix her breakfast, in bed; I had to—"

"When I was delivering to her she was crying."

Turning to his keyboard, Asher punched out and punched out and then read the display. "There's a thirty to forty percent cure rate for multiple sclerosis."

Patiently, the foodman said, "Not out here. M.E.D. can't get to her out here. I told her to demand a transfer back home. That's what I'd sure as hell do. She won't do it."

"She's crazy," Asher said.

"You're right. She's rattled up crazy. Everybody out here is crazy."

"I just got told that once today already."

"You want proof of it? She's proof of it. Wouldn't you go back home if you knew you were very sick?"

"We're never supposed to surrender our domes. Anyhow it's against the law to emigrate back. No, it's not," he corrected himself. "Not if you're sick. But our job here—"

"Oh yeah; that's right—what you monitor here is so important. Like Linda Fox. Who told you that once today?"

"A Clem," Asher said. "A Clem walked in here and told me I'm crazy. And now you climb down my ladder and tell me the same thing. I'm being diagnosed by Clems and foodmen. Do you hear that sappy string music or don't you? It's all over my dome; I can't locate the source and I'm sick of it. Okay, I'm sick and I'm crazy; how could I benefit Ms. Rommey? You said it yourself. I'm in here totally rattled up; I'm no good to anyone."

The foodman set down his cup. "I have to go."

"Fine," Asher said. "I'm sorry; you upset me by telling me about Ms. Rommey."

"Call her and talk to her. She needs someone to talk to and you're the closest dome. I'm surprised she didn't tell you."

Herb Asher thought, I didn't ask.

"It is the law, you know," the foodman said.

"What law?"

"If a domer is in distress the nearest neighbor—"

"Oh." He nodded. "Well, it's never come up before in my case. I mean—yeah, it is the law. I forgot. Did she tell you to remind me of the law?"

"No," the foodman said.

After the foodman had departed, Herb Asher got the code for Rybys Rommey's dome, started to run it into his transmitter and then hesitated. His wall clock showed 18:30 hours. At this point in his forty-two-hour cycle he was supposed to accept a sequence of high-speed entertainment, audio- and video-taped signals emanating from a slave satellite at CY30 III; upon storing them he was to run them back at normal and select the material suitable for the overall dome system on his own planet.

He took a look at the log. Fox was doing a concert that ran two hours. Linda Fox, he thought. You and your synthesis of old-time rock, modern-day streng and the lute music of John Dowland. Jesus, he thought; if I don't transcribe the relay of your live concert every domer on the planet will come storming in here and kill me. Outside of emergencies—which really didn't occur—this is what I'm paid to handle: information traffic between planets, information that connects us with home and keeps us human. The tape drums have to turn.

He started the tape transport at its high-speed mode, set the module's controls for receive, locked it in at the satellite's operating frequency, checked the wave form on the visual scope to be sure that the carrier was coming in undistorted and then patched into an audio transduction of what he was getting.

The voice of Linda Fox emerged from the strip of drivers mounted above him. As the scope showed, there was no distortion. No noise. No clipping. All channels, in fact, were balanced; his meters indicated that.

Sometimes I could cry myself when I hear her, he thought. Speaking of crying.

Wandering all across this land,
My band.
In the worlds that pass above,
I love.
Play for me you spirits who are weightless.
I believe in drinking to your greatness.
My band.

And, behind Linda Fox's vocal, the vibrolutes which were her trademark. Until Fox no one had ever thought of bringing back that sixteenth-century instrument for which Dowland had written so beautifully and so effectively.

Shall I sue? shall I seek for grace?
Shall I pray? shall I prove?
Shall I strive to a heavenly joy
With an earthly love?
Are there worlds? Are there moons
Where the lost shall endure?
Shall I find for a heart that is pure?

These remasterings of the old lute songs, he said to himself; they bind us. Some new thing, for scattered people as flung as if they had been dropped in haste: here and there, disarranged, in domes, on the backs of miserable worlds and in satellites and arks—victimized by the power of oppressive migration, and with no end in sight.

Now the Fox was singing one of his favorites:

Silly wretch, let me rail
At a voyage that is blind.
Holy hopes do require

A flurry of static. Herb Asher grimaced and cursed; the next line had been effaced. Damn, he thought.

Again the Fox repeated the lines.

Silly wretch, let me rail
At a voyage that is blind.
Holy hopes do require

Again the static. He knew the missing line. It went:

Greater find.

Angrily, he signaled the source to replay the last ten seconds of its transmission; obligingly, it rewound, paused, gave him the signal back, and repeated the quatrain. This time he could make out the final line, despite the eerie static.

Silly wretch, let me rail
At a voyage that is blind.
Holy hopes do require
Your behind.

"Christ!" Asher said, and shut his tape transport down. Could he have heard that? "Your behind"?

It was Yah. Screwing up his reception. This was not the first time.

The local throng of Clems had explained it to him when the interference had first set in several months ago. In the old days before humans had migrated to the CY30-CY30B star system, the autochthonic population had worshiped a mountain deity named Yah, whose abode, the autochthons had explained, was the little mountain on which Herb Asher's dome had been erected.

His incoming microwave and psychotronic signals had gotten cooked by Yah every now and then, much to his displeasure. And when no signals were coming in, Yah lit up his screens with faint but obviously sentient driblets of information. Herb Asher had spent a long time fussing with his equipment, trying to screen out this interference, but with no success. He had studied his manuals and erected shields, but to no avail.

This, however, was the first time that Yah had wrecked a Linda Fox tune. Which, as far as Asher was concerned, put the matter over a crucial line.

The fact of the matter was, whether it was healthy or not, he was totally dependent on the Fox.

He had long maintained an active fantasy life dealing with the Fox. He and Linda Fox lived on Earth, in California, at one of the beach towns in the Southland (unspecified beyond that). Herb Asher surfed and the Fox thought he was wonderful. It was like a living commercial for beer. They had campouts on the beach with their friends; the girls walked around nude from the waist up; the portable radio was always tuned to a twenty-four-hour no-commercials-at-all rock station.

However, the truly spiritual was what mattered most; the topless girls at the beach were simply—well, not vital but pleasant. The total package was highly spiritual. It was amazing how spiritual an elaborated beer commercial could get.

And, at the peak of it all, the Dowland songs. The beauty of the universe lay not in the stars figured into it but in the music generated by human minds, human voices, human hands. Vibrolutes mixed on an intricate board by experts, and the voice of Fox. He thought, I know what I must have to keep on going. My job is my delight: I transcribe this and I broadcast it and they pay me.

"This is the Fox," Linda Fox said.

Herb Asher switched the video to holo, and a cube formed in which Linda Fox smiled at him. Meanwhile, the drums spun at furious speed, getting hour upon hour into his permanent possession.

"You are with the Fox," she declared, "and the Fox is with *you.*" She pinned him with her gaze, the hard, bright eyes. The diamond face, feral and wise, feral and true; this is the Fox / Speaking to you. He smiled back.

"Hi, Fox," he said.

"Your behind," the Fox said.

Well, that explained the soupy string music, the endless *Fiddler on the Roof.* Yah was responsible. Herb Asher's dome had been infiltrated by the ancient local deity who obviously begrudged the human settlers the electronic activity that they had brought. I got bugs all in my meal, Herb Asher thought, and I got deities all in my reception. I ought to move off this mountain. What a rinky-dink mountain it is anyhow—no more, really, than a slight hill. Let Yah have it back. The autochthons can start serving up roasted goat meat to the deity once more. Except that all the autochthonic goats had died out, and, along with them, the ritual.

Anyhow his incoming transmission was ruined. He did not have to replay it to know. Yah had cooked the signal before it reached the recording heads; this was not the first time, and the contamination always got onto the tape.

Thus I might as well say fuck it, he said to himself. And ring up the sick girl in the next dome.

He dialed her code, feeling no enthusiasm.

It took Rybys Rommey an amazingly long time to respond to his signal, and as he sat noting the signal-register on his own board he thought, Is she finished? Or did they come and forcibly evacuate her?

His microscreen showed vague colors. Visual static, nothing more. And then there she was.

"Did I wake you up?" he said. She seemed so slowed down, so torpid. Perhaps, he thought, she's sedated.

"No. I was shooting myself in the ass."

"What?" he said, startled. Was Yah screwing him over once again, cooking his signal? But she had said it, all right.

Rybys said, "Chemotherapy. I'm not doing too well."

But what an uncanny coincidence, he thought. *Your behind* and *shooting myself in the ass*. I'm in an eerie world, he thought. Things are behaving funny.

"I just now taped a terrific Linda Fox concert," he said. "I'll be broadcasting it in the next few days. It'll cheer you up."

Her slightly swollen face showed no response. "It's too bad we're stuck in these domes. I wish we could visit one another. The foodman was just here. In fact he brought me my medication. It's effective but it makes me throw up."

Herb Asher thought, I wish I hadn't called.

"Is there any way you could visit me?" Rybys said.

"I have no portable air, none at all." It was of course a lie.

"I have," Rybys said.

In panic he said, "But if you're sick—"

"I can make it over to your dome."

"What about your station? What if data come in that—"

"I've got a beeper I can bring with me."

Presently he said, "OK."

"It would mean a lot to me, someone to sit with for a little while. The foodman stays like half an hour, but that's as long as he can. You know what he told me? There's been an outbreak of a form of amyotrophic lateral sclerosis on CY30 VI. It must be a virus. This whole condition is a virus. Christ, I'd hate to have amyotrophic lateral sclerosis. This is like the Mariana form."

"Is it contagious?" Herb Asher said.

She did not answer directly; she said, "What I have can be cured." Obviously she wanted to reassure him. "If the virus is around . . . I won't come over; it's okay." She nodded and reached to shut off her transmitter. "I'm going to lie down," she said, "and get more sleep. With this you're supposed to sleep as much as you can. I'll talk to you tomorrow. Good-bye."

"Come over," he said.

Brightening, she said, "Thank you."

"But be sure you bring your beeper. I have a hunch a lot of telemetric confirms are going to—"

"Oh, fuck the telemetric confirms!" Rybys said, with venom. "I'm so sick of being stuck in this goddam dome! Aren't you going bugward sitting around watching tape-drums turn and little meters and gauges and shit?"

"I think you should go back home," he said. "To the Sol System."

"No," she said, more calmly. "I'm going to follow exactly the M.E.D. instructions for my chemotherapy and beat this fucking M.S. I'm not going home. I'll come over and fix you dinner. I'm a good cook. My mother was Italian and my father is Chicano so I spice everything I fix, except you can't get the spices out here. But I figured out how to beat that with different synthetics. I've been experimenting."

Herb Asher said, "In this concert I'm going to be broadcasting, the Fox does a version of Dowland's 'Shall I Sue.' "

"A song about litigation?"

"No. 'Sue' in the sense of to pay court to or woo. In matters of love." And then he realized that she was putting him on.

"Do you want to know what I think of the Fox?" Rybys said. "Recycled sentimentality, which is the worst kind of sentimentality; it isn't even original. And she looks like her face is on upside down. She has a mean mouth."

"I like her," he said, stiffly; he felt himself becoming mad, really mad. I'm supposed to help you? he asked himself. Run the risk of catching what you have so you can insult the Fox?

"I'll fix you beef Stroganoff with parsley noodles," Rybys said.

"I'm doing fine," he said.

Hesitating, she said in a low, faltering voice, "Then you don't want me to come over?"

"I—" he said.

Rybys said, "I'm very frightened, Mr. Asher. Fifteen minutes from now I'm going to be throwing up from the I-V Neurotoxite. But I don't want to be alone. I don't want to give up my dome and I don't want to be by myself. I'm sorry if I offended you. It's just that to me the Fox is a joke. She is a joke media personality. She is pure hype. I won't say anything more; I promise."

"Do you have the—" He amended what he intended to say. "Are you sure it won't be too much for you, fixing dinner?"

"I'm stronger now than I will be," she said. "I'll be getting weaker for a long time."

"How long?"

"There's no way to tell."

He thought, You are going to die. He knew it and she knew it. They did not have to talk about it. The complicity of silence was there, the agreement. A dying girl wants to cook me a dinner, he thought. A dinner I don't want to eat. *I've got to say no to her. I've got to keep her out of my dome.* The insistence of the weak, he thought; their dreadful power. It is so much easier to throw a body block against the strong!

"Thank you," he said. "I'd like it very much if we had dinner together. But make sure you keep in radio contact with me on your way over here—so I'll know you're okay. Promise?"

"Well, sure," she said. "Otherwise—" She smiled. "They'd find me a century from now, frozen with pots, pans and food, as well as synthetic spices. You do have portable air, don't you?"

"No, I really don't," he said.

And knew that his lie was palpable to her.

3

The meal smelled good and tasted good but halfway through, Rybys Rommey excused herself and made her way unsteadily from the central matrix of the dome—his dome—into the bathroom. He tried not to listen; he arranged it with his percept system not to hear and with his cognition not to know. In the bathroom the girl, violently sick, cried out and he gritted his teeth and pushed his plate away and then all at once he got up and set in motion his in-dome audio system; he played an early album of the Fox.

> Come again!
> Sweet love doth now invite
> Thy graces, that refrain
> To do me due delight . . .

"Do you by any chance have some milk?" Rybys said, standing at the bathroom door, her face pale.

Silently, he got her a glass of milk, or what passed for milk on their planet.

"I have anti-emetics," Rybys said as she held the glass of milk, "but I didn't remember to bring any with me. They're back at my dome."

"I could get them for you," he said.

"You know what M.E.D. told me?" she said, her voice heavy with indignation. "They said that this chemotherapy won't make my hair fall out but already it's coming out in—"

"Okay," he interrupted.

" 'Okay'?"

"I'm sorry," he said.

Rybys said, "This is upsetting you. The meal is spoiled and you're—I don't know what. If I'd remembered to bring my anti-emetics I'd be able to keep from—" She became silent. "Next time I'll bring them. I promise. This is one of the few albums of the Fox that I like. She was really good then, don't you think?"

"Yes," he said tightly.

"Linda Box," Rybys said.

"What?" he said.

"Linda the box. That's what my sister and I used to call her." She tried to smile.

He said, "Please go back to your dome."

"Oh," she said. "Well—" She smoothed her hair, her hand shaking. "Will you come with me? I don't think I can make it by myself right now. I'm really weak. I really am sick."

He thought, You are taking me with you. That's what this is. That is what is happening. You will not go alone; you will take my spirit with you. And you know. You know it as well as you know the name of the medication you are taking, and you hate me as you hate the medication, as you hate M.E.D. and your illness; it is all hate, for each and every thing under these two suns. I know you. I understand you. I see what is coming. In fact it has begun.

And, he thought, I don't blame you. But I will hang on to the Fox; the Fox will outlast you. And so will I. You are not going to shoot down the luminiferous ether which animates our souls.

I will hang onto the Fox and the Fox will hold me in her arms and hang on to me. The two of us—we can't be pried apart. I have dozens of hours of the Fox on audio and video tape, and the tapes are not just for me but for everyone. You think you can kill that? he said to himself. It's been tried before. The power of the weak, he thought, is an imperfect power; it loses in the end. Hence its name. We call it weak for a reason.

"Sentimentality," Rybys said.

"Right," he said sardonically.

"Recycled at that."

"And mixed metaphors."

"Her lyrics?"

"What I'm thinking. When I get really angry I mix—"

"Let me tell you something," Rybys said. "One thing. If I am going to survive I can't be sentimental. I have to be very harsh. If I've made you angry I'm sorry but that is how it is. It is my life. Someday you may be in the spot I am in and then you'll know. Wait for that and then judge me. If it ever happens. Meanwhile this stuff you're playing on your in-dome audio system is crap. It has to be crap, for me. Do you see? You can forget about me; you can send me back to my dome, where I probably really belong, but if you have anything to do with me—"

"Okay," he said. "I understand."

"Thank you. May I have some more milk? Turn down the audio and we'll finish eating. Okay?"

Amazed, he said, "You're going to keep on trying to—"

"All those creatures—and species—who gave up trying to eat aren't with us anymore." She seated herself shakily, holding on to the table.

"I admire you."

"No," she said, "I admire *you*. It's harder on you. I know."

"Death—" he began.

"This isn't death. You know what this is? In contrast to what's coming out of your audio system? This is life. The milk, please; I really need it."

As he got her more milk he said, "I guess you can't shoot down ether. Luminiferous or otherwise."

"No," she agreed, "since it doesn't exist."

"How old are you?" he said.

"Twenty-seven."

"You emigrated voluntarily?"

Rybys said, "Who can say? I can't reconstruct my earlier thinking, now, at this point in my life. Basically I felt there was a spiritual component to emigrating. It was either emigrate or go into the priesthood. I was raised Scientific Legate but—"

"The Party," Herb Asher said. He still thought of it by its old name, the Communist Party.

"But in college I began to get involved in church work. I made the decision. I chose God over the material universe."

"So you're Catholic."

"C.I.C., yes. You're using a term that's under ban. As I'm sure you know."

"It makes no difference to me," Herb Asher said. "I have no involvement with the Church."

"Maybe you'd like to borrow some C. S. Lewis."

"No thanks."

"This illness that I have," Rybys said, "is something that made me wonder about—" She paused. "You have to experience everything in terms of the ultimate picture. As of itself my illness would seem to be evil, but it serves a higher purpose we can't see. Or can't see yet, anyhow."

"That's why I don't read C. S. Lewis," Herb Asher said.

She glanced at him dispassionately. "Is it true that the Clems used to worship a pagan deity on this little hill?"

"Apparently so," he said. "Called Yah."

"Hallelujah," Rybys said.

"What?" he said, startled.

"It means 'Praise ye Yah.' The Hebrew is *Halleluyah.*"

"Yahweh, then."

"You never say that name. That's the sacred Tetragrammaton. *Elohim,* which is not plural but singular, means 'God,' and then later on in the Bible the Divine Name appears with *Adonay,* so you get 'Lord God.' You can choose between *Elohim* or *Adonay* or use both together but you can never say Yahweh."

"You just said it."

Rybys smiled. "So nobody's perfect. Kill me."

"Do you believe all that?"

"I'm just stating matters of fact." She gestured. "Historic fact."

"But you do believe it. I mean, you believe in God."

"Yes."

"Did God will your M.S.?"

Hesitating, Rybys said slowly, "He permitted it. But I believe he's healing me. There's something I have to learn and this way I'll learn it."

"Couldn't he teach you some easier way?"

"Apparently not."

Herb Asher said, "Yah has been communicating with me."

"No, no; that's a mistake. Originally the Hebrews believed that the pagan gods existed but were evil; later they realized that the pagan gods didn't exist."

"My incoming signals and my tapes," Asher said.

"Are you serious?"

"Of course I am."

"There's a life form here besides the Clems?"

"There is where my dome is; yes. It's on the order of C.B. interference, except that it's sentient. It's selective."

Rybys said, "Play me one of the tapes."

"Sure." Herb Asher walked over to his computer terminal and began to punch keys. A moment later he had the correct tape playing.

Silly wretch, let me rail
At a voyage that is blind.
Holy hopes do require
Your behind.

Rybys giggled. "I'm sorry," she said, laughing. "Is that Yah who did that? Not some wise guy on the mother ship or over on Fomalhaut? I mean, it sounds exactly *like* the Fox. The tone, I mean; not the words. The intonation. Somebody's playing a joke on you, Herb. That isn't a deity. Maybe it's the Clems."

"I had one of them in here," Asher said sourly. "I think we should have used nerve gas on them when we settled here originally. I thought you only encountered God after you die."

"God is God of history and of nations. Also of nature. Originally Yahweh was probably a volcanic deity. But he periodically enters history, the best example being when he intervened to bring the Hebrew slaves out of Egypt and to the Promised Land.

They were shepherds and accustomed to freedom; it was terrible for them to be making bricks. And the Pharaoh had them gathering the straw as well and still being required to meet their quota of bricks per day. It is an archetypal timeless situation, God bringing men out of slavery and into freedom. Pharaoh represents all tyrants at all times." Her voice was calm and reasonable; Asher felt impressed.

"So you can encounter God while you're alive," he said.

"Under exceptional circumstances. Originally God and Moses talked together as a man talks with his friend."

"What went wrong?"

"Wrong in what way?"

"Nobody hears God's voice anymore."

Rybys said, "You do."

"My audio and video systems do."

"That's better than nothing." She eyed him. "You don't seem to enjoy it."

"It's interfering with my life."

She said, "So am I."

To that he could think of no response; it was true.

"What do you normally do all the time?" Rybys asked. "Lie in your bunk listening to the Fox? The foodman told me that; is it true? That doesn't sound to me like much of a life."

Anger touched him, a weary anger. He was tired of defending his life-style. So he said nothing.

"I think what I'll lend you first," Rybys said, "is C. S. Lewis's *The Problem of Pain*. In that book he—"

"I read *Out of the Silent Planet*," Asher said.

"Did you like it?"

"It was OK."

Rybys said, "And you should read *The Screwtape Letters*. I have two copies of that."

To himself, Asher thought, Can't I just watch you slowly die, and learn about God from that? "Look," he said. "I *am* Scientific Legate. The Party. You understand? That's my decision; that's the side I found. Pain and illness are something to be eradicated, not understood. There is no afterlife and there is no God, except maybe a freak ionospheric disturbance that's fucking up my equipment here on this dipshit mountain. If when I die I find out I'm wrong I'll plead ignorance and a bad upbringing. Meanwhile I'm more interested in shielding my cables and eliminating the interference than I am in talking back and forth with this Yah. I have no goats to sacrifice and anyway I have other things to do. I resent my Fox tapes being ruined; they are precious to me and some of them I can't replace. Anyhow God doesn't insert such phrases as 'your behind' in otherwise beautiful songs. Not any god I can imagine."

Rybys said, "He's trying to get your attention."

"He would do better to say, 'Look, let's talk.' "

"This apparently is a furtive life form. It's not isomorphic with us. It doesn't think the way we do."

"It's a pest."

Rybys said, pondering, "It may be modifying its manifestations to protect you."

"From what?"

"From it." Suddenly she shuddered wildly, in evident pain. "Oh goddam it! My hair *is* falling out!" She got to her feet. "I have to go back to my dome and put on that wig they gave me. This is awful. Will you go with me? *Please?*"

He thought, I don't see how someone whose hair is falling out can believe in God. "I can't," he said. "I just can't go with you. I'm sorry. I don't have any portable air and I have to person my equipment. It's the truth."

Gazing at him unhappily, Rybys nodded. Apparently she believed him. He felt a little guilty, but, more than that, he experienced overwhelming relief that she was leaving. The burden of dealing with her would be off him, at least for a time. And perhaps if he got lucky he could make the relief permanent. If he had any prayer at all it was, I hope I never see her enter this dome again. As long as she lives.

A pleased sense of relaxation stole over him as he watched her suit up for the trip back to her dome. And he inquired of himself which of his trove of Fox tapes he would play when Rybys and her cruel verbal snipings had departed, and he would be free again: free to be what he truly was, the connoisseur of the undying lovely. The beauty and perfection toward which all things moved: Linda Fox.

That night as he lay sleeping a voice said softly to him, "Herbert, Herbert."

He opened his eyes. "I'm not on standby," he said, thinking it was the mother ship. "Dome Nine is active. Let me sleep."

"Look," the voice said.

He looked—and saw that his control board, which governed all his communications gear, was on fire. "Jesus Christ," he said, and reached for the wall switch that would turn on the emergency fire extinguisher. But then he realized something. Something perplexing. Although the control board was burning, it was not consumed.

The fire dazzled him and burned his eyes. He shut his eyes and put his arm over his face. "Who is it?" he said.

The voice said, "It is Ehyeh."

"Well," Herb Asher said, amazed. It was the deity of the mountain, speaking to him openly, without an electronic interface. A strange sense of his own worthlessness overcame Herb Asher, and he kept his face covered. "What do you want?" he said. "I mean, it's late. This is my sleep cycle."

"Sleep no more," Yah said.

"I've had a hard day." He was frightened.

Yah said, "I command you to take care of the ailing girl. She is all alone. If you do not hasten to her side I will burn down your dome and all the equipment in it, as well as all you own besides. I will scorch you with flame until you wake up. You are not awake, Herbert, not yet, but I will cause you to be awake; I will make you rise up from your bunk and go and help her. Later I will tell her and you why, but now you are not to know."

"I don't think you have the right person," Asher said. "I think you should be talking to M.E.D. It's their responsibility."

At that moment an acrid stench reached his nose. And, as he watched in dismay, his control board burned down to the floor, into a little pile of slag.

Shit, he thought.

"Were you to lie again to her about your portable air," Yah said, "I would afflict you terribly, beyond repair, just as this equipment is now beyond repair. Now I shall destroy your Linda Fox tapes." Immediately the cabinet in which Herb Asher kept his video and audio tapes began to burn.

"Please," he said.

The flames disappeared. The tapes were undamaged. Herb Asher got up from his bunk and went over to the cabinet; reaching out his hand he touched the cabinet—and instantly yanked his hand away; the cabinet was searingly hot.

"Touch it again," Yah said.

"I will not," Asher said.

"You will trust the Lord your God."

He reached out again and this time found the cabinet cold. So he ran his fingers over the plastic boxes containing the tapes. They, too, were cold. "Well, goodness," he said, at a loss.

"Play one of the tapes," Yah said.

"Which one?"

"Any one."

He selected a tape at random and placed it into the deck. He turned his audio system on.

The tape was blank.

"You erased my Fox tapes," he said.

"That is what I have done," Yah said.

"Forever?"

"Until you hasten to the side of the ailing girl and care for her."

"Now? She's probably asleep."

Yah said, "She is sitting crying."

The sense of worthlessness within Herb Asher burgeoned; in shame he shut his eyes. "I'm sorry," he said.

"It is not too late. If you hurry you can reach her in time."

"What do you mean, 'in time'?"

Yah did not answer, but in Herb Asher's mind appeared a picture, resembling a hologram; it was in color and it was in depth. Rybys Rommey sat at her kitchen table in a blue robe; on the table was a bottle of medication and a glass of water. In dejection she sat resting her chin on her fist; in her fist she clutched a wadded-up handkerchief.

"I'll get my suit on," Asher said; he popped the suit-compartment door open, and his suit—little used and long neglected—tumbled out onto the floor.

Ten minutes later he stood outside his dome, in the bulky suit, his lamp sweeping out over the expanse of frozen methane before him; he trembled, feeling the cold even through the suit—which was a delusion, he realized, since the suit was absolutely insulating. What an experience, he said to himself as he started walking down the slope. Roused out of my sleep in the middle of the night, my equipment burned down, my tapes erased—bulk erased in their totality.

The methane crystals crunched under his boots as he walked down the slope, homing in on the automatic signal emitted by Rybys Rommey's dome; the signal would guide him. Pictures inside my head, he thought. Pictures of a girl about to take her own life. It's a good thing Yah woke me. She probably would have done it.

He was still frightened, and as he descended the slope he sang to himself an old Communist Party marching song.

Because he fought for freedom
He was forced to leave his home.
Near the blood-stained Manzanares,
Where he led the fight to hold Madrid,
Died Hans, the Commissar,
Died Hans, the Commissar.
With heart and hand I pledge you,
While I load my gun again,
You will never be forgotten,
Nor the enemy forgiven,
Hans Beimler, our Commissar,
Hans Beimler, our Commissar.

4

As Herb Asher descended the slope the meter in his hand showed the homing signal growing in strength. She ascended this hill to get to my dome, he realized. I made her walk uphill, since I wouldn't go to her. I made a sick girl toil her way up step by step, carrying an armload of supplies. I will fry in hell.

But, he realized, it's not too late.

He made me take her seriously, Asher realized. I simply was not taking her seriously. It was as if I imagined that she was making up her illness. Telling a tale to get attention. What does that say about me? he asked himself. Because in point of fact I really knew she was sick, truly sick, not faking it. I have been asleep, he said to himself. And, while I slept, a girl has been dying.

And then he thought about Yah, and he trembled. I can get my rig repaired, he thought. The gear that Yah burned down. That won't be hard; all I have to do is notify the mother ship and inform them that I suffered a meltdown. And Yah promised to restore to me my Fox tapes—which undoubtedly he can do. But I've got to go back to that dome and live there. How can I live there? I can't live there. It's impossible.

Yah has plans for me, he thought. And he felt fear, realizing this. He can make me do anything.

Rybys greeted him impassively. She did have on a blue robe and she did hold a wadded-up handkerchief, and, he saw, her eyes were red from crying. "Come in," she said, although he was already in the dome; she seemed a little dazed. "I was thinking about you," she said. "Sitting and thinking."

On the kitchen table stood a medicine bottle. Full.

"Oh, that," she said. "I was having trouble sleeping and I was thinking about taking a sleeping pill."

"Put it away," he said.

Obediently, she returned the bottle to her bathroom cabinet.

"I owe you an apology," he said.

"No you don't. Want something to drink? What time is it?" She turned to look at her wall clock. "I was up anyhow; you didn't wake me. Some telemetric data was coming in." She pointed to her gear; lights showed, indicating activity.

He said, "I mean I had air. Portable air."

"I know that. Everyone has portable air. Sit down; I'll fix you tea." She rooted in an overflowing drawer beside her stove. "Somewhere I have teabags."

Now, for the first time, he became aware of the condition of her dome. It was shocking. Dirty dishes, pots and pans and even glasses of spoiled food, soiled clothing strewn everywhere, litter and debris . . . Troubled, he gazed around, wondering if he should offer to clean up the place. And she moved so slowly, with such evident fatigue. He had an intuition, suddenly, that she was far sicker than she had originally led him to believe.

"It's a sty," she said.

He said, "You are very tired."

"Well, it wears me out to heave up my guts every day of the week. Here's a teabag. Shit; it's been used once. I use them and then dry them out. It's OK once, but sometimes I find I'm reusing the same bag again and again. I'll try to find a fresh one." She continued to rummage.

The TV screen showed a picture. It was an animated horror: a vast hemorrhoid that swelled and pulsed angrily. "What are you watching?" Asher asked. He averted his gaze from the animation.

"There's a new soap opera on. It just began the other day. 'The Splendor of—' I forget. Somebody or something. It's really interesting. They've been running it a lot."

"You like the soaps?" he said.

"They keep me company. Turn up the sound."

He turned up the sound. The soap opera had now resumed, replacing the animated hemorrhoid. An elderly bearded man, an exceedingly hairy old man, struggled with two popeyed arachnids who sought, apparently, to decapitate him. "Get your fucking mandibles off me!" the elderly man shouted, flailing about. The flash of laser beams ignited the screen. Herb Asher remembered once again the burning down of his communications gear by Yah; he felt his heart race in anxiety.

"If you don't want to watch it—" Rybys said.

"It's not that." Telling her about Yah would be hard; he doubted if he could do it. "Something happened to me. Something woke me." He rubbed his eyes.

"I'll bring you up to date," Rybys said. "Elias Tate—"

"Who is Elias Tate?" Asher interrupted.

"The old bearded man; I remember what the program is called, now. 'The Splendor of Elias Tate.' Elias has fallen into the hands—although they don't have hands, actually—of the antmen of Sychron Two. There's this queen who is really evil, named—I forget." She reflected. "Hudwillub, I think. Yes, that's it. Anyhow, Hudwillub wants Elias Tate dead. She's really awful; you'll see her. She has one eye."

"Gracious," Asher said, not interested. "Rybys," he said, "listen to me."

As if she had not heard him, Rybys plodded on, "However, Elias has this friend Elisha McVane; they're really good friends and they always help each other out. It's sort of—" She glanced at Asher. "Like you and me. You know; helping each other. I fixed you dinner and you came over here because you were worried about me."

"I came over here," he said, "because I was told to."

"But you were worried."

"Yes," he said.

"Elisha McVane is a lot younger than Elias. He's really good-looking. Anyhow, Hudwillub wants—"

"Yah sent me," Asher said.

"Sent you what?"

"Here." His heart continued to labor.

"Did he? That's really interesting. Anyhow, Hudwillub is very beautiful. You'll like her. I mean, you'll like her physically. Well, let me put it this way; she's objectively *obviously* attractive, but spiritually she's lost. Elias Tate is a sort of external conscience for her. What do you take in your tea?"

"Did you hear—" he began and then gave up.

"Milk?" Rybys examined the contents of her refrigerator, got out a carton of milk, poured some of the milk into a glass, tasted it and made a face. "It's sour. Goddam." She poured the milk down the sink drain.

"What I am telling you," Asher said, "is important. The deity of my hill woke me up in the night to tell me that you were in trouble. He burned down half my equipment. He erased all my Fox tapes."

"You can get more from the mother ship."

Asher stared at her.

"Why are you staring at me?" Quickly, Rybys inspected the buttons of her robe. "I'm not unfastened, am I?"

Only mentally, he thought.

"Sugar?" she said.

"Okay," he said. "I should notify the C-in-C on the mother ship. This is a major matter."

Rybys said, "You do that. Contact the C-in-C and tell him that God talked to you."

"Can I use your gear? I'll report my meltdown at the same time. That's my proof."

"No," she said.

"No?" He glared at her, baffled.

"That's inductive reasoning, which is suspect. You can't reason back from effects to causes."

"What the hell are you talking about?"

Calmly, Rybys said, "Your meltdown doesn't prove that God

exists. Here; I'll write it down in symbolic logic for you. If I can find my pen. Look for it; it's red. The pen, not the ink. I used to —"

"Give me a minute. Just one goddam minute. To think. Okay? Will you do that?" He heard his voice rising.

"There's someone outside," Rybys said. She pointed to an indicator; it blinked rapidly. "A Clem stealing my trash. I keep my trash outside. That's because—"

"Let the Clem in," Asher said, "and I'll tell *it*."

"About Yah? Okay, and then they'll start coming to your little hill with offerings, and they'll be consulting Yah all day and all night; you'll never get any peace. You won't be able to lie in your bunk and listen to Linda Fox. The tea is ready." She filled two cups with boiling water.

Asher dialed the mother ship. A moment later he had the ship's operator circuit. "I want to report a contact with God," he said. "This is for the Commander-in-Chief personally. God spoke to me an hour ago. An autochthonic deity called Yah."

"Just a moment." A pause and then the ship's operator circuit said, "This wouldn't be the Linda Fox man, would it? Station Five?"

"Yes," he said.

"We have your video tape of *Fiddler on the Roof* that you requested. We tried to transmit it to your dome but your receiving manifold appears to be malfunctioning. We have notified repair and they will be out shortly. The tape features the original cast starring Topol, Norma Crane, Molly Picon—"

"Just a minute," Asher said. Rybys had put her hand on his arm, to attract his attention. "What is it?" he said.

"There's a human being outside; I got a look at it. Do something."

To the mother ship's operator circuit, Asher said, "I'll call you back." He rang off.

Rybys had turned on the external floodlight. Through the dome's port Asher saw a strange sight: a human being, but not wearing a standard suit; instead the man wore what looked like a robe, a very heavy robe, and leather apron. His boots had a rustic, much-mended quality about them. Even his helmet seemed antique. What the hell is this? Asher asked himself.

"Thank God you're here," Rybys said. From the locker by her bunk she brought out a gun. "I'm going to shoot him," she said. "Tell him to come in; use the bullhorn. You make sure you're out of the way."

I'm dealing with lunatics, Asher thought. "Let's simply not let him in."

"Fuck that! He'll wait until you're gone. Tell him to come in. He's going to rape me and kill me and kill you, if we don't get him first. You know what he is? I recognize what he is; I know that gray robe. He's a Wild Beggar. You know what a Wild Beggar is?"

"I know what a Wild Beggar is," Asher said.

"They're criminals!"

"They're renegades," Asher said. "They don't have domes any more."

"Criminals." She cocked the gun.

He did not know whether to laugh or be dismayed; Rybys stood there swollen with indignation, in her blue bathrobe and furry slippers; she had put her hair up in curlers and her face was puffy and red with indignation. "I don't want him skulking around my dome. It's *my* dome! Hell, I'll call the mother ship and they'll send out a party of cops, if you're not going to do anything."

Turning on the external bullhorn, Asher said into it, "You, out there."

The Wild Beggar glanced up, blinked, shielded his eyes, then waved at Asher through the port. A wrinkled, weathered, hairy old man, grinning at Asher.

"Who are you?" Asher said into the bullhorn.

The old man's lips moved, but of course Asher heard nothing. Rybys's outside mike either wasn't turned on or it wasn't working. To Rybys Asher said, "Please don't shoot him. OK? I'm going to let him in. I think I know who he is."

Slowly and carefully Rybys disarmed her gun.

"Come inside," Asher said into the bullhorn. He activated

the hatch mechanism and the intermediate membrane dropped into place. With vigorous steps the Wild Beggar disappeared inside.

"Who is he?" Rybys said.

Asher said, "It's Elias Tate."

"Oh, then that soap opera isn't a soap opera." She turned to the screen of the TV. "I've been intercepting a psychotronic information-transfer. I must have plugged in the wrong cable. Damn. Well, what the hell. I thought it was on the air an awful lot of the time."

Shaking off methane crystals, Elias Tate appeared before them, wild and hairy and gray, and happy to be inside out of the cold. He began at once to remove his helmet and vast robe.

"How are you feeling?" he asked Rybys. "Any better? Has this donkey been taking good care of you? His ass is grass if he hasn't."

Wind blew about him, as if he were the center of a storm.

To the girl in the white frock Emmanuel said, "I am new. I do not understand where I am."

The bamboo rustled. The children played. And Mr. Plaudet stood with Elias Tate watching the boy and girl. "Do you know me?" the girl said to Emmanuel.

"No," he said. He did not. And yet she seemed familiar. Her face was small and pale and she had long dark hair. Her eyes, Emmanuel thought. They are old. The eyes of wisdom.

To him in a low voice the girl said, " 'When there was yet no ocean I was born.' " She waited a moment, studying him, searching for something, a response perhaps; he did not know. " 'I was fashioned in times long past,' " the girl said. " 'At the beginning, long before earth itself.' "

Mr. Plaudet called to her reprovingly, "Tell him your name. Introduce yourself."

"I am Zina," the girl said.

"Emmanuel," Mr. Plaudet said, "this is Zina Pallas."

"I don't know her," Emmanuel said.

"You two are going to go and play on the swings," Mr. Plaudet said, "while Mr. Tate and I talk. Go on. Go."

Elias came over to the boy, bent down and said, "What did she say to you just now? This little girl, Zina; what did she tell you?" He looked angry, but Emmanuel was accustomed to the old man's anger; it flashed forth constantly. "I couldn't hear."

"You grow deaf," Emmanuel said.

"No, she lowered her voice," Elias said.

"I said nothing that was not said long ago," Zina said.

Perplexed, Elias glanced from Emmanuel to the girl. "What nationality are you?" he asked the girl.

"Let's go," Zina said. She took Emmanuel by the hand and led him away; the two of them walked in silence.

"Is this a nice school?" Emmanuel asked her presently.

"It's OK. The computers are outdated. And the government monitors everything. The computers are government computers; you must keep that in mind. How old is Mr. Tate?"

"Very old," Emmanuel said. "About four thousand years old, I guess. He goes away and comes back."

"You've seen me before," Zina said.

"No I haven't."

"Your memory is missing."

"Yes," he said, surprised that she knew. "Elias tells me it will return."

"Your mother is dead?"

He nodded.

"Can you see her?" Zina said.

"Sometimes."

"Tap your father's memories. Then you can be with her in retrotime."

"Maybe."

"He has it all stored."

Emmanuel said, "It frightens me. Because of the crash. I think they did it on purpose."

"Of course they did, but it was you they wanted, even if they didn't know it."

"They may kill me now."

"There is no way they can find you," Zina said.

"How do you know that?"

"Because I am that which knows. I will know for you until you remember, and even then I will stay with you. You always wanted that. I was at your side every day; I was your darling and your delight, playing always in your presence. And when you had finished, my chief delight was in them."

Emmanuel asked, "How old are you?"

"Older than Elias."

"Older than me?"

"No," Zina said.

"You look older than me."

"That's because you have forgotten. I am here to cause you to remember, but you are not to tell anyone that, even Elias."

Emmanuel said, "I tell him everything."

"Not about me," Zina said. "Don't tell him about me. You have to promise me that. If you tell anyone about me the government will find out."

"Show me the computers."

"Here they are." Zina led him into a large room. "You can ask them anything but they give you modified answers. Maybe you can trick them. I like to trick them. They're really stupid."

He said to her, "You can do magic."

At that Zina smiled. "How did you know?"

"Your name. I know what it means."

"It's only a name."

"No," he said. "Zina is not your name; Zina is what you *are*."

"Tell me what that is," the girl said, "but tell me very quietly. Because if you know what I am then some of your memory is returning. But be careful; the government listens and watches."

"Do the magic first," Emmanuel said.

"They will know; the government will know."

Going across the room, Emmanuel stopped by a cage with a rabbit in it. "No," he said. "Not that. Is there another animal here that you could be?"

"Careful, Emmanuel," Zina said.

"A bird," Emmanuel said.

"A cat," Zina said. "Just a second." She paused, moved her lips. The cat came in, then, from outside, a gray-striped female. "Shall I be the cat?"

"I want to be the cat," Emmanuel said.

"The cat will die."

"Let the cat die."

"Why?"

"They were created for that."

Zina said, "Once a calf about to be slaughtered ran to a Rabbi for protection and put its head between the Rabbi's knees. The Rabbi said, 'Go! For this you were created,' meaning, 'You were created to be slaughtered.' "

"And then?" Emmanuel said.

Zina said, "God greatly afflicted the Rabbi for a long time."

"I understand," Emmanuel said. "You have taught me. I will not be the cat."

"Then I will be the cat," Zina said, "and it will not die because I am not like you." She bent down, her hands on her knees, to address the cat. Emmanuel watched, and presently the cat came to him and asked to speak to him. He lifted it up and held it in his arms and the cat placed its paw against his face. With its paw it told him that mice were annoying and a bother and yet the cat did not wish to see an end of mice because, as annoying as they were, still there was something about them that was fascinating, more fascinating than annoying; and so the cat sought out mice, although the cat did not respect the mice. The cat wanted there to be mice and yet the cat despised mice.

All this the cat communicated by means of its paw against the boy's cheek.

"All right," Emmanuel said.

Zina said, "Do you know where any mice are right now?"

"You are the cat," Emmanuel said.

"Do you know where any mice are right now?" she repeated.

"You are a kind of mechanism," Emmanuel said.

"Do you know—"

"You have to find them yourself," Emmanuel said.

"But you could help me. You could chase them my way." The girl opened her mouth and showed him her teeth. He laughed.

Against his cheek the paw conveyed more thoughts; that Mr. Plaudet was coming into the building. The cat could hear his steps. Put me down, the cat communicated.

Emmanuel set the cat down.

"Are there any mice?" Zina said.

"Stop," Emmanuel said. "Mr. Plaudet is here."

"Oh," Zina said, and nodded.

Entering the room, Mr. Plaudet said, "I see you've found Misty, Emmanuel. Isn't she a nice little animal? Zina, what's wrong with you? Why are you staring at me?"

Emmanuel laughed; Zina was having trouble disentangling herself from the cat. "Be careful, Mr. Plaudet," he said. "Zina'll scratch you."

"You mean Misty," Mr. Plaudet said.

"That's not the kind of brain damage I have," Emmanuel said. "To—" He broke off; he could feel Zina telling him *no*.

"He's not very good at names, Mr. Plaudet," Zina said. She had managed to separate herself from the cat, now, and Misty, perplexed, walked slowly away. Obviously Misty had not been able to fathom why, all at once, she found herself in two different places.

"Do you remember my name, Emmanuel?" Mr. Plaudet asked.

"Mr. Talk," Emmanuel said.

"No," Mr. Plaudet said. He frowned. " 'Plaudet' is German for 'talk,' though."

"I told Emmanuel that," Zina said. "About your name."

After Mr. Plaudet left, Emmanuel said to the girl, "Can you summon the bells? For dancing?"

"Of course." And then she flushed. "That was a trick question."

"But you play tricks. You always play tricks. I'd like to hear the bells, but I don't want to dance. I'd like to watch the dancing, though."

"Some other time," Zina said. "You do remember something, then. If you know about the dancing."

"I think I remember. I asked Elias to take me to see my father, where they have him stored. I want to see what he looks like. If I saw him, maybe I'd remember a lot more. I've seen pictures of him."

Zina said, "There's something you want from me even more than the dancing."

"I want to know about the time power you have. I want to see you make time stop and then run backward. That's the best trick of all."

"I said you should see your father about that."

"But you can do it," Emmanuel said. "Right here."

"I'm not going to. It disturbs too many things. They never line up again. Once they're out of synch— Well, someday I'll do it for you. I could take you back to before the collision. But I'm not sure that's wise because you might have to live it over, and that would make you worse. Your mother was very sick, you know. She probably would not have lived anyhow. And your father will be out of cryonic suspension in four more years."

"You're sure?" Emmanuel said excitedly.

"When you're ten years old you'll see him. He's back with your mother right now; he likes to retrotime to when he first met her. She was very sloppy; he had to clean up her dome."

"What is a 'dome'?" Emmanuel asked.

"They don't have them here; that's for outspace. The colonists. Where you were *born*. I know Elias told you. Why don't you listen to him more?"

"He's a man," Emmanuel said. "A human being."

"No he's not."

"He was born as a man. And then I—" He paused, and a segment of memory came back to him. "I didn't want him to die. Did I? So I took him, all at once. When he and—" He tried to think, to frame the word in his mind.

"Elisha," Zina said.

"They were walking together," Emmanuel said, "and I took

him up, and he sent part of himself back to Elisha. So he never died; Elias, I mean. But that's not his real name."

"That's his Greek name."

"I do remember some things, then," Emmanuel said.

"You'll remember more. You see, you set up a disinhibiting stimulus that would remind you before—well, when the right time came. You're the only one who knows what the stimulus is. Even Elias doesn't know it. *I* don't know it; you hid it from me, back when you were what you were."

"I am what I am now," Emmanuel said.

"Yes, except that you have an impaired memory," Zina said, pragmatically. "So it isn't the same."

"I guess not," the boy said. "I thought you said you could make me remember."

"There are different kinds of remembering. Elias can make you remember a little, and I can make you remember more; but only your own disinhibiting stimulus can make you *be*. The word is . . . you have to bend close to me to listen; only you should hear this word. No, I'll write it." Zina took a piece of paper from a nearby desk, and a length of chalk, and wrote one word.

HAYAH

Gazing down at the word, Emmanuel felt memory come to him, but only for a nanosecond; at once—almost at once—it departed.

"*Hayah,*" he said, aloud.

"That is the Divine Tongue," Zina said.

"Yes," he said. "I know." The word was Hebrew, a Hebrew root word. And the Divine Name itself came from that word. He felt a vast and terrible awe; he felt afraid.

"Fear not," Zina said quietly.

"I am afraid," Emmanuel said, "because for a moment I remembered." *Knew,* he thought, *who I am.*

But he forgot again. By the time he and the girl had gone outside into the yard he no longer knew. And yet—strange!—he knew that he had known, known and forgotten again almost at once. As if, he thought, I have two minds inside me, one on the surface and the other in the depths. The surface one has been injured but the deep one has not. And yet the deep one can't speak; it is closed up. Forever? No; there would be the stimulus, one day. His own device.

Probably it was necessary that he not remember. Had he been able to recall into consciousness everything, the basis of it all, then the government would have killed him. There existed two heads of the beast, the religious one, a Cardinal Fulton Statler Harms, and then a scientific one named N. Bulkowsky. But these were phantoms. To Emmanuel the Christian-Islamic Church and the Scientific Legate did not constitute reality. He knew what lay behind them. Elias had told him. But even had Elias not told him he would have known anyhow; he would everywhere and at every time be able to identify the Adversary.

What did puzzle him was the girl Zina. Something in the situation did not ring right. Yet she had not lied; she could not lie. He had not made it possible for her to deceive; that constituted her fundamental nature: her veracity. All he had to do was ask her.

Meanwhile, he would assume that she was one of the *zine;* she herself had admitted that she danced. Her name, of course, came from *dziana,* and sometimes it appeared as she used it, as Zina.

Going up to her, stopping behind her but standing very close to her, he said in her ear, "Diana."

At once she turned. And as she turned he saw her change. Her nose became different and instead of a girl he saw now a grown woman wearing a metal mask pushed back so that it revealed her face, a Greek face; and the mask, he realized, was the war mask. That would be Pallas. He was seeing Pallas, now, not Zina. But, he knew, neither one told him the truth about her. These were only images. Forms that she took. Still, the metal mask of war impressed him. It faded, now, this image, and he knew that no one but himself had seen it. She would never reveal it to other people.

"Why did you call me 'Diana'?" Zina asked.

"Because that is one of your names."

Zina said, "We will go to the Garden one of these days. So you can see the animals."

"I would like that," he said. "Where is the Garden?"

"The Garden is here," Zina said.

"I can't see it."

"You made the Garden," Zina said.

"I can't remember." His head hurt; he put his hands against the sides of his face. Like my father, he thought; he used to do what I am doing. Except that he is not my father.

To himself he said, I have no father.

Pain filled him, the pain of isolation; suddenly Zina had disappeared, and the school yard, the building, the city—everything vanished. He tried to make it return but it would not return. No time passed. Even time had been abolished. *I have completely forgotten,* he realized. *And because I have forgotten, it is all gone.* Even Zina, his darling and delight, could not remind him now; he had returned to the void.

A low murmuring sound moved slowly across the face of the void, across the deep. Heat could be seen; at this transformation of frequency heat appeared as light, but only as a dull red light, a somber light. He found it ugly.

My father, he thought. You are not.

His lips moved and he pronounced one word.

HAYAH

The world returned.

5

Elias Tate, throwing himself down on a heap of Rybys's dirty clothes, said, "Do you have any real coffee? Not that joke stuff the mother ship peddles to you." He grimaced.

"I have some," Rybys said, "but I don't know where it is."

"Have you been throwing up frequently?" Elias said to her, eyeing her. "Every day or so?"

"Yes." She glanced at Herb Asher, amazed.

"You're pregnant," Elias Tate said.

"I'm in chemo!" Rybys said angrily, her face dark red with fury. "I'm heaving up my guts because of the goddam Neurotox-ite and the Prednoferic—"

"Consult your computer terminal," Elias said.

There was silence.

"Who are you?" Herb Asher said.

"A Wild Beggar," Elias said.

"Why do you know so much about me?" Rybys said.

Elias said, "I came to be with you. I'll be with you from now on. Consult your terminal."

Seating herself at her computer terminal, Rybys placed her arm in the M.E.D. slot. "I hate to put it to you this way," she said to Elias and Herb Asher, "but I'm a virgin."

"Get out of here," Herb Asher said quietly to the old man.

"Wait until M.E.D. gives her the test result," Elias said.

Tears filled Rybys's eyes. "Shit. This is just terrible. I have M.S. and then now this, as if M.S. isn't enough."

To Herb Asher, Elias said, "She must return to Earth. The authorities will permit it; her illness will be sufficient legal cause."

To the computer terminal, which had now locked onto the M.E.D. channel, Rybys said brokenly, "Am I pregnant?"

Silence.

The terminal said, "You are three months pregnant, Ms. Rommey."

Rising, Rybys walked to the port of the dome and stared fixedly out at the methane panorama. No one spoke.

"It's Yah, isn't it?" Rybys said presently.

"Yes," Elias said.

"This was planned out a long time ago," Rybys said.

"Yes," Elias said.

"And my M.S. is so there is a legal pretext for me to return to Earth."

"To get you past Immigration," Elias said.

Rybys said, "And you know all about it." She pointed at Herb Asher. "He's going to say he's the father."

"He will," Elias said, "and he will go with you. So will I. You'll be checking in at Bethesda Naval Hospital at Chevy Chase. We'll go by emergency axial flight, high-velocity flight, because of the seriousness of your physical condition. We should start as soon as possible. You already have the papers in your possession, the necessary legal papers requesting a transfer back home."

"Yah made me sick?" Rybys said.

After a pause Elias nodded.

"What is this?" Rybys said furiously. "A coup of some kind? You're going to smuggle—"

Interrupting her, Elias said in a low, harsh voice, "The Roman X Fretensis."

"Masada," Rybys said. "Seventy-three C.E. Right? I thought so. I started thinking so when a Clem told me about the mountain deity at our Station Five."

"He lost," Elias said. "The Tenth Legion was made up of fifteen thousand experienced soldiers. But Masada held out for almost two years. And there were less than a thousand Jews at Masada, including women and children."

To Herb Asher, Rybys said, "Only seven women and children survived the fall of Masada. It was a Jewish fortress. They had hidden in a water conduit." To Elias Tate she said, "And Yahweh was driven from the Earth."

"And the hopes of man," Elias said, "faded away."

Herb Asher said, "What are you two talking about?"

"A fiasco," Elias Tate said briefly.

"So he—Yah—first makes me sick, and then he—" She broke off. "Did he start out from this star system originally? Or was he driven here?"

"He was driven here," Elias said. "There is a zone around Earth now. A zone of evil. It keeps him out."

"The *Lord?*" Rybys said. "The Lord is kept out? Away from Earth?" She stared at Elias Tate.

"The people of Earth do not know," Elias Tate said.

"But you know," Herb Asher said. "Right? How do you know all these things? How do you know so much? Who are you?"

Elias Tate said, "My name is Elijah."

The three of them sat together drinking tea. Rybys's face had an embittered, stark expression on it, a look of fury; she said almost nothing.

"What bothers you the most?" Elias Tate said. "The fact that Yah was driven off Earth, that he was defeated by the Adversary, or that you have to go back to Earth carrying him inside you?"

She laughed. "Leaving my station."

"You have been honored," Elias said.

"Honored with illness," Rybys said; her hand shook as she lifted her cup to her lips.

"Do you realize who it is that you carry in your womb?" Elias said.

"Sure," Rybys said.

"You are not impressed," Elias said.

"I had my life all planned out," Rybys said.

"I think you're taking a small view of this," Herb Asher said. Both Elias and Rybys glanced at him with distaste, as if he had intruded. "Maybe I don't understand," he said, weakly.

Reaching out her hand, Rybys patted him. "It's OK. I don't understand either. Why me? I asked that when I came down with the M.S. Why the hell me? Why the hell you? You have to leave your station, too; *and* your Fox tapes. *And* lying all day and night in your bunk doing nothing, with your gear on auto. Christ. Well, I guess Job had it right. God afflicts those he loves."

"The three of us will travel to Earth," Elias said, "and there you will give birth to your son, Emmanuel. Yah planned this at the beginning of the age, before the defeat at Masada, before the fall of the Temple. He foresaw his defeat and moved to rectify the situation. God can be defeated but only temporarily. *With God the remedy is greater than the malady.*"

" *'Felix culpa,'* " Rybys said.

"Yes," Elias agreed. To Herb Asher he explained, "It means 'happy fault,' referring to the fall, the original fall. Had there been no fall perhaps there would have been no Incarnation. No birth of Christ."

"Catholic doctrine," Rybys said remotely. "I never thought it would apply to me personally."

Herb Asher said, "But didn't Christ conquer the forces of evil? He said, 'I have overcome the world.' "

"Well," Rybys said, "apparently he was wrong."

"When Masada fell," Elias said, "all was lost. God did not enter history in the first century C.E.; he left history. Christ's mission was a failure."

"You are very old," Rybys said. "How old are you, Elias? Almost four thousand years, I guess. You can take a long-term view but I can't. You've known this about the First Advent all this time? For two thousand years?"

"As God foresaw the original fall," Elias said, "he also foresaw that Jesus would not be acceptable. It was known to God before it happened."

"What does he know about this now?" Rybys said. "What we are going to do?"

Elias was silent.

"He doesn't know," Rybys said.

"This—" Elias hesitated.

"The final battle," Rybys said. "It could go either way. Couldn't it?"

"In the end," Elias said, "God wins. He has absolute foresight."

"He can know," Rybys said, "but does that mean he can— Look, I really don't feel well. It's late and I'm sick and I'm worn out and I feel as if . . ." She gestured. "I'm a virgin and I'm pregnant. The Immigration doctors will never believe it."

Herb Asher said, "I think that's the point. That's why I'm supposed to marry you and come along."

"I'm not going to marry you; I don't even know you." She stared at him. "Are you kidding? *Marry* you? I've got M.S. and I'm pregnant— Damn it, both of you; go away and leave me alone. I mean it. Why didn't I take that bottle of Seconax when I had the chance? I never had the chance; Yah was watching. He sees even the fallen sparrow. I forgot."

"Do you have any whiskey?" Herb Asher said.

"Oh fine," Rybys said bitterly. "You can get drunk but can I? With M.S. and some kind of baby inside me? There I was"—she glared hatefully at Elias Tate—"picking up your thoughts visually on my TV set, and I imagined in my deluded folly that it was a corny soap opera dreamed up by writers at Fomalhaut—pure fiction. Arachnids were going to decapitate you? Is that what your unconscious fantasies consist of? And you're Yahweh's spokesperson?" She blanched. "I spoke the Sacred Name. Sorry."

"Christians speak it all the time," Elias said.

Rybys said, "But I'm a Jew. I *would* be a Jew; that's what got me into this. If I was a Gentile Yah wouldn't have picked me. If I'd ever been laid I'd—" She broke off. "The Divine Machinery has a peculiar brutality to it," she finished. "It isn't romantic. It's cruel; it really is."

"Because there is so much at stake," Elias said.

"What is at stake?" Rybys said.

"The universe exists because Yah remembers it," Elias said.

Both Herb Asher and Rybys stared at him.

"If Yah forgets, the universe ceases," Elias said.

"Can he forget?" Rybys said.

"He has yet to forget," Elias said elliptically.

"Meaning he could forget," Rybys said. "Then that's what this is about. You just spelled it out. I see. Well—" She shrugged and then reflexively sipped at her cup of tea. "Then I wouldn't exist in the first place except for Yah. Nothing would exist."

Elias said, "His name means 'He Brings into Existence Whatever Exists.' "

"Including evil?" Herb Asher asked.

"It says in Scripture," Elias said, "thus:

". . . So that men from the rising and the setting sun
May know that there is none but I:
I am the LORD, there is no other;
I make the light, I create darkness,
author alike of prosperity and trouble.
I, the LORD, do all these things."

"Where does it say that?" Rybys said.

"Isaiah forty-five," Elias said.

" 'Prosperity and trouble,' " Rybys echoed. " 'Weal and woe.' "

"Then you know the passage." Elias regarded her.

"It's hard to believe," she said.

"It is monotheism," Elias said harshly.

"Yes," she said, "I guess it is. But it's brutal. What's happening to me is brutal. And there's more ahead. I want out and I can't get out. Nobody asked me originally. Nobody is asking me now. Yah foresees what lies ahead but I don't, except that there's more cruelty and pain and throwing up. Serving God seems to mean throwing up and shooting yourself with a needle every day. I am a diseased rat in a kind of cage. That's what he's made me into. I have no faith and no hope and he has no love, only power. God is a symptom of power, nothing else. The hell with it. I give up. I don't care. I'll do what I have to but it will kill me and I know it. OK?"

The two men were silent. They did not look at her or at each other.

Herb Asher said finally, "He saved your life tonight. He sent me over here."

"That and five credpops will get you a cupee of Kaff," Rybys said. "He gave me the illness in the first place!"

"And he's guiding you through," Herb said.

"To what end?" she said.

"To emancipate an infinitude of lives," Elias said.

"Egypt," she said. "And the brick makers. Over and over again. Why doesn't the emancipation last? Why does it fade out? Isn't there any final resolution?"

"This," Elias said, "is that final resolution."

"I am not one of the emancipated," Rybys said. "I fell along the way."

"Not yet," Elias said.

"But it's coming."

"Perhaps." The expression on Elias Tate's face could not be read.

As the three of them sat, there came a low, murmuring voice which said, "Rybys, Rybys."

Rybys gave a muffled cry and looked around her.

"Fear not," the voice said. "You will live on in your son. You cannot now die, nor even unto the end of the age."

Silently, her face buried in her hands, Rybys began to cry.

Late in the day, when school had ended, Emmanuel decided to try the Hermetic transform once again, so that he would know the world around him.

First he speeded up his internal biological clock so that his thoughts raced faster and faster; he felt himself rushing down the tunnel of linear time until his rate of movement along that axis was enormous. First, therefore, he saw vague floating colors and then he suddenly encountered the Watcher, which is to say the Grigon, who barred the way between the Lower and Upper Realms. The Grigon presented itself to him as a nude female torso that he could reach out and touch, so close was it. Beyond this point he began to travel at the rate of the Upper Realm, so that the Lower Realm ceased to be something but became, instead, a process; it evolved in accretional layers at a rate of 31.5 million to one in terms of the Upper Realm's time scale.

Thereupon he saw the Lower Realm—not as a place—but as transparent pictures permutating at immense velocity. These pictures were the Forms outside of space being fed into the Lower Realm to become reality. He was one step away, now, from the Hermetic transform.

The final picture froze and time ceased for him. With his eyes shut he could still see the room around him; the flight had ended; he had eluded that which pursued him. That meant that his neural firing was perfect, and his pineal body registered the presence of light carried up its branch of the optic conduit.

He sat for a little while, although "little while" no longer signified anything. Then, by degrees, the transform took place. He saw outside him the pattern, the print, of his own brain; he was within a world made up of his brain, with living information carried here and there like little rivers of shining red that were alive. He could reach out, therefore, and touch his own thoughts in their original nature, before they became thoughts. The room was filled with their fire, and immense spaces stretched out, the volume of his own brain external to him.

Meanwhile he introjected the outer world so that he contained it within him. He now had the universe inside him and his own brain outside everywhere. His brain extended into the vast spaces, far larger than the universe had been. Therefore he knew the extent of all things that were himself, and, because he had incorporated the world, he knew it *and controlled it.*

He soothed himself and relaxed, and then could see the outlines of the room, the coffee table, a chair, walls, pictures on the walls: the ghost of the external universe lingering outside him. Presently he picked up a book from the table and opened it. Inside the book he found, written there, his own thoughts, now in a printed form. The printed thoughts lay arranged along the time axis which had become spacial and the only axis along which motion was possible. He could see, as in a hologram, the different ages of his thoughts, the most recent ones being closest to the surface, the older ones lower and deeper in many successive layers.

He regarded the world outside him which now had become reduced to spare geometric shapes, squares mostly, and the Golden Rectangle as a doorway. Nothing moved except the scene beyond the doorway, where his mother rushed happily among tangled old rosebushes and a farmland she had known as a child; she was smiling and her eyes were bright with joy.

Now, Emmanuel thought, I will change the universe that I have taken inside me. He regarded the geometric shapes and allowed them to fill up a little with matter. Across from him the ratty blue couch that Elias prized began to warp away from plumb; its lines changed. He had taken away the causality that guided it and it stopped being a ratty blue couch with Kaff stains on it and became instead a Hepplewhite cabinet, with fine bone china plates and cups and saucers behind its doors.

He restored a certain measure of time—and saw Elias Tate come and go about the room, enter and leave; he saw accretional layers laminated together in sequence along the linear time axis. The Hepplewhite cupboard remained for a short series of layers; it held its passive or off or rest mode, and then it was whisked over into its active or on or motion mode and joined the permanent world of the phylogons, participating now in all those of its class that had come before. In his projected world brain the Hepplewhite cabinet, and its bone china pieces, became incorporated into true reality forever. It would now undergo no more changes, and no one would see it but he. It was, to everyone else, in the past.

He completed the transform with the formulary of Hermes Trismegistus:

Verum est . . . quod superius est sicut quod inferius et quod inferius est sicut quod superius, ad perpetrando miracula rei unius.

That is:

The truth is that what is above is like what is below and what is below is like what is above, to accomplish the miracles of the one thing.

This was the Emerald Tablet, presented to Maria Prophetissa, the sister of Moses, by Tehuti himself, who gave names to all created things in the beginning, before he was expelled from the Palm Tree Garden.

That which was below, his own brain, the microcosm, had become the macrocosm, and, inside him as microcosm now, he contained the macrocosm, which is to say, what is above.

I now occupy the entire universe, Emmanuel realized; I am now everywhere equally. Therefore I have become Adam Kadmon, the First Man. Motion along the three spacial axes was impossible for him because he was already wherever he wished to go. The only motion possible for him or for changing reality lay along the temporal axis; he sat contemplating the world of the phylogons, billions of them in process, continually growing and completing themselves, driven by the dialectic that underlay all transformation. It pleased him; the sight of the interconnected network of phylogons was beautiful to behold. This was the *kosmos* of Pythagorias, the harmonious fitting-together of all things, each in its right way and each imperishable.

I see now what Plotinus saw, he realized. But, more than that, I have rejoined the sundered realms within me; *I have restored the Shekhina to En Sof.* But only for a little while and only locally. Only in microform. It would return to what it had been as soon as he released it.

"Just thinking," he said aloud.

Elias came into the room, saying as he came, "What are you doing, Manny?"

Causality had been reversed; he had done what Zina could do: make time run backward. He laughed in delight. And heard the sound of bells.

"I saw Chinvat," Emmanuel said. "The narrow bridge. I could have crossed it."

"You must not do that," Elias said.

Emmanuel said, "What do the bells mean? Bells ringing far off."

"When you hear the distant bells it means that the Saoshyant is present."

"The Saviour," Emmanuel said. "Who is the Saviour, Elias?"

"It must be yourself," Elias said.

"Sometimes I despair of remembering."

He could still hear the bells, very far off, ringing slowly, blown, he knew, by the desert wind. It was the desert itself speaking to him. The desert, by means of the bells, was trying to remind him. To Elias he said, "Who am I?"

"I can't say," Elias said.

"But you know."

Elias nodded.

"You could make everything very simple," Emmanuel said, "by saying."

"You must say it yourself," Elias said. "When the time comes you will know and you will say it."

"I am—" the boy said hesitantly.

Elias smiled.

She had heard the voice issue forth from her own womb. For a time she felt afraid and then she felt sad; sometimes she cried, and still the nausea continued—it never let up. I don't recall reading about that in the Bible, she thought. Mary being afflicted with morning sickness. I'll probably get edema and stretch marks. I don't remember reading about that either.

It would make a good graffito on some wall, she said to herself. THE VIRGIN MARY HAD STRETCH MARKS. She fixed herself a little meal of synthetic lamb and green beans; seated alone at her table she gazed out listlessly through the dome's port at the landscape. I really should clean up this place, she realized. Before Elias and Herb come back. In fact, I should make a list of what I have to do.

Most of all, she thought, I have to understand this situation. He is already inside me. It has happened.

I need another wig, she decided. For the trip. A better one. I think I'll try out a blond one that's longer. Goddam chemo, she thought. If the ailment doesn't kill you the therapy will. The remedy, she thought acidly, is worse than the malady. Look; I turned it around. God, I feel sick.

And then, as she picked at her plate of cold, synthetic food, a strange idea came to her. What if this is a maneuver by the Clems? she said to herself. We invaded their planet; now they're fighting back. They figured out what our conception of God involves. They're simulating that conception!

I wish mine was simulated, she ruminated.

But to get back to the point, she said to herself. They read our minds or study our books—never mind how they did it—and they fake us out. So what I have inside me is a computer terminal or something, a glorified radio. I can see me going through Immigration. "Anything to declare, Miss?" "Only a radio." Well, she thought, where is this radio? I don't see any radio. Well, you have to look real hard. No, she thought; it's a matter for Customs, not Immigration. What is the declared value of this radio, Miss? That would be hard to say, she answered in her mind. You're not going to believe me but—it's one of a kind. You don't see radios like this every day.

I should probably pray, she decided.

"Yah," she said, "myself, I am weak and sick and afraid, and I really don't want to be involved in this." Contraband, she thought. I'm going to smuggle in contraband. "Lady, come with me. We're going to conduct a complete body search. The matron will be in here in a minute; just sit down and read a magazine." I'll tell them it's an outrage, she thought. "What a surprise!" Feigned amazement. "I have *what* inside me? You're kidding. No, I have no idea how it got there. Will wonders never cease."

A strange lethargy came over her, a kind of hypnagogic state, even as she sat reflexively eating. The embryo inside her had begun to unfold a picture before her, a view by a mind totally different from hers.

She realized, This is how they will view it. The powers of the world.

What she saw, through their eyes, was a monster. The Christian-Islamic Church and the Scientific Legate—their fear did not resemble her fear; hers had to do with effort and danger, with what was required of her. But they— She saw them consulting Big Noodle, the AI System that processed Earth's information, the vast artificial intelligence on which the government relied.

Big Noodle, after analyzing the data, informed the authorities that something sinister had been smuggled past Immigration and onto Earth; she felt their recoil, their aversion. Incredible, she thought. To see the Lord of the universe through their eyes; to see him as foreign. How could the Lord who created everything be a foreign thing? *They are not in his image, then,* she realized. This is what Yah is telling me. I always assumed—we were always taught—that man is the image of God. It is like calling to like. Then they really believe in themselves! They sincerely do not understand.

The monster from outer space, she thought. We must be on guard perpetually lest it show up and sneak through Immigration. How deranged they are. How far off the mark. Then they would kill my baby, she thought. It is impossible but it is true. And no one could make them understand what they had done. The Sanhedrin thought the same way, she said to herself, about Jesus. This is another Zealot. She shut her eyes.

They are living in a cheap horror film, she thought. There is something wrong when you fear little children. When you view them, any one of them, as weird and awful. I don't want this insight, she said to herself, drawing back in aversion. Take it away, please; I've seen enough.

I understand.

She thought, This is why it has to be done. Because they see as they do. They pray; they make decisions; they shield their world—they keep out hostile intrusions. To them this is a hostile intrusion. They are demented; they would kill the God who made them. No rational thing does that. Christ did not die on the cross to render men spotless; he was crucified because they were crazy; they saw as I see now. It is a vista of lunacy.

They think they are doing the right thing.

6

The girl Zina said, ''I have something for you.''

''A present?'' He held out his hand, trustingly.

Only a child's toy. An information slate, such as every young person had. He felt keen disappointment.

''We made it for you,'' Zina said.

''Who is that?'' He examined the slate. Self-governing factories turned out hundreds of thousands of such slates. Each slate contained common microcircuitry. ''Mr. Plaudet gave me one of these already,'' he said. ''They're plugged into the school.''

''We make ours differently,'' Zina said. ''Keep it. Tell Mr. Plaudet this is the one he gave you. He won't be able to distinguish them from each other. See? We even have the brand name on it.'' With her finger she traced the letters I.B.M.

''This one isn't really I.B.M.,'' he said.

''Definitely not. Turn it on.''

He pressed the tab of the slate. On the slate, on the pale gray surface, a single word in illuminated red appeared.

VALIS

''That's your question for right now,'' Zina said. ''To figure out what 'Valis' is. The slate is posing the problem for you at a class-one level . . . which means it'll give you further clues, if you want them.''

"Mother Goose," Emmanuel said.

On the slate the word VALIS disappeared. Now it read:

HEPHAISTOS

"Kyklopes," Emmanuel said instantly.

Zina laughed. "You're as fast as it is."

"What's it connected to? Not Big Noodle." He did not like Big Noodle.

"Maybe it'll tell you," Zina said.

The slate now read:

SHIVA

"Kyklopes," Emmanuel repeated. "It's a trick. This was built by the troop of Diana."

At once the girl's smile faded.

"I'm sorry," Emmanuel said. "I won't say it again out loud even one more time."

"Give me the slate back." She held out her hand.

Emmanuel said, "I will give it back if it says for me to give it back. He pressed the tab.

NO

"All right," Zina said. "I'll let you keep it. But you don't know what it is; you don't understand it. The troop didn't build it. Press the tab."

Again he pressed the tab.

LONG BEFORE CREATION

"I—" Emmanuel faltered.

"It will come back to you," Zina said. "Through this. Use it. I don't think you should tell Elias either. He might not understand."

Emmanuel said nothing. This was a matter that he himself would decide. It was important not to let others make his choices for him. And, basically, he trusted Elias. Did he also trust Zina? He was not sure. He sensed the multitude of natures within her, the profusion of identities. Ultimately he would seek out the real one; he knew it was there, but the tricks obscured it. Who is it, he asked himself, who plays tricks like this? What being is the trickster? He pressed the tab.

DANCING

To that, he gave a nod of assent. Dancing certainly was the right answer; in his mind he could see her dancing, with all the troop, burning the grass beneath their feet, leaving it scorched, and the minds of men disoriented. You cannot disorient me, he said to himself. Even though you control time. Because I control time, too. Perhaps even more than you.

That night at dinner he discussed Valis with Elias Tate.

"Take me to see it," Emmanuel said.

"It's a very old movie," Elias said.

"But at least we could rent a cassette. From the library. What does 'Valis' mean?"

"Vast Active Living Intelligence System," Elias said. "The movie is mostly fiction. It was made by a rock singer in the latter part of the twentieth century. His name was Eric Lampton but he called himself Mother Goose. The film contained Mini's Synchronicity Music, which had considerable impact on all modern music to this day. Much of the information in the film is conveyed subliminally by the music. The setting is an alternate U.S.A. where a man named Ferris F. Fremount is president."

Emmanuel said, "But what is Valis?"

"An artificial satellite that projects a hologram that they take to be reality."

"Then it's a reality generator."

"Yes," Elias said.

"Is the reality genuine?"

"No; I said it's a hologram. It can make them see whatever it wants them to see. That's the whole point of the film. It's a study of the power of illusion."

Going to his room, Emmanuel picked up the slate that Zina had given him and pressed the tab.

"What are you doing?" Elias said, coming in behind him.

The slate showed one word:

NO

"That's plugged into the government," Elias said. "There's no point in using it. I knew Plaudet would give you one of those." He reached for it. "Give it to me."

"I want to keep it," Emmanuel said.

"Good grief; it says I.B.M. right on it! What do you expect it to tell you? The truth? When has the government ever told anyone the truth? They killed your mother and put your father into cryonic suspension. Let me have it, damn it."

"If this is taken from me," Emmanuel said, "they will give me another."

"I suppose so." Elias withdrew his hand. "But don't believe what it says."

"It says you're wrong about Valis," Emmanuel said.

"In what way?"

Emmanuel said, "It just said 'no.' It didn't say anything more." He pressed the tab again.

YOU

"What the hell does that mean?" Elias said, mystified.

"I don't know," Emmanuel said truthfully. He thought, I will keep using it.

And then he thought, It is tricking me. It dances along the path like a bobbing light, leading me and leading me, away, further, further, into the darkness. And then when the darkness is everywhere the bobbing light will wink out. I know you, he thought at the slate. I know how you work. I will not follow; you must come to *me*.

He pressed the tab.

FOLLOW ME

"Where no one ever returns," Emmanuel said.

After dinner he spent some time with the holoscope, studying Elias's most precious possession: the Bible expressed as layers at different depths within the hologram, each layer according to age. The total structure of Scripture formed, then, a three-dimensional cosmos that could be viewed from any angle and its contents read. According to the tilt of the axis of observation, differing messages could be extracted. Thus Scripture yielded up an infinitude of knowledge that ceaselessly changed. It became a wondrous work of art, beautiful to the eye, and incredible in its pulsations of color. Throughout it red and gold pulsed, with strands of blue.

The color symbolism was not arbitrary but extended back in time to the early medieval Romanesque paintings. Red always represented the Father. Blue the color of the Son. And gold, of course, that of the Holy Spirit. Green stood for the new life of the elect; violet the color of mourning; brown the color of endurance and suffering; white, the color of light; and, finally, black, the color of the Powers of Darkness, of death and sin.

All these colors could be found in the hologram formed by the Bible along the temporal axis. In conjunction with sections of text, complex messages formed, permutated, re-formed. Emmanuel never tired of gazing into the hologram; for him as well as Elias it was the master hologram, surpassing all others. The Christian-Islamic Church did not approve of transmuting the Bible into a color-coded hologram, and forbade the manufacture and sale. Hence Elias had constructed this hologram himself, without approval.

It was an open hologram. New information could be fed into it. Emmanuel wondered about that but he said nothing. He sensed a secret. Elias could not answer him, so he did not ask.

What he could do, however, was type out on the keyboard linked to the hologram a few crucial words of Scripture, whereupon the hologram would align itself from the vantage point of the citation, along all its spacial axes. Thus the entire text of the Bible would be focused in relationship to the typed-out information.

"What if I fed something new into it?" he had asked Elias one day.

Elias had said severely, "Never do that."

"But it's technically possible."

"It is not done."

About that the boy wondered often.

He knew, of course, why the Christian-Islamic Church did not allow the transmuting of the Bible into a color-coded hologram. If you learned how you could gradually tilt the temporal axis, the axis of true depth, until successive layers were superimposed and a vertical message—a new message—could be read out. In this way you entered into a dialogue with Scripture; it became alive. It became a sentient organism that was never twice the same. The Christian-Islamic Church, of course, wanted both the Bible and the Koran frozen forever. If Scripture escaped out from under the church its monopoly departed.

Superimposition was the critical factor. And this sophisticated superimposition could only be achieved in a hologram. And yet he knew that once, long ago, Scripture had been deciphered this way. Elias, when asked, was reticent about the matter. The boy let the topic drop.

There had been an acutely embarrassing incident at church the year before. Elias had taken the boy to Thursday morning mass. Since he had not been confirmed, Emmanuel could not receive the host; while the others in the congregation gathered at the rail Emmanuel remained bent in prayer. All at once, as the priest carried the chalice from person to person, dipping the wafers in the consecrated wine and saying, "The Blood of Our Lord Jesus Christ, which was shed for thee—" all at once Emmanuel had stood up where he was in his pew and stated clearly and calmly:

"The blood is not there nor the body either."

The priest paused and looked to see who had spoken.

"You do not have the authority," Emmanuel said. And, upon saying that, he turned and walked out of the church. Elias found him in their car, listening to the radio.

"You can't do that," Elias had said as they drove home. "You can't tell them things like that. They'll open a file on you and that's what we don't want." He was furious.

"I saw," Emmanuel said. "It was a wafer and wine only."

"You mean the accidents. The external form. But the essence was—"

"There was no essence other than the visible appearance," Emmanuel answered. "The miracle did not occur because the priest was not a priest."

They drove in silence after that.

"Do you deny the miracle of transubstantiation?" Elias asked that night as he put the boy to bed.

"I deny that it took place today," Emmanuel said. "There in that place. I will not go there again."

"What I want," Elias said, "is for you to be as wise as a serpent and as innocent as a dove."

Emmanuel regarded him.

"They killed—"

"They have no power over me," Emmanuel said.

"They can destroy you. They can arrange another accident. Next year I'm required to put you in school. Fortunately because of your brain damage you won't have to go to a regular school. I'm counting on them to—" Elias hesitated.

Emmanuel finished, "—Consign anything they see about me that is different to the brain damage."

"Right."

"Was the brain damage arranged?"

"I— Perhaps."

"It seems useful." But, he thought, *if only I knew my real name*. "Why can't you say my name?" he said to Elias.

"Your mother did," Elias said obliquely.

"My mother is dead."

"You will say it yourself, eventually."

"I'm impatient." A strange thought came to him. "Did she die because she said my name?"

"Maybe," Elias said.

"And that's why you won't say it? Because it would kill you if you did? And it wouldn't kill me."

"It is not a name in the usual sense. It is a command."

All these matters remained in his mind. A name that was not a name but a command. It made him think of Adam who named the animals. He wondered about that. Scripture said:

. . . and brought them unto the man to see
what he would call them . . .

"Did God not know what the man would call them?" he asked Elias one day.

"Only man has language," Elias explained. "Only man can give birth to language. Also—" He eyed the boy. "When man gave names to creatures he established his dominion over them."

What you name you control, Emmanuel realized. Hence no one is to speak my name because no one is to have—or can have —control over me. "God played a game with Adam, then," he said. "He wanted to see if the man knew their correct names. He was testing the man. God enjoys games."

"I'm not sure I know the answer to that," Elias said.

"I did not ask. I said."

"It is not something usually associated with God."

"Then the nature of God is known."

"His nature is *not* known."

Emmanuel said, "He enjoys games and play. It says in Scripture that he rested but I say that he played."

He wanted to feed that into the hologram of the Bible, as an addendum, but he knew that he should not. How would it alter the total hologram? he wondered. To add to the Torah that God enjoys joyful sport . . . Strange, he thought, that I can't add that. Someone must add it; it has to be there, in Scripture. Someday.

He learned about pain and death from an ugly dying dog. It had been run over and lay by the side of the road, its chest crushed, bloody foam bubbling from its mouth. When he bent over it the dog gazed at him with glasslike eyes, eyes that already saw into the next world.

To understand what the dog was saying he put his hand on its stumpy tail. "Who mandated this death for you?" he asked the dog. "What have you done?"

"I did nothing," the dog replied.

"But this is a harsh death."

"Nonetheless," the dog told him, "I am blameless."

"Have you ever killed?"

"Oh yes. My jaws are designed to kill. I was constructed to kill smaller things."

"Do you kill for food or pleasure?"

"I kill out of joy," the dog told him. "It is a game; it is the game I play."

Emmanuel said, "I did not know about such games. Why do dogs kill and why do dogs die? Why are there such games?"

"These subtleties mean nothing to me," the dog told him. "I kill to kill; I die because I must. It is necessity, the rule that is the final rule. Don't you live and kill and die by that rule? Surely you do. You are a creature, too."

"I do what I wish."

"You lie to yourself," the dog said. "Only God does as he wishes."

"Then I must be God."

"If you are God, heal me."

"But you are under the law."

"You are not God."

"God willed the law, dog."

"You have said it, then, yourself; you have answered your own question. Now let me die."

When he told Elias about the dog who died, Elias said:

Go, stranger, and to Lacedaemon tell
That here, obeying her behests, we fell.

"That was for the Spartans who died at Thermopylae," Elias said.

"Why do you tell me that?" Emmanuel said.

Elias said:

Go tell the Spartans, thou that passeth by,
That here, obedient to their laws, we lie.

"You mean the dog," Emmanuel said.

"I mean the dog," Elias said.

"There is no difference between a dead dog in a ditch and the Spartans who died at Thermopylae." He understood. "None," he said. "I see."

"If you can understand why the Spartans died you can understand it all," Elias said.

You who pass by, a moment pause;
We, here, obey the Spartan laws.

"Is there no couplet for the dog?" Emmanuel asked.

Elias said:

Passer, this enter in your log:
As Spartan was, so, too, the dog.

"Thank you," Emmanuel said.

"What was the last thing the dog said?" Elias said.

"The dog said, 'Now let me die.' "

Elias said:

Lasciatemi morire!
E chi volete voi che mi conforte
In cosi dura sorte,
In cosi gran martire?

"What is that?" Emmanuel said.

"The most beautiful piece of music written before Bach," Elias said. "Monteverdi's madrigal 'Lamento D'Arianna.' Thus:

Let me die!
And who do you think can comfort me
in my harsh misfortune,
in such grievous torment?

"Then the dog's death is high art," Emmanuel said. "The highest art of the world. Or at least celebrated, recorded, in and by high art. Am I to see nobility in an old ugly dying dog with a crushed chest?"

"If you believe Monteverdi, yes," Elias said. "And those who revere Monteverdi."

"Is there more to the lament?"

"Yes, but it does not apply. Theseus has left Ariadne; it is unrequited love."

"Which is more awesome?" Emmanuel said. "A dying dog in a ditch or Ariadne spurned?"

Elias said, "Ariadne imagines her torment, but the dog's is real."

"Then the dog's torment is worse," Emmanuel said. "It is the greater tragedy." He understood. And, strangely, he felt content. It was a good universe in which an ugly dying dog was of more worth than a classic figure from ancient Greece. He felt the tilted balance right itself, the scales that weighed it all. He felt the honesty of the universe, and his confusion left him. But, more important, the dog understood its own death. After all, the dog would never hear Monteverdi's music or read the couplet on the stone column at Thermopylae. High art was for those who saw death rather than lived death. For the dying creature a cup of water was more important.

"Your mother detested certain art forms," Elias said. "In particular she loathed Linda Fox."

"Play me some Linda Fox," Emmanuel said.

Elias put an audio cassette into the tape transport, and he and Emmanuel listened.

Flow not so fast, ye fountains,
What

"Enough," Emmanuel said. "Shut it off." He put his hands over his ears. "It's dreadful." He shuddered.

"What's wrong?" Elias put his arm around the boy and lifted him up to hold him. "I've never seen you so upset."

"He listened to that while my mother was dying!" Emmanuel stared into Elias's bearded face.

I remember, Emmanuel said to himself. I am beginning to remember who I am.

Elias said, "What is it?" He held the boy tight.

It is happening, Emmanuel realized. At last. That was the first of the signal that I—I myself—prepared. Knowing it would eventually fire.

The two of them gazed into each other's faces. Neither the boy nor the man spoke. Trembling, Emmanuel clung to the old bearded man; he did not let himself fall.

"Do not fear," Elias said.

"Elijah," Emmanuel said. "You are Elijah who comes first. Before the great and terrible day."

Elias, holding the boy and rocking him gently, said, "You have nothing to fear on that day."

"But *he* does," Emmanuel said. "The Adversary whom we hate. His time has come. I fear for him, knowing as I do, now, what is ahead."

"Listen," Elias said quietly.

How you have fallen from heaven, bright morning star,
felled to the earth, sprawling helpless across the nations!
You thought in your own mind,
  I will scale the heavens;
I will set my throne high above the stars of God,
I will sit on the mountain where the gods meet
  in the far recesses of the north.
I will rise high above the cloud-banks
  and make myself like the Most High.
Yet you shall be brought down to Sheol,
  to the depths of the abyss.
Those who see you will stare at you,
  they will look at you and ponder . . .

"You see?" Elias said. "*He is here.* This is his place, this little world. He made it his fortress two thousand years ago, and set up a prison for the people as he did in Egypt. For two thousand years the people have been crying and there was no response, no aid. He has them all. And thinks he is safe."

Emmanuel, clutching the old man, began to cry.

"Still afraid?" Elias said.

Emmanuel said, "I cry with them. I cry with my mother. I cry with the dying dog who did not cry. I cry *for* them. And for Belial who fell, the bright morning star. Fell from heaven and began it all."

And, he thought, I cry for myself. I am my mother; I am the dying dog and the suffering people, and I, he thought, am that bright morning star, too . . . even Belial; I am that and what it has become.

The old man held him fast.

7

Cardinal Fulton Statler Harms, Chief Prelate of the vast organizational network that comprised the Christian-Islamic Church, could not for the life of him figure out why there wasn't a sufficient amount of money in his Special Discretionary Fund to cover his mistress's expenses.

Perhaps, he pondered as his barber shaved him slowly and carefully, he had too dim a notion of the extent of Deirdre's needs.

Originally she had approached him—no small task in itself, since it involved ascending the C.I.C. hierarchy rung by rung—ascending without falling entirely off before reaching the top. Deirdre, at that time, represented the W.C.L.F., the World Civil Liberties Forum, and she had a list of abuses—it was hazy to him then and it was still hazy to him, but anyhow the two of them had wound up in bed, and now, officially, Dierdre had become his executive secretary.

For her work she blotted up two salaries: the visible one that came with her job and the invisible one doled out from the substantial account that he was free to dispense as he saw fit. Where all this money went after it reached Deirdre he hadn't the foggiest idea. Bookkeeping had never been his strong suit.

"You want the yellow removed from this gray on the side, don't you?" his barber said, shaking up the contents of a bottle.

"Please," Harms said; he nodded.

"You think the Lakers are going to snap their losing streak?" his barber said. "I mean, they acquired that What's-his-name; he's nine feet two inches. If they hadn't raised the—"

Tapping his ear, Harms said, "I'm listening to the news, Arnold."

"Well, yeah, I can see that, Father," Arnold the barber said as he splashed bleach onto the Chief Prelate's graying hair. "But there's something I wanted to ask you, about homosexual priests. Doesn't the Bible forbid homosexuality? So I don't see how a priest can be a practicing homosexual."

The news that Harms was attempting to hear had to do with the health of the Procurator Maximus of the Scientific Legate, Nicholas Bulkowsky. A solemn prayer vigil had been formally called into being but nonetheless Bulkowsky continued to decline. Harms had, sub rosa, dispatched his personal physician to join the team of specialists attending to the Procurator's urgent condition.

Bulkowsky, as not only Cardinal Harms but the entire curia knew, was a devout Christian. He had been converted by the evangelical, charismatic Dr. Colin Passim who, at his revival meetings, often flew through the air in dramatic demonstration of the power of the Holy Spirit within him.

Of course, Dr. Passim had not been the same since he sailed through a vast stained-glass window of the cathedral at Metz, France. Formerly he had talked occasionally in tongues and now he talked only in tongues. This had inspired a popular TV comic to suggest that an English-Glossolalia dictionary be brought out, so that folks could understand Dr. Passim. This in turn had given rise to such indignation in the pious that Cardinal Harms had it jotted down on his desk calendar somewhere that, when possible, he should pronounce the comic anathema. But, as usual, he had not gotten around to such petty matters.

Much of Cardinal Harms's time was spent in a secret activity: he had been feeding St. Anselm's *Proslogion* to the great Artificial Intelligence system Big Noodle with the idea of resurrecting the long-discredited Ontological Proof for the existence of God.

He had gone right back to Anselm and the original statement of the argument, unsoiled by the accretions of time:

> Anything understood must be in the intelligence. Certainly, too, the being greater than which none can be conceived cannot exist in the intellect alone; for if it were only in the intellect it could be conceived as existing also in reality and this would be to conceive a still greater being. In such a case, if the being greater than which none can be conceived is merely in the intelligence (and not in reality), then this same being is something than which one could still conceive a greater (i.e., one which exists both in the intelligence and in reality). This is a contradiction. Consequently, there can be no doubt that the being greater than which none can be conceived must exist both in the intelligence and in reality.

However, Big Noodle knew all about Aquinas and Descartes and Kant and Russell and their criticisms, and the A.I. system also possessed common sense. It informed Harms that Anselm's argument did not hold water, and presented him with page after page of analysis as to why. Harms's response was to edit out Big Noodle's analysis and seize upon Hartshorne and Malcolm's defense of Anselm; viz: that God's existence is either logically necessary or logically impossible. Since it has not been demonstrated to be impossible—which is to say, the concept of such an entity has not been shown to be self-contradictory—then it follows that we must of necessity conclude that God exists.

Upon fastening onto this weary argument, Harms had dispatched a copy via his direct line to the ailing Procurator Maximus as a means of instilling new vigor in his co-ruler.

"Now take the Giants," Arnold the barber was saying as he valiantly tried to bleach the yellow from the cardinal's hair. "I say you can't count them out. Look at Eddy Tubb's ERA for last year. So he has a sore arm; pitchers always get sore arms."

The day had begun for the Chief Prelate Cardinal Fulton Statler Harms; trying to hear the news, meditating simultaneously on his enterprise vis-à-vis St. Anselm, fending off Arnold's baseball statistics—this constituted his morning confrontation with reality, his routine. All that remained to make it the Platonic archetypal beginning of his activity phase was the mandatory—and futile—attempt to pin down Deirdre regarding her cost over-run.

He was prepared for that; he had a new girl waiting in the wings. Dierdre, who did not know it, was about to go.

At his resort city on the Black Sea the Procurator Maximus walked in slow circles as he read Deirdre Connell's most recent report on the chief prelate. No health problems assailed the procurator; he had allowed news of his "medical condition" to leak its way into the media so as to ensnare his co-ruler in a web of self-serving lies. This gave him time to study his intelligence staff's appraisal of Deirdre Connell's daily reports. So far it was the educated opinion of everyone who intimately served the procurator that Cardinal Harms had lost touch with reality and was lost in harebrained theological quests—journeys that led him further and further away from any control over the political and economic situation that was pro forma his purview.

The fake reports also gave him time to fish and relax and sun himself and figure out how to depose the cardinal in order to get one of his own people into the position of chief prelate of the C.I.C. Bulkowsky had a number of S.L. functionaries in the curia, well-trained and eager. As long as Deirdre Connell held down the post of executive secretary and mistress to the cardinal, Bulkowsky had the edge. He felt reasonably certain that Harms owned no one in the Scientific Legate's top positions, owned no reciprocal access. Bulkowsky had no mistress; he was a family man with a plump, middle-aged wife, and three children all attending private schools in Switzerland. In addition, his conversion to Dr. Passim's enthusiastic nonsense—the miracle of flying had of course been achieved by technological means—was a strategic fraud, designed to lull the cardinal deeper into his grand dreams.

The procurator knew all about the attempt to induce Big Noodle to come up with verification of St. Anselm's Ontological Proof for the existence of God; the topic was a joke in regions dominated by the Scientific Legate. Deirdre Connell had been instructed to recommend to her aging lover that he spend more and more time in his lofty venture.

Nonetheless, although wholly rooted in reality, Bulkowsky had not been able to solve certain problems of his own—matters which he concealed from his co-ruler. Decisions for the S.L. had fallen off among the youth cadres during recent months; more and more college students, even those in the hard sciences, were finding for the C.I.C., throwing aside the hammer-and-sickle pin and donning the cross. Specifically there had developed a paucity of ark engineers, with the result that three S.L. orbiting arks, with their inhabitants, had had to be abandoned. This news had *not* reached the media, since the inhabitants had perished. To shield the public from the grim news the designations of the remaining S.L. arks had been changed. On computer printouts the malfunctions did not appear; the situation gave the semblance of normality.

At least we did eliminate Colin Passim, Bulkowsky reflected. A man who talks like an aud-tape of a duck played backward is no threat. The evangelist had, without suspecting it, succumbed to S.L. advanced weaponry. The balance of world power had thus been made to shift ever so slightly. Little things like that added up. Take, for instance, the presence of the S.L. agent duked in as the cardinal's mistress and secretary. Without that—

Bulkowsky felt supremely confident. The dialectical force of historic necessity was on his side. He could retire to his floating bed, half an hour from now, with a knowledge that the world situation was in hand.

"Cognac," he said to a robot attendant. "Courvoisier Napoleon."

As he stood by his desk warming the snifter with the palms of his hands his wife, Galina, entered the room. "Make no appointments for Thursday night," she said. "General Yakir has planned a recital for the Moscow corps. The American chanteuse Linda Fox will be singing. Yakir expects us."

"Certainly," Bulkowsky said. "Have roses prepared for the end of the recital." To a pair of robot servants he said, "Have my valet de chambre remind me."

"Don't nod off during the recital," Galina said. "Mrs. Yakir will be hurt. You remember the last time."

"The Penderecki abomination," Bulkowsky said, remembering well. He had snored through the "Quia Fecit" of the "Magnificat" and then read about his behavior in intelligence documents a week later.

"Remember that as far as informed circles know, you are a born-again Christian," Galina said. "What did you do about those responsible for the loss of the three arks?"

"They are all dead," Bulkowsky said. He had had them shot.

"You could recruit replacement from the U.K."

"We will have our own soon. I don't trust what the U.K. sends us. Everyone is for sale. For instance, how much is that chanteuse now asking for her decision?"

"The situation is confused," Galina said. "I have read the intelligence reports; the cardinal is offering her a large sum to decide for the C.I.C. I don't think we should try to meet it."

"But if an entertainer that popular were to step forth and announce that she had seen the white light and accepted sweet Jesus into her life—"

"You did."

"But," Bulkowsky said, "you know why." As he had accepted Jesus solemnly, with much pomp, he would presently declare that he had renounced Jesus and returned, wiser now, to the S.L. This would have a dire effect on the curia and, hopefully, even on the cardinal himself. The chief prelate's morale, according to S.L. psychologists, would be shattered. The man actually supposed that one day everyone associated with the S.L. would march up to the various offices of the C.I.C. and convert.

"What are you doing about that doctor he sent?" Galina said. "Are there any difficulties?"

"No." He shook his head. "The forged medical reports keep

him busy." Actually the medical information presented regularly to the physician whom the cardinal had sent were not forged. They simply pertained to someone other than Bulkowsky, some minor S.L. person genuinely sick. Bulkowsky had sworn Harms's physician to secrecy, pleading medical ethics as the issue, but of course Dr. Duffey covertly dispatched detailed reports on the procurator's health to the cardinal's staff at every opportunity. S.L. intelligence routinely intercepted them, checked to make sure they painted a sufficiently grave picture, copied them and sent them on. By and large the medical reports traveled by microwave signal to an orbiting C.I.C. communications satellite and from there were beamed down to Washington, D.C. However, Dr. Duffey, in a periodic fit of cleverness, sometimes simply mailed the information. This was harder to control.

Imagining that he was dealing with an ailing man, and one who had decided for Jesus, the cardinal had relaxed his stance of vigil regarding the higher activities of the S.L. The cardinal now supposed the procurator to be hopelessly incompetent.

"If Linda Fox will not decide for the S.L.," Galina said, "why don't you draw her aside and tell her that one day on her way to a concert engagement her private rocket—that gaudy plush thing she flies herself—will go up in a flash of flaming fire?"

Gloomily, Bulkowsky said, "Because the cardinal got to her first. He has already passed the word to her that if she doesn't accept sweet Jesus into her life bichlorides will find her whether she wants to accept them or not."

The tactic of poisoning Linda Fox with small doses of mercury was an artful one. Long before she died (if she did die) she would be as mad as a hatter—literally, since it had been mercury poisoning, mercury used to process felt hats, that had driven the English hatters of the nineteenth century into famous organic psychosis.

I wish I had thought of that, Bulkowsky said to himself. Intelligence reports stated that the chanteuse had become hysterical when informed by a C.I.C. agent of what the cardinal intended if she did not decide for Jesus—hysteria and then temporary hypothermia, followed by a refusal to sing "Rock of Ages" in her next concert, as had been scheduled.

On the other hand, he reflected, cadmium would be better than mercury because it would be more difficult to detect. The S.L. secret police had used trace amounts of cadmium on unpersons for some time, and to good effect.

"Then money won't influence her," Galina said.

"I wouldn't dismiss it. It's her ambition to own Greater Los Angeles."

Galina said, "But if she's destroyed, the colonists will grumble. They're dependent on her."

"Linda Fox is not a person. She is a *class* of persons, a type. She is a sound that electronic equipment, very sophisticated electronic equipment, makes. There are more of her. There will always be. She can be stamped out like tires."

"Well, then don't offer her very much money." Galina laughed.

"I feel sorry for her," Bulkowsky said. How must it feel, he asked himself, not to exist? That's a contradiction. To feel is to exist. Then, he thought, probably she does not feel. Because it is a fact that she does not exist, not really. We ought to know. We were the first to imagine her.

Or rather—Big Noodle had first imagined the Fox. The A.I. system had invented her, told her what to sing and how to sing it; Big Noodle set up her arrangements . . . even down to the mixing. And the package was a complete success.

Big Noodle had correctly analyzed the emotional needs of the colonists and had come up with a formula to meet those needs. The A.I. system maintained an ongoing survey, deriving feedback; when the needs changed, Linda Fox changed. It constituted a closed loop. If, suddenly, all the colonists disappeared, Linda Fox would wink out of existence. Big Noodle would have canceled her, like paper run through a paper shredder.

"Procurator," a robot serving assembly said, coasting up to Bulkowsky.

"What is it?" he said irritably; he did not like to be interrupted when he was conversing with his wife.

The robot serving assembly said, "Hawk."

To Galina he said, "Big Noodle wants me. It's urgent. You'll excuse me." He walked away from her rapidly and into his complex of private offices where he would find the carefully protected terminal of the A.I. system.

The terminal indeed pulsed, waiting for him.

"Troop movements?" Bulkowsky said as he seated himself facing the screen of the terminal.

"No," the artificial voice of Big Noodle came, with its characteristic ambiance. "A conspiracy to smuggle a monster baby through Immigration. Three colonists are involved. I monitored the fetus of the woman. Details to follow." Big Noodle broke the circuit.

"Details when?" Bulkowsky said, but the A.I. system did not hear him, having cut itself off. Damn, he thought. It shows me little courtesy. Too busy deconstructing the Ontological Proof of the Existence of God.

Cardinal Fulton Statler Harms received the news from Big Noodle with his customary aplomb. "Thank you very much," he said as the A.I. system signed off. Something alien, he said to himself. Some sport that God never intended should exist. This is the truly dreadful aspect of space migration: we do not get back what we send out. We get in return the unnatural.

Well, he thought, we shall have it killed; however I will be interested to see its brain-print. I wonder what this one is like. A snake within an egg, he thought. A fetus within a woman. The original story retold: a creature that is subtle.

> The serpent was more crafty than any wild
> creature that the LORD God had made.

Genesis chapter three, verse one. What happened before is not going to happen again. We will destroy it this time, the evil one. In whatever form it now has taken.

He thought, I shall pray on it.

"Excuse me," he said to his small audience of visiting priests who waited outside in the vast lounge. "I must retire to my chapel for a little while. A serious matter has come up."

Presently he knelt in silence and gloom, with burning candles off in the far corners, the chamber and himself hallowed.

"Father," he prayed, "teach us to know thy ways and to emulate thee. Help us to protect ourselves and guard against the evil one. May we foresee and understand his wiles. For his wiles are great; his cunning also. Give us the strength—lend us thy holy power—to ferret him out wherever he is."

He heard nothing in response. It did not surprise him. Pious people spoke to God, and crazy people imagined that God spoke back. His answers had to come from within himself, from his own heart. But, of course, the Spirit guided him. It was always thus.

Within him the Spirit, in the form of his own proclivities, ratified his original insight. "Thou shalt not suffer a witch to live" included in its domain the smuggled mutation. "Witch" equaled "monster." He therefore had scriptural support.

And anyhow he was God's regent on Earth.

Just to be on the safe side he consulted his huge copy of the Bible, rereading Exodus twenty-two, verse seventeen.

Thou shalt not suffer a sorceress to live.

And then for good measure he read the next verse.

Whosoever lieth with a beast shall surely
be put to death.

Then he read the notes.

Ancient witchcraft was steeped in crime, immorality and imposture; and it debased the populace by hideous practices and superstitions. It is preceded by provisions against sexual license and followed by condemnation of unnatural vice and idolatry.

Well, that certainly applied here. Hideous practices and superstitions. Things spawned by intercourse with nonhumans on far off foreign planets. They shall not invade this sacred world, he said to himself. I'm sure my colleague the Procurator Maximus will agree.

Suddenly illumination washed over him. We're being invaded! he realized. The thing we've been talking about for two centuries. The Holy Spirit is telling me; it has happened!

Accursed spawn of filth, he thought; rapidly he made his way to his master chamber where the direct—and highly shielded—line to the procurator could be found.

"Is this about the baby?" Bulkowsky said, when contact—in an instant—had been established. "I have retired for the night. It can wait until tomorrow."

"There is an abomination out there," Cardinal Harms said. "Exodus twenty-two, verse seventeen. 'Thou—' "

"Big Noodle won't let it reach Earth. It must have been intercepted at one of the outer rings of Immigration."

"God does not wish monsters on this his primary world. You as a born-again Christian should realize that."

"Certainly I do," Bulkowsky said, with indignation.

"What shall I instruct Big Noodle to do?"

Bulkowsky said, "It's what will Big Noodle instruct *us* to do, rather. Don't you think?"

"We will have to pray our way through this crisis," Harms said. "Join me now in a prayer. Bow your head."

"My wife is calling me," Bulkowsky said. "We can pray tomorrow. Good-night." He hung up.

Oh God of Israel, Harms prayed, his head bowed. Protect us from procrastination and from the evil that has descended on it. Awaken the Procurator's soul to the urgency of this our hour of ordeal.

We are being spiritually tested, he prayed. I know that is the case. We must prove our worth by casting out this satanic presence. Make us worthy, Lord; lend us thy sword of might. Give us thy saddle of righteousness to mount the steed of . . . He could not finish the thought; it was too intense. Hasten to our aid, he finished, and raised his head. A sense of triumph filled him; as if, he thought, we have trapped something to be killed. We have hunted it down. And it will die. Praise be to God!

8

The high-velocity axial flight made Rybys Rommey deathly ill. United Spaceways had arranged for five adjoining seats for her, so that she could lie outstretched; even so, she was barely able to speak. She lay on her side, a blanket up to her chin.

Somberly, as he gazed down at the woman, Elias Tate said, "The damn legal technicalities. If we hadn't been held up—" He grimaced.

Within Rybys's body the fetus, now six months along, had been silent for a vast amount of time. What if the fetus dies? Herb Asher asked himself. The death of God . . . but not under circumstances anyone ever anticipated. And no one, except himself, Rybys and Elias Tate would ever know.

Can God die? he wondered. And with him my wife.

The marriage ceremony had been lucid and brief, a transaction by the deepspace authorities, with no religious or moral overtones. Both he and Rybys had been required to undergo extensive physical examinations, and, of course, her pregnancy had been discovered.

"You're the father?" the doctor asked him.

"Yes," Herb Asher said.

The doctor grinned and noted that on his chart.

"We felt we had to get married," Herb said.

"It's a good attitude." The doctor was elderly and well

groomed, and totally impersonal. "Are you aware that it's a boy?"

"Yes," he said. He certainly was.

"There is one thing I do not understand," the doctor said. "Was this impregnation natural? It wasn't artificial insemination, by any chance? Because the hymen is intact."

"Really," Herb Asher said.

"It's rare but it can happen. So technically your wife is still a virgin."

"Really," Herb Asher said.

The doctor said, "She is quite ill, you know. From the multiple sclerosis."

"I know," he answered stoically.

"There is no guarantee of a cure. You realize that. I think it's an excellent idea to return her to Earth, and I heartily approve of your going along with her. But it may be for nothing. M.S. is a peculiar ailment. The myelin sheath of the nerve fibers develops hard patches and this eventually results in permanent paralysis. We have finally isolated two causal factors, after decades of intensive effort. There is a microorganism, but, and this is a major factor, a form of allergy is involved. Much of the treatment involves transforming the immune system so that—" The doctor continued on, and Herb Asher listened as well as he could. He knew it all already; Rybys had told him several times, and had shown him texts that she had obtained from M.E.D. Like her, he had become an authority on the disease.

"Could I have some water?" Rybys murmured, lifting her head; her face was blotched and swollen, and Herb Asher could understand her only with difficulty.

A stewardess brought Rybys a paper cup of water; Elias and Herb lifted her to a sitting position and she took the cup in her hands. Her arms, her body, trembled.

"It won't be much longer," Herb Asher said.

"Christ," Rybys murmured. "I don't think I'm going to make it. Tell the stewardess I'm going to throw up again; make her bring back that bowl. Jesus." She sat up fully, her face stricken with pain.

The stewardess, bending down beside her, said, "We'll be firing the retrojets in two hours, so if you can just hold on—"

"Hold on?" Rybys said. "I can't even hold on to what I drank. Are you sure that Coke wasn't tainted or something? I think it made me worse. Don't you have any ginger ale? If I had some ginger ale maybe I could keep from—" She cursed with venom and rage. "Damn this," she said. "Damn all this. It isn't worth it!" She stared at Herb Asher and then Elias.

Yah, Herb Asher thought. Can't you do anything? It's sadistic to let her suffer this way.

Within his mind a voice spoke. He could not at first fathom what it meant; he heard the words but they seemed to make no sense. The voice said, "Take her to the Garden."

He thought, What Garden?

"Take her by the hand."

Herb Asher, reaching down, fumbling in the folds of the blanket, took his wife's hand.

"Thank you," Rybys said. Feebly, she squeezed his hand.

Now, as he sat leaning over her, he saw her eyes shine; he saw spaces beyond her eyes, and if he were looking into something empty, containing huge stretches of space. Where are you? he wondered. It is a universe in there, within your skull; it is a different universe from this: not a mirror reflection but another land. He saw stars, and clusters of stars; he saw nebulae and great clouds of gases that glowed darkly and yet still with a white light, not a ruddy light. He felt wind billow about him and he heard something rustle. Leaves or branches, he thought; I hear plants. The air felt warm. That amazed him. It seemed to be fresh air, not the stale, recirculated air of the spaceship.

The sound of birds, and, when he looked up, blue sky. He saw bamboo, and the rustling sound came from the wind blowing through the canes of bamboo. He saw a fence, and there were children. And yet at the same time he still held his wife's weak hand. Strange, he thought. The air so dry, as if it comes sweeping off the desert. He saw a boy with brown curly hair; the boy's hair reminded him of Rybys's hair before she had lost it, before, from the chemotherapy, it had fallen out and disappeared.

Where am I? he wondered. At a school?

Beside him fussy Mr. Plaudet told him pointless stories having to do with the school's financial needs, the school's problems—he wasn't interested in the school's problems; he was interested in his son. His son's brain damage; he wanted to know all about it.

"What I can't understand," Plaudet was saying, "is why they kept you in suspension for ten years for a spleen. For heaven's sake, a splenectomy is a normal and regular type of surgery, and there is frequently a splenolus that can be—"

"Which hemisphere of his brain is damaged?" Herb Asher interrupted.

"Mr. Tate has all the medical reports. But I'll go to our computer and ask for a printout. Manny seems a little afraid of you, but I suppose it's because he's never seen his father before."

"I'll stay out here with him," Herb said, "while you get me the printout. I want to know as much as possible about the injury."

"Herb," Rybys said.

Startled, he realized where he was; aboard the United Spaceways XR4 axial flight from Fomalhaut to the Sol System. In two hours the first Immigration party would board the ship and make their preliminary inspection.

"Herb," his wife whispered, "I just saw my son."

"A school," Herb Asher said, "where he's going to go."

"I don't think I'll live to be there," Rybys said. "I have a feeling . . . He was there and you were there, and a noisy little ratlike man who babbled on, but I wasn't anywhere around. I looked; I kept looking. This really is going to kill me but it won't kill my son. That's what he told me, remember? Yah told me I would live on through my son, so I guess I will die; I mean, this body will die, but they'll save him. Were you there when Yah said that? I don't remember. That was a garden we were in, wasn't it? Bamboo. I saw the wind blowing. The wind talked to me; it was like voices."

"Yes," he said.

"They used to go out in the desert for forty days and forty

nights. Elijah and then Jesus. Elias?" She looked around. "You ate locusts and wild honey and called on men to repent. You told King Ahab there would be no dew nor rain these years . . . thus says the Lord. According to my word." She shut her eyes.

She is really sick, Herb Asher said to himself. But I saw her son. Beautiful and wild and—something more. Timid. Very human, he thought; that was a human child. Maybe this is all in our minds. Maybe the Clems have occluded our perceptions so that we believe and see and experience but it is not real. I give up, he thought. I just don't know.

Something to do with time. He seems able to transform time. Now I am here in the ship but then I am in the Garden with the child and the other children, her child, years from now. What is the true time? he asked himself. Me here in the ship or back in my dome before I met Rybys or after she is dead and Emmanuel is in school? And I have been in cryonic suspension, for a matter of years. It has to do or had to do or will have to do with my spleen. Did they shoot me? he wondered. Rybys died from her illness but how did I die? And what became or will become of Elias?

Leaning toward him Elias said, "I want to talk to you." He motioned Herb Asher away from Rybys and away from the other passengers. "We are not to mention Yah. We will use the word 'Jehovah' from now on. It's a word coined in 1530; it's all right to say it. You understand the situation. Immigration will try to tap our minds with psychotronic listening devices, but Jehovah will cloud our minds and they will get little or nothing. But this is the part that is hard to say. Jehovah's power wanes from here on. The zone of Belial begins soon."

"OK." He nodded.

"You know all this."

"And a lot more." From what Elias had told him and from what Rybys had told him—and Jehovah had told him much, in his sleep, in vivid dreams. Jehovah had been teaching all of them; they would know what to do.

Elias said, "He is with us, and can address us from her womb. But there is always the possibility that very advanced electronic scanning devices, monitoring devices, might pick it up. He will converse with us sparingly." After a pause he added, "If at all."

"A strange idea," Herb Asher said. "I wonder what the authorities would think if their intelligence-gathering circuitry picked up the thoughts of God."

"Well," Elias said, "they wouldn't know what it was. I know the authorities of Earth; I have dealt with them for four thousand years, in situation after situation. Country after country. War after war. I was with Graf Egemont in the Dutch wars of independence, the Thirty Years War; I was present the day he was executed. I knew Beethoven . . . but perhaps 'knew' is not the word."

"You were Beethoven," Herb Asher said.

"Part of my spirit returned to Earth and to him," Elias said.

Vulgar and fiery, Herb thought. Passionately dedicated to the cause of human freedom. Walking hand-in-hand with his friend Goethe, the two men stirring the new life of the German Enlightenment. "Who else were you?" he said.

"Many people in history."

"Tom Paine?"

"We engineered the American Revolution," Elias said. "A group of us. We were the Friends of God at one time, and the Brothers of the Rosy Cross in 1615 . . . I was Jakob Boehme, but you wouldn't know of him. My spirit doesn't dwell alone in a man; it is not incarnation. It is part of my spirit returning to Earth to bond with a human whom God has selected. There are always such humans and I am there. Martin Buber was one such man, God rest his noble soul. That dear and gentle man. The Arabs, too, placed flowers on his grave. Even the Arabs loved him." Elias fell silent. "Some of the men I sent myself to were better men than I was. But I have the power to return. God granted it to me to—well, it was for Israel's sake. A hint of immortality for the dearest people of all. You know, Herb, God offered the Torah, it is said, to every people in the world, back in ancient times, before he offered it to the Jews, and every nation rejected it for one reason or another. The Torah said, 'Thou shalt not kill' and many could not live by that; they wanted religion to be separate from morality—they didn't want religion to hobble their desires. Finally God offered it to the Jews, who accepted it."

"The Torah is the Law?" Herb said.

"It is more than the Law. The word 'Law' is inadequate. Even though the New Testament of the Christians always uses the word 'Law' for Torah. Torah is the totality of divine disclosure by God; it is alive; it existed before creation. It is a mystic, almost cosmic, entity. The Torah is the Creator's instrument. With it he created the universe and for it he created the universe. It is the highest idea and the living soul of the world. Without it the world could not exist and would have no right to exist. I am quoting the great Hebrew poet Hayyim Nahman Bialik who lived from the latter part of the nineteenth century into the mid-twentieth century. You should read him sometime."

"Can you tell me anything else about the Torah?"

"Resh Lakish said, 'If one's intent is pure, the Torah for him becomes a life-giving medicine, purifying him to life. But if one's intent is not pure, it becomes a death-giving drug, purifying him to death.' "

The two men remained silent for a time.

"I will tell you something more," Elias said. "A man came to the great Rabbi Hillel—he lived in the first century, C.E.—and said, 'I will become a proselyte on the condition that you teach me the entire Torah while I stand on one foot.' Hillel said, 'Whatever is hateful to you, do not do it to your neighbor. That is the entire Torah. The rest is commentary; go and learn it.' " He smiled at Herb Asher.

"Is the injunction actually in the Torah?" Herb Asher said. "The first five books of the Bible?"

"Yes. Leviticus nineteen, eighteen. God says, 'You shall love your neighbor as a man like yourself.' You did not know that, did you? Almost two thousand years before Jesus."

"Then the Golden Rule derives from Judaism," Herb said.

"Yes, it does, and early Judaism. The Rule was presented to man by God Himself."

"I have a lot to learn," Herb said.

"Read," Elias said. " *'Cape, lege,'* the two words Augustine heard. Latin for 'Take, read.' You do that, Herb. Take the book and read it. It is there for you. *It is alive.*"

As their journey continued, Elias disclosed to him further intriguing aspects of the Torah, qualities regarding the Torah that few men knew.

"I tell you these matters," Elias said, "because I trust you. Be careful whom you relate them to."

Four ways existed by which to read the Torah, the fourth being a study of its hidden, innermost side. When God said, "Let there be light," he meant the mystery that shone in the Torah. This was the concealed primordial light of Creation itself, it being of such nobility that it could not be debased by the use of mortals; so God wrapped it up within the heart of the Torah. This was an inexhaustible light, related to the divine sparks which the Gnostics had believed in, the fragments of the Godhead which were now scattered throughout Creation, enclosed—unfortunately—in material shells, that of physical bodies.

Most interesting of all, some Medieval Jewish mystics held the view that there had been 600,000 Jews who went out of Egypt and received the Torah at Mount Sinai. Reincarnated at each succeeding generation, these 600,000 souls continually live. Each soul or spark is related to the Torah in a different way; thus, 600,000 separate, unique meanings of the Torah exist. The idea is as follows: that for each of these 600,000 persons the Torah is different, and each person has his own specific letter in the Torah, to which his own soul is attached. So in a sense 600,000 Torahs exist.

Also, three aeons or epochs in time exist, the first in order being an age of grace, the second or current one being of severe justice and limitation, and the next, yet to come, being of mercy. A different Torah exists for each of the three ages. And yet there is only one Torah. A primal or matrix Torah exists in which there is no punctuation nor any spaces between the words; in fact all the letters are jumbled together. In each of the three ages the letters form themselves into alternative words, as events unfold.

The current age, that of severe justice and limitation, Elias explained, is marred by the fact that in its Torah one of the letters was defective, the consonant *shin*. This letter was always written with three prongs but it should have had four. Thus the Torah produced for this age was defective. Another view held by Medieval Jewish mystics was that a letter is actually missing in our alphabet. Because of this our Torah contains negative laws as well as positive. In the next aeon the missing or invisible letter will be restored, and every negative prohibition in the Torah will disappear. Hence this next aeon or, as it is called in Hebrew, the next *shemittah,* will lack restrictions imposed on humans; freedom will replace severe justice and limitation.

Out of this notion comes the idea (Elias said) that there are invisible portions of the Torah—invisible to us now, but to be visible in the Messianic Age that is to come. The cosmic cycle will bring this age inevitably: it will be the next *shemittah,* very much like the first; the Torah will again rearrange itself out of its jumbled matrix.

Herb Asher thought, It sounds like a computer. The universe is programmed—and then more accurately reprogrammed. Fantastic.

Two hours later an official government ship clamped itself to their ship, and, after a time, Immigration agents began to move among them, beginning their inspection. And their interrogation.

Filled with fear, Herb Asher held Rybys against him, and he sat as close to Elias as possible, obtaining strength from the older man. "Tell me, Elias," Herb said quietly, "the most beautiful thing you know about God." His heart pounded harshly within him and he could scarcely breathe.

Elias said, "All right. 'Rabbi Judah said, quoting Rav:

> The day consists of twelve hours. During the first three hours, the Holy One (God), praised be He, is engaged in the study of Torah. During the second three He sits in judgment over His entire world. When He realizes that the world is deserving of destruction, He rises from the Throne of Justice, to sit on the Throne of Mercy. During the third group of three hours, He

provides sustenance for the entire world, from huge beasts to lice. During the fourth, He sports with the Leviathan, as it is written, "Leviathan, which you did form to sport with" (Ps. 104:26) . . . During the fourth group of three hours (according to others) He teaches schoolchildren.' "

"Thank you," Herb Asher said. Three Immigration agents were moving toward them, now, their uniforms bright, shiny; and they carried weapons.

Elias said, "Even God consults the Torah as the formula and blueprint of the universe." An Immigration agent held out his hand for Elias's identification; the old man passed the packet of documents to him. "And even God cannot act contrary to it."

"You are Elias Tate," the senior Immigration agent said, examining the documents. "What is your purpose in returning to the Sol System?"

"This woman is very ill," Elias said. "She is entering the naval hospital at—"

"I asked you your purpose, not hers." He gazed down at Herb Asher. "Who are you?"

"I'm her husband," Herb said. He handed over his identification and permits and documentation.

"She is certified as not contagious?" the senior Immigration agent said.

"It's multiple sclerosis," Herb said, "which is not—"

"I didn't ask you what she has; I asked you if it is contagious."

"I'm telling you," he said. "I'm answering your question."

"Get up."

He stood.

"Come with me." The senior Immigration agent motioned Herb Asher to follow him up the aisle. Elias started to follow but the agent shoved him back, bodily. "Not you."

Following the Immigration agent, Herb Asher made his way step by step up the aisle to the rear of the ship. None of the other passengers was standing; he alone had been singled out.

In a small compartment marked CREW ONLY the senior Immigration agent faced Herb Asher, staring at him silently; the man's eyes bulged as if he were unable to speak, as if what he had to say could not be said. Time passed. What the hell is he doing? Herb Asher asked himself. Silence. The raging stare continued.

"Okay," the Immigration agent said. "I give up. What *is* your purpose in returning to Earth?"

"I told you."

"Is she really sick?"

"Very. She's dying."

"Then she's too sick to travel. It makes no sense."

"Only on Earth are there facilities where—"

"You are under Terran law *now,*" the Immigration agent said. "Do you want to serve time for giving false information to a federal officer? I'm sending you back to Fomalhaut. The three of you. I don't have any more time. Go back to where you were sitting and remain there until you're told what to do."

A voice, a neutral, dispassionate voice, neither male nor female, a kind of perfect intelligence, spoke inside Herb Asher's head. "At Bethesda they want to study her disease."

He started visibly. The agent regarded him.

"At Bethesda," he said, "they want to study her disease."

"Research?"

"It's a microorganism."

"You said it isn't contagious."

The neutral voice said, "Not at this stage."

"Not at this stage," he said aloud.

"Are they afraid of plague?" the Immigration agent said abruptly.

Herb Asher nodded.

"Go back to your seat." The agent, irritably, waved him away. "This is out of my jurisdiction. You have a pink form, form 368? Properly filled out and signed by a doctor?"

"Yes." It was true.

"Are either you or the older man with you infected?"

The voice inside his head said, "Only Bethesda can determine that." He had, suddenly, a vivid inner glimpse of the person whose voice he heard; he saw in his own mind a visage, female, a placid but strong face. A metal mask had been pushed back from that visage, exposing wise, impassive eyes; a beautiful classic face, like Athena; he was staggered with astonishment. This could not be Yahweh. This was a woman. But like no woman he had ever seen. He did not know her. He did not understand who this was. Her voice was not Yah's voice, and this could not be Yah's visage. He did not know what to make of it. He was perplexed beyond the telling of it. Who had taken on the task of advising him?

"Only Bethesda can determine that," he managed to say.

The Immigration agent paused uncertainly. His exterior harshness had evaporated.

The female voice whispered again, and this time, in his mind, he saw her lips move. "Time is of the essence."

"Time is of the essence," Herb Asher said. His voice grated in his own ears.

"Shouldn't you be quarantined? You probably shouldn't be with other people. Those other passengers— We should have you on a special ship. It can be arranged. It might be better . . . we could get her there faster."

"OK," he said. Reasonably.

"I'll put in a call," the Immigration agent said. "What's the name of this microorganism? It's a virus?"

"The nerve sheathing—"

"Never mind. Go back to your seat. Look." The Immigration agent followed after him. "I don't know whose idea it was to send you on a commercial carrier, but I'm getting you off of it right now. There are strict statutes that haven't been observed, here. Bethesda is expecting you? Do you want me to put in a call ahead, or is that all taken care of?"

"She is registered with them already." This was so. The arrangements had been made.

"This is really nuts," the Immigration agent said, "to put you on a public carrier. They should have known better back at Fomalhaut."

"CY30-CY30B," Herb Asher said.

"Whatever. I don't want any part of this. A mistake of this kind—" The Immigration agent cursed. "Some dumb fool back at Fomalhaut probably figured it'd save the taxpayers a few bucks— Take your seat and I'll see that you're notified when your ship is ready. It should— Christ."

Herb Asher, shaking, returned to his seat.

Elias eyed him. Rybys lay with her eyes shut; she was oblivious to what was happening.

"Let me ask you a question," Herb said to Elias. "Have you ever tasted Laphroaig Scotch?"

"No," Elias said, puzzled.

"It is the finest of all Scotches," Herb said. "Ten years old, very expensive. The distillery opened in 1815. They use traditional copper stills. It requires two distillations—"

"What went on in there?" Elias said.

"Just let me finish. Laphroaig is Gaelic for 'the beautiful hollow by the broad bay.' It's distilled on Islay in the Western Isles of Scotland. Malted barley—they dry it in a kiln over a peat fire, a genuine peat fire. It's the only Scotch made that way now. The peat can only be found on the island of Islay. Maturation takes place in oak casks. It's incredible Scotch. It's the finest liquor in the world. It's—" He broke off.

An Immigration agent came over to them. "Your ship is here, Mr. Asher. Come with me. Can your wife walk? You want some help?"

"Already?" He was dumbfounded. And then he realized that the ship had been there all this time. Immigration was routinely prepared to deal with emergency situations. Especially of this kind. Or rather, what they supposed this situation to be.

"Who wears a metal mask?" Herb said to Elias as he drew the blanket from Rybys. "Pushed back up over her hair. And has a straight nose, a very strong nose—well, let it go. Give me a hand." Together, he and Elias got Rybys to her feet. The Immigration agent watched sympathetically.

"I don't know," Elias said.

"There is someone else," Herb said as they moved Rybys step by step up the aisle.

"I'm going to throw up," Rybys said weakly.

"Just hang on," Herb Asher said. "We're almost there."

Big Noodle notified Cardinal Fulton Statler Harms and the Procurator Maximus, and then, to all the heads of states in the world it printed out the following mystifying statement:

> ON THE STANDARD OF FIFTY THEY SHALL WRITE: FINISHED IS THE STAND OF THE FROWARD THROUGH THE MIGHTY ACTS OF GOD, TOGETHER WITH THE NAMES OF THE COMMANDERS OF THE FIFTY AND OF ITS TENS. WHEN THEY GO OUT TO BATTLE, THEY SHALL WRITE UPON THEIR WPSOX TO FORM A COMPLETE FRONT. THE LINE IS TO CONSIST OF A THOUSAND MEN MEN MEN MEN MEN EACH FRONT LINE IS TO BE SEVEN SEVEN SEVEN DEEP, ONE MAN STANDING BEHIND THE OTHER STOP REPEAT ALL OF THEM ARE TO HOLD SHIELDS OF POLISHED BRONZE REPEAT BRONZE RESEMBLING MIRRORS THESE SHIELDS

The statement ended there. Technicians swarmed over the A.I. system in a matter of minutes.

Their verdict: the A.I. system would have to be shut down for a time. Something basic had gone wrong with it. The last coherent information it had processed was the message that the pregnant woman Rybys Rommey-Asher, her husband, Herbert Asher, and their companion, Elias Tate, had been cleared by Immigration at Ring III and had been transferred from a commercial axial carrier to a government-owned speedship, whose destination was Washington, D.C.

Standing at his no longer pulsing terminal, Cardinal Harms thought, A mistake has been made. Immigration was supposed to intercept them, not facilitate their flight. It doesn't make any sense. And now we've lost our primary data-processing entity, on which we are totally dependent.

He rang up the procurator maximus, and was told by an underling that the procurator had gone to bed.

The son of a bitch, Harms said to himself. The idiot. We have one more station at which to intercept them: Immigration proper, at Washington, D.C. And if they got this far— My good God, he thought. The monster is using its paranormal powers!

Once more he called the procurator maximus. "Is Galina available?" he said, but he knew it was hopeless. Bulkowsky had given up. Going to bed at this point amounted to that.

"Mrs. Bulkowsky?" the S.L. official said, incredulous. "Of course not."

"Your general staff? One of your marshals?"

"The procurator will return your call," the S.L. functionary informed him; obviously they had orders from Bulkowsky not to disturb him.

Christ! Harms said to himself as he slammed down the phone mechanism. The screen faded.

Something has gone wrong, Harms realized. They should not have gotten this far *and Big Noodle knew it*. The A.I. system had literally gone insane. That was not a technical breakdown, he realized; that was a psychotic fugue. Big Noodle understood something but could not communicate it. Or had the A.I. system in fact communicated it? What, Harms asked himself, was that gibberish?

He contacted the highest order of computers remaining, the one at Cal Tech. After transmitting the puzzling material to it he gave instructions that the material be identified.

The Cal Tech computer identified it five minutes later.

QUMRAN SCROLL "THE WAR OF THE SONS OF LIGHT AND THE SONS OF DARKNESS." SOURCE: JEWISH ASCETIC SECT ESSENES

Strange, Harms thought. He knew of the Essenes. Many theologians had speculated that Jesus was an Essene, and certainly there was evidence that John the Baptist was an Essene. The sect had anticipated an early end to the world, with the Battle of Armageddon taking place within the first century, C.E. The sect had shown strong Zoroastrian influences.

He reflected, John the Baptist. Stipulated by Christ to have been Elijah returned, as promised by Jehovah in Malachi:

> Look, I will send you the prophet Elijah before the great and terrible day of the Lord comes. He will reconcile fathers to sons and sons to fathers, lest I come and put the land under a ban to destroy it.

The final verse of the Old Testament; there the Old Testament ended and the New Testament began.

Armageddon, he pondered. The final battle between the Sons of Darkness and the Sons of Light. Between Jehovah and—what had the Essenes called the evil power? Belial. That was it. That was their term for Satan. Belial would lead the Sons of Darkness; Jehovah would lead the Sons of Light. This would be the seventh battle.

There will be six battles, three of which the Sons of Light will win and three of which the Sons of Darkness will win. Leaving Belial in power. But then Jehovah himself takes command in what amounts to a tie breaker.

The monster in her womb is Belial, Cardinal Harms realized. He has returned to overthrow us. To overthrow Jehovah, whom we serve.

The Divine Power itself is now in jeopardy, he declared; he felt great wrath.

It seemed to the cardinal, at this point, that meditation and prayer were called for. And a strategy by which the invaders would be destroyed when they reached Washington, D.C.

If only Big Noodle had not broken down!

Glumly, he made his way to his private chapel.

9

The procurator said, "We will wreck their ship. There is no particular problem. An accident will take place; the three of them —four, if you include the fetus—will be killed." To him it seemed simple.

At his end of the line Cardinal Harms said, "They will evade it. Don't ask me how." His gloom had not departed.

"You have jurisdiction in Washington, D.C.," the procurator said. "Order their ship destroyed; *order it now.*"

"Now" was eight hours later. Eight precious hours during which the procurator had peacefully slept. Cardinal Harms glared at his co-ruler. Or, he thought suddenly, had Bulkowsky been struggling to find a solution? Perhaps he had not slept at all. This solution sounded like Galina's. They had conferred, the two of them; they worked as a team.

"What a stale solution," he said. "Your typical answer, to dispatch a warhead."

"Mrs. Bulkowsky likes it," the procurator said.

"I dare say. The two of you sat up all night working *that* out?"

"We did not sit up. I slept soundly, although Galina had strange dreams. There's one she told me that—well, I think it worth relating. Do you want to hear Galina's dream? I'd like your opinion about it, since it seems to have religious overtones."

"Shoot," Harms said.

"A huge white fish lies in the ocean. Near the surface, as a whale does. It is a friendly fish. It swims toward us; I mean, toward Galina. There is a series of canals with locks. The great white fish makes its way into the canal system with extreme difficulty. Finally it is caught, away from the ocean, near the people watching. It has done this on purpose; it wants to offer itself to the people as food. A metal saw is produced, one of those two-man band saws that lumberjacks use to cut down trees. Galina said that the teeth on the saw were dreadful. People began to saw slices of flesh from the great fish, who is still alive. They saw slice after slice of the living flesh of the great white fish that is so friendly. In the dream Galina thinks, 'This is wrong. We are injuring the fish too much.' " Bulkowsky paused. "Well? What do you say?"

"The fish is Christ," Cardinal Harms said, "who offers his flesh to man so that man may have eternal life."

"That's all very well, but it was unfair to the fish. She said it was a wrong thing to do. Even though the fish offered itself. Its pain was too much. Oh yes; in the dream she thought, 'We must find another kind of food, which doesn't cause the great fish suffering.' And then there were some blurred episodes where she was looking in a refrigerator; she saw a pitcher of water, a pitcher wrapped in straw or reeds or something . . . and a cube of pink food like a cube of butter. Words were written on the wrapper but she couldn't read them. The refrigerator was the common property of some kind of small settlement of people, off in a remote area. What happened, the way it worked, was that this pitcher of water and this pink cube belonged to the whole colony and you only ate the food and drank the water when you realized you were approaching your moment of death."

"What did drinking the water—"

"Then you came back later. Reborn."

Harms said, "That is the host under the two species. The consecrated wine and wafer. The blood and body of our Lord. The food of eternal life. 'This is my body. Take—' "

"The settlement seemed to exist at another time entirely. A long time ago. As in antiquity."

"Interesting," Harms said, "but we still have our problem to face, what to do about the monster baby."

"As I said," the procurator said, "we will arrange an accident. Their ship won't reach Washington, D.C. When, precisely, does it arrive? How much time do we have?"

"Just a moment." Harms pressed keys on the board of a small computer terminal. "Christ!" he said.

"What's the matter? It only takes seconds to dispatch a small missile. You have them in that area."

Harms said, "Their ship has landed. While you slept. They are already being processed by Immigration at Washington, D.C."

"It is normal to sleep," the procurator said.

"The monster made you sleep."

"I've been sleeping all my life!" Angrily, the procurator added, "I am here at this resort for rest; my health is bad."

"I wonder," Harms said.

"Notify Immigration, at once, to hold them. Do it *now*."

Harms rang off, and contacted Immigration. I will take that woman, that Rybys Rommey-Asher, and break her neck, he said to himself. I will chop her into little pieces, and her fetus along with her. I will chop up all of them and feed them to the animals at the zoo.

Surprised, he asked himself; Did I think that? The ferocity of his ratiocination amazed him. I really hate them, he realized. I am furious. I am furious with Bulkowsky for logging eight full hours of sleep in the midst of this crisis; if I had the power I would chop him up, too.

When he had the director of Washington, D.C. Immigration on the line he asked first of all if the woman Rybys Rommey-Asher, her husband and Elias Tate were still there.

"I'll check, your Eminence," the bureau chief said. A pause, a very long pause. Harms counted off the seconds, cursing and praying by turns. Then the director returned. "We are still processing them."

"Hold them. Don't let them go for any reason whatsoever. The woman is pregnant. Inform her—do you know who I'm talking about? Rybys Rommey-Asher—inform her that there will be a mandatory abortion of the fetus. Have your people make up any excuse they want."

"Do you actually want an abortion performed on her? Or is this a pretext—"

"I want abortion induced within the next hour," Harms said. "A saline abortion. I want the fetus killed. I'm going to take you into our confidence. I have been conferring with the procurator maximus; this is global policy. The fetus is a freak. A radiation sport. Possibly even the monster offspring of interspecies symbiosis. Do you understand?"

"Oh," the Immigration director said. "Interspecies symbiosis. Yes. We'll kill it with localized heat. Inject radioactive dye directly into it through the abdominal wall. I'll tell one of our doctors—"

"Tell him to abort her or tell him to kill it inside her," Harms said, "but kill it and kill it now."

"I'll need a signature," the Immigration director said. "I can't do this without authorization."

"Transmit the forms." He sighed.

From his terminal pages oozed; he took hold of them, found the lines where his signature was required, signed and fed the pages back into the fone terminal.

As he sat in the Immigration lounge with Rybys, Herb Asher wondered where Elias Tate had gone. Elias had excused himself to go to the men's room, but he had not returned.

"When can I lie down?" Rybys murmured.

"Soon," he said. "They're putting us right through." He did not amplify because undoubtedly the lounge was bugged.

"Where's Elias?" she said.

"He'll be back."

An Immigration official, not in uniform but wearing a badge, approached them. "Where is the third member of your party?" He consulted his clipboard. "Elias Tate."

"In the men's room," Herb Asher said. "Could you please process this woman? You can see how sick she is."

"We want a medical examination made on her," the Immigration official said dispassionately. "We require a medical determination before we can put you through."

"It's been done already! By her own doctor originally and then by—"

"This is standard procedure," the official said.

"That doesn't matter," Herb Asher said. "It's cruel and it's useless."

"The doctor will be with you shortly," the official said, "and while she's being examined by him you will be interrogated. To save you time. We won't interrogate her, at least not very extensively. I'm aware of her grave medical condition."

"My God," Herb said, "you can *see* it!"

The official departed, but returned almost at once, his face grim. "Tate isn't in the men's room."

"Then I don't know where he is."

"They may have processed him. Put him through." The official hurried off, speaking into a hand-held intercom unit.

I guess Elias got away, Herb Asher thought.

"Come in here," a voice said. It was a woman doctor, in a white smock. Young, wearing glasses, her hair tied back in a bun, she briskly escorted Herb Asher and his wife down a short sterile-looking and sterile-smelling corridor into an examination room. "Lie down, Mrs. Asher," the doctor said, helping Rybys to an examination table.

"Rommey-Asher," Rybys said as she got up painfully onto the table. "Can you give me an I-V anti-emetic? And soon? I mean soon. I mean now."

"In view of your wife's illness," the doctor said to Herb Asher as she seated herself at her desk, "why wasn't her pregnancy terminated?"

"We've been through all this," he said savagely.

"We may still require her to abort. We do not wish a deformed infant born; it's against public policy."

Staring at the doctor in fear, Herb said, "But she's six months into her pregnancy!"

"We have it down as five months," the doctor said. "Well within the legal period."

"You can't do it without her consent," Herb said; his fear became wild.

"The decision," the doctor told him, "is no longer yours to make, now that you have returned to Earth. A medical board will study the matter."

It was obvious to Herb Asher that there would be a mandatory abortion. He knew what the board would decide—had decided.

In the corner of the room a piped-in music source gave forth the odious background noise of soupy strings. The same sound, he realized, that he had heard off and on at his dome. But now the music changed, and he realized that a popular number of the Fox's was coming up. As the doctor sat filling out medical forms the Fox's voice could distantly be heard. It gave him comfort.

Come again!
Sweet love doth now invite
Thy graces, that refrain
To do me due delight.

The lady doctor's lips moved reflexively in synchronization with the Fox's familiar Dowland song.

All at once Herb Asher became aware that the voice from the speaker only resembled the Fox's. The voice was no longer singing; it was speaking.

The faint voice said distinctly:

There will be no abortion. There will be a birth.

At her desk the doctor seemed unaware of the transition. Yah has cooked the audio signal, Herb Asher realized. As he watched he saw the doctor pause, pen lifted from the page before her.

Subliminal, he said to himself as he watched the doctor hesitate. The woman still imagines she is hearing a familiar song. Familiar lyrics. She is in a kind of spell. As if hypnotized.

The song resumed.

"We can't abort her legally if she's six months along," the doctor said hesitantly. "Mr. Asher, there must be an error. We have her down as five. Five months into her pregnancy. But if you say six, then—"

"Examine her if you want," Herb Asher said. "It's at least six. Make your own determination."

"I—" The doctor rubbed her forehead, wincing; she shut her eyes and grimaced, as in pain. "I see no reason to—" She broke off, as if unable to remember what she intended to say. "I see no reason," she resumed after a moment, "to dispute this." She pressed a button on her desk intercom.

The door opened and a uniformed Immigration official stood there. A moment later he was joined by a uniformed Customs agent.

"The matter is settled," the doctor said to the Immigration official. "We can't force her to abort; she's too far along."

The Immigration official gazed down at her fixedly.

"It's the law," the doctor said.

"Mr. Asher," the Customs agent said, "let me ask you something. In your wife's declaration prepared for Customs clearance she lists two phylacteries. What is a phylactery?"

"I don't know," Herb Asher said.

"Aren't you Jewish?" the Customs agent said. "Every Jew knows what a phylactery is. Your wife, then, is Jewish and you are not?"

"Well," Herb Asher said, "she is C.I.C. but—" He paused. He sensed himself moving step by step into a trap. It was patently impossible that a husband would not know his wife's religion. They are getting into an area I do not want to discuss, he said to himself. "I'm a Christian," he said, then. "Although I was raised Scientific Legate. I belonged to the Party's Youth Corps. But now—"

"But Mrs. Asher is Jewish. Hence the phylacteries. You've never seen her put them on? One goes on the head; one goes on the left arm. They're small square leathern boxes containing sections of Hebrew scripture. It strikes me as odd that you don't know anything about this. How long have you known each other?"

"A long time," Herb Asher said.

"Is she really your wife?" the Immigration official said. "If she is six months along in her pregnancy—" He consulted with some of the documents lying on the doctor's desk. "She was pregnant when you married her. Are you the father of the child?"

"Of course," he said.

"What blood type are you? Well, I have it here." The Immigration official began going through the filled-out legal and medical forms. "It's somewhere . . ."

The fone on the desk rang; the lady doctor picked it up and identified herself. "For you." She handed the receiver to the Immigration official.

The Immigration official, raptly attentive, listened in silence; then, putting his hand over the audio sender, he said irritably to Herb Asher, "The blood type checks out. You two are cleared. But we want to talk to Tate, the older man who—" He broke off and again listened to his fone.

"You can call a cab from the payfone in the lounge," the Customs agent said.

"We're free to go?" Herb Asher said.

The Customs agent nodded.

"Something is wrong," the doctor said; again she had removed her glasses and sat rubbing her eyes.

"There's this other matter," the Customs agent said to her, and bent down to present her with a stack of documents.

"Do you know where Tate is?" the Immigration official called after Herb Asher as he and Rybys made their way from the examination room.

"No, I don't," Herb said, and found himself in the corridor; supporting Rybys he walked step by step back down the corridor to the lounge. "Sit down," he said to her, depositing her in a heap on a couch. Several waiting people gazed at them dully. "I'll fone. I'll be right back. Do you have any change? I need a five-dollar piece."

"Christ," Rybys murmured. "No, I don't have."

"We got through," he said to her in a low voice.

"OK!" she said angrily.

"I'll fone for a cab." Going through his pockets, searching for a five-dollar piece, he felt elated. Yah had intervened, distantly and feebly, but it had been enough.

Ten minutes later they and their luggage were aboard a Yellow flycab, rising up from the Washington, D.C. spaceport, heading in the direction of Bethesda–Chevy Chase.

"Where the hell is Elias?" Rybys managed to say.

"He drew their attention," Herb said. "He diverted them. Away from us."

"Great," she said. "So now he could be anywhere."

All at once a large commercial flycar came hurtling toward them at reckless speed.

The robot driver of the cab cried out in dismay. And then the massive flycar sideswiped them; it happened in an instant. Violent waves of concussion hurled the cab in a downward spiral; Herb Asher clutched his wife against him—buildings bloomed into hugeness, and he knew, he knew absolutely and utterly, what had happened. The bastards, he thought in pain; he hurt physically; he ached from the realization. Warning beepers in the cab had gone off—"

Yah's protection wasn't enough, he realized as the cab spun lower and lower like a falling, withered leaf.

It's too weak. Too weak here.

The cab struck the edge of a high-rise building.

Darkness came and Herb Asher knew no more.

He lay in a hospital bed, wired up and tubed up to countless devices like a cyborg entity.

"Mr. Asher?" a voice was saying, a male voice. "Mr. Asher, can you hear me?"

He tried to nod but could not.

"You have suffered serious internal damage," the male voice said. "I am Dr. Pope. You've been unconscious for five days. Surgery was performed on you but your ruptured spleen had to be removed. That's only a part of it. You are going to be put into cryonic suspension until replacement organs— Can you hear me?"

"Yes," he said.

"—Until replacement organs, available from donors, can be procured. The waiting list isn't very long; you should be in suspension for only a few weeks. How long, specifically—"

"My wife."

"Your wife is dead. She lost brain function for too long a time. We had to rule out cryonic suspension for her. It wouldn't have been of any use."

"The baby."

"The fetus is alive," Dr. Pope said. "Your wife's uncle, Mr. Tate, has arrived and has taken legal responsibility. We've removed the fetus from her body and placed it in a synthowomb. According to all our tests it was not damaged by the trauma, which is something of a miracle."

Grimly, Herb Asher thought, Exactly.

"Your wife asked that he be called Emmanuel," Dr. Pope said.

"I know."

As he lost consciousness Herb Asher said to himself, Yah's plans have not been completely wrecked. Yah has not been defeated entirely. There is still hope.

But not very much.

"Belial," he whispered.

"Pardon me?" Dr. Pope leaned close to hear. "Belial? Is that someone you want us to contact? Someone who should know?"

Herb Asher said, "He knows."

The chief prelate of the Christian-Islamic Church said to the procurator maximus of the Scientific Legate, "Something went wrong. They got past Immigration."

"Where did they go? They have to have gone somewhere."

"Elias Tate disappeared even before the Customs inspection. We have no idea where he is. As for the Ashers—" The cardinal hesitated. "They were last seen leaving in a cab. I'm sorry."

Bulkowsky said, "We will find them."

"With God's help," the cardinal said, and crossed himself. Bulkowsky, seeing that, did likewise.

"The power of evil," Bulkowsky said.

"Yes," the cardinal said. "That is what we are up against."

"But it loses in the end."

"Yes, absolutely. I am going to the chapel, now. To pray. I advise you to do the same."

Raising an eyebrow, Bulkowsky regarded him. His expression could not be read; it was intricate.

10

When Herb Asher awoke he was told perplexing facts. He had spent—not weeks—but years in cryonic suspension. The doctors could not explain why it had taken so long to obtain replacement organs. Circumstances, they told him, beyond our control. Procedural problems.

He said, "What about Emmanuel?"

Dr. Pope, who looked older and grayer and more distinguished than before, said, "Someone broke into the hospital and removed your son from the synthowomb."

"When?"

"Almost at once. The fetus was in the synthowomb for only a day, according to our records."

"Do you know who did it?"

"According to our video tapes—we monitor our synthowombs constantly—it was an elderly bearded man." After a pause Dr. Pope added, "Deranged in appearance. You must face the very high probability factor that your son is dead, has in fact been dead for ten years, either from natural causes, which is to say from being taken out of his synthowomb . . . or due to the actions of the elderly bearded man. Either deliberate or accidental. The police could not locate either of them. I'm sorry."

Elias Tate, Herb said to himself. Spiriting Emmanuel away, to safety. He shut his eyes and felt overwhelming gratitude.

"How do you feel?" Dr. Pope inquired.

"I dreamed. I didn't know that people in cryonic suspension were conscious."

"You weren't."

"I dreamed again and again about my wife." He felt bitter grief hover over him and then descend on him, filling him; the grief was too much. "Always I found myself back there with her. When we met, before we met. The trip to Earth. Little things. Dishes of spoiled food . . . she was sloppy."

"But you do have your son."

"Yes," he said. He wondered how he would be able to find Elias and Emmanuel. They will have to find me, he realized.

For a month he remained at the hospital, undergoing remedial therapy to build up his strength, and then, on a cool morning in mid-March, the hospital discharged him. Suitcase in hand he walked down the front steps, shaky and afraid but happy to be free. Every day during his therapy he had expected the authorities to come swooping down on him. They did not. He wondered why.

As he stood with a throng of people trying to flag down a flycar Yellow cab he noticed a blind beggar standing off to one side, an ancient, white-haired, very large man wearing soiled clothing; the old man held a cup.

"Elias," Herb Asher said.

Going over to him he regarded his old friend. Neither of them spoke for a time and then Elias Tate said, "Hello, Herbert."

"Rybys told me you often take the form of a beggar," Herb Asher said. He reached out to put his arms around the old man, but Elias shook his head.

"It is Passover," Elias said. "And I am here. The power of my spirit is too great; you should not touch me. It is all my spirit, now, at this moment."

"You are not a man," Herb Asher said, awed.

"I am many men," Elias said. "It's good to see you again. Emmanuel said you would be released today."

"The boy is all right?"

"He is beautiful."

"I saw him," Herb Asher said. "Once, a while ago. In a vision that—" He paused. "Jehovah sent to me. To help me."

"Did you dream?" Elias asked.

"About Rybys. And about you as well. About everything that happened. I lived it over and over again."

"But now you are alive again," Elias said. "Welcome back, Herbert Asher. We have much to do."

"Do we have a chance? Do we have any real chance?"

"The boy is ten years old," Elias said. "He has confused their wits, scrambled up their thinking. He has made them forget. But—" Elias was silent a moment. "He, too, has forgotten. You will see. A few years ago he began to remember; he heard a song and some of his memories came back. Enough, perhaps, or maybe not enough. You may bring back more. He programmed himself, originally, before the accident."

With extreme difficulty Herb Asher said, "He was injured, then? In the accident?"

Elias nodded. Somberly.

"Brain damage," Herb Asher said; he saw the expression on his friend's face.

Again the old man nodded, the elderly beggar with the cup. The immortal Elijah, here at Passover. As always. The eternal, helping friend of man. Tattered and shabby, and very wise.

Zina said, "Your father is coming, isn't he?"

Together they sat on a bench in Rock Creek Park, near the frozen-over water. Trees shaded them with bare, stark branches. The air had turned cold, and both children wore heavy clothing. But the sky overhead was clear. Emmanuel gazed up for a time.

"What does your slate say?" Zina asked.

"I don't have to consult my slate."

"He isn't your father."

Emmanuel said, "He's a good person. It's not his fault that my mother died. I'll be happy to see him once more. I've missed him." He thought, It's been a long time. According to the scale by which they reckon here in the Lower Realm.

What a tragic realm this is, he reflected. Those down here are prisoners, and the ultimate tragedy is that they don't know it; they think they are free because they have never been free, and do not understand what it means. *This is a prison,* and few men have guessed. But I know, he said to himself. Because that is why I am here. To burst the walls, to tear down the metal gates, to break each chain. Thou shalt not muzzle the ox as he treadeth out the corn, he thought, remembering the Torah. You will not imprison a free creature; you will not bind it. Thus says the Lord your God. Thus I say.

They do not know whom they serve. This is the heart of their misfortune: service in error, to a wrong thing. They are poisoned as if with metal, he thought. Metal confining them and metal in their blood; this is a metal world. Driven by cogs, a machine that grinds along, dealing out suffering and death . . . They are so accustomed to death, he realized, as if death, too, were natural. How long it has been since they knew the Garden. The place of resting animals and flowers. When can I find for them that place again?

There are two realities, he said to himself. The Black Iron Prison, which is called the Cave of Treasures, in which they now live, and the Palm Tree Garden with its enormous spaces, its light, where they originally dwelt. Now they are literally blind, he thought. Literally unable to see more than a short distance; far-away objects are invisible to them now. Once in a while one of them guesses that formerly they had faculties now gone; once in a while one of them discerns the truth, that they are not now what they were and not now where they were. But they forget again, exactly as I forgot. And I still forget somewhat, he realized. I still have only a partial vision. I am occluded, too.

But I will not be, soon.

"You want a Pepsi?" Zina said.

"It's too cold. I just want to sit."

"Don't be unhappy." She put her mittened hand on his arm. "Be joyful."

Emmanuel said, "I'm tired. I'll be okay. There's a lot that has to be done. I'm sorry. It weighs on me."

"You're not afraid, are you?"

"Not any more," Emmanuel said.

"You are sad."

He nodded.

Zina said, "You'll feel better when you see Mr. Asher again."

"I see him now," Emmanuel said.

"Very good," she said, pleased. "And even without your slate."

"I use it less and less," he said, "because the knowledge is progressively more and more in me. As you know. And you know why."

To that, Zina said nothing.

"We are close, you and I," Emmanuel said. "I have always loved you the most. I always will. You are going to stay on with me and advise me, aren't you?" He knew the answer; he knew that she would. She had been with him from the beginning—as she said, his darling and delight. And her delight, as Scripture said, was in mankind. So, through her, he himself loved mankind; it was his delight as well.

"We could get something hot to drink," Zina said.

He murmured, "I just want to sit." I shall sit here until it is time to go to meet Herb Asher, he said to himself. He can tell me about Rybys; his many memories of her will give me joy, the joy that, right now, I lack.

I love him, he realized. I love my mother's husband, my legal father. Like other men he is a good human being. He is a man of merit, and to be cherished.

But, unlike other men, Herb Asher knows who I am. Thus I can talk openly with him, as I do with Elias. And with Zina. It will help, he thought. I will be less weary. No longer as I am now, pinned by my cares; weighed down. The burden, to some extent, will lift. Because it will be shared.

And, he thought, there is still so much that I do not remember. I am not as I was. Like them, like the people, I have fallen. The bright morning star which fell did not fall alone, it tore down everything else with it, including me. Part of my own being fell with it, and I am that fallen being now.

But then, as he sat there on the bench with Zina, in the park, on this cold day so near the vernal equinox, he thought, But Herbert Asher lay dreaming in his bunk, dreaming of a phantom life with Linda Fox, while my mother struggled to survive. Not once did he try to help her; not once did he inquire into her trouble and seek remedy. Not until I, I myself, forced him to go to her, not until then did he do anything. I do not love the man, he said to himself. I know the man and he forfeited his right to my love—he lost my love because he did not care.

I cannot, thereupon, care about him. In response.

Why should I help any of them? he asked himself. They do what is right only when forced to, when there is no alternative. They fell of their own accord and are fallen now, of their own accord, by what they have voluntarily done. My mother is dead because of them; they murdered her. They would murder me if they could figure out where I am; only because I have confused their wits do they leave me alone. High and low they seek my life, just as Ahab sought Elijah's life, so long ago. They are a worthless race, and I do not care if they fall. I do not care at all. To save them I must fight what they themselves are. And have always been.

"You look so downcast," Zina said.

"What is this for?" he said. "They are what they are. I grow more and more weary. And I care less and less, as I begin to remember. For ten years I have lived on this world, now, and for ten years they have hunted me. Let them die. Did I not say to them the talion law: 'An eye for an eye, a tooth for a tooth'? Is that not in the Torah? They drove me off this world two thousand years ago; I return; they wish me dead. Under the talion law I should wish them dead. It is the sacred law of Israel. It is *my* law, my word."

Zina was silent.

"Advise me," Emmanuel said. "I have always listened to your advice."

Zina said:

> One day Elijah the prophet appeared to Rabbi Baruka in the market of Lapet. Rabbi Baruka asked him, "Is there any one among the people of this market who is destined to share in

the world to come?" . . . Two men appeared on the scene and Elijah said, "These two will share in the world to come." Rabbi Baruka asked them, "What is your occupation?" They said, "We are merrymakers. When we see a man who is downcast, we cheer him up. When we see two people quarreling with one another, we endeavor to make peace between them."

"You make me less sad," Emmanuel said. "And less weary. As you always have. As Scripture says of you:

Then I was at his side every day,
his darling and delight,
playing in his presence continually,
playing on the earth, when he had finished it,
while my delight was in mankind.

And Scripture says:

Wisdom I loved; I sought her out when I was young and longed to win her for my bride, and I fell in love with her beauty.

But that was Solomon, not me.

So I determined to bring her home to live with me, knowing that she would be my counsellor in prosperity and my comfort in anxiety and grief.

Solomon was a wise man, to love you so."

Beside him the girl smiled. She said nothing, but her dark eyes shone.

"Why are you smiling?" he asked.

"Because you have shown the truth of Scripture when it says:

I will betroth you to Me forever. I will betroth you to Me in righteousness and in justice, in love and in mercy. I will betroth you to Me in faithfulness, and you shall love the Lord.

Remember that you made the Covenant with man. And you made man in your own image. You cannot break the Covenant; you have made man that promise, that you will never break it."

Emmanuel said, "That is so. You advise me well." He thought, And you cheer my heart. You above all else, you who came before creation. Like the two merrymakers, he thought, who Elijah said would be saved. Your dancing, your singing, and the sound of bells. "I know," he said, "what your name means."

"Zina?" she said. "It's just a name."

"It is the Roumanian word for—" He ceased speaking; the girl had trembled visibly, and her eyes were now wide.

"How long have you known it?" she said.

"Years. Listen:

I know a bank where the wild thyme blows,
Where oxlips and the nodding violet grows;
Quite over-canopied with luscious woodbine,
With sweet musk-roses, and with eglantine:
There sleeps Titania sometime of the night,
Lull'd in these flowers with dances and delight;
And there the snake throws her enamell'd skin,
Weed wide enough

I will finish; listen:

To wrap a fairy in.

And I have known this," he finished, "all this time."

Staring at him, Zina said, "Yes, Zina means *fairy*."

"You are not Holy Wisdom," he said, "you are Diana, the fairy queen."

Cold wind rustled the branches of the trees. And, across the frozen creek, a few dry leaves scuttled.

"I see," Zina said.

About the two of them the wind rustled, as if speaking. He could hear the wind as words. And the wind said:

BEWARE!

He wondered if she heard it, too.

But they were still friends. Zina told Emmanuel about an early identity that she had once had. Thousands of years ago, she said, she had been Ma'at, the Egyptian goddess who represented the cosmic order and justice. When someone died his heart was weighed against Ma'at's ostrich feather. By this the person's burden of sins was determined.

The principle by which the sinfulness of the person was determined consisted of the degree of his truthfulness. To the extent that he was truthful the judgment went in his favor. This judgment was presided over by Osiris, but since Ma'at was the goddess of truthfulness, then it followed that the determination was hers to make.

"After that," Zina said, "the idea of the judgment of human souls passed over into Persia." In the ancient Persian religion, Zoroastrianism, a sifting bridge had to be crossed by the newly dead person. If he was evil the bridge got narrower and narrower until he toppled off and plunged into the fiery pit of hell. Judaism in its later stages and Christianity had gotten their ideas of the Final Days from this.

The good person, who managed to cross the sifting bridge, was met by the spirit of his religion: a beautiful young woman with superb, large breasts. However, if the person was evil the spirit of his religion consisted of a dried-up old hag with sagging paps. You could tell at a glance, therefore, which category you belonged to.

"Were you the spirit of religion for the good persons?" Emmanuel asked.

Zina did not answer the question; she passed on to another matter which she was more anxious to communicate to him.

In these judgments of the dead, stemming from Egypt and

Persia, the scrutiny was pitiless and the sinful soul was de facto doomed. Upon your death the books listing your good deeds and bad deeds closed, and no one, even the gods, could alter the tabulation. In a sense the procedure of judgment was mechanical. A bill of particulars, in essence, had been drawn up against you, compiled during your lifetime, and now this bill of particulars was fed into a mechanism of retribution. Once the mechanism received the list, it was all over for you. The mechanism ground you to shreds, and the gods merely watched, impassively.

But one day (Zina said) a new figure made its appearance at the path leading to the sifting bridge. This was an enigmatic figure who seemed to consist of a shifting succession of aspects or roles. Sometimes he was called Comforter. Sometimes Advocate. Sometimes Beside-Helper. Sometimes Support. Sometimes Advisor. No one knew where he had come from. For thousands of years he had not been there, and then one day he had appeared. He stood at the edge of the busy path, and as the souls made their way to the sifting bridge this complex figure—who sometimes, but rarely, seemed to be a woman—signaled to the persons, each in turn, to attract their attention. It was essential that the Beside-Helper got their attention before they stepped onto the sifting bridge, because after that it was too late.

"Too late for what?" Emmanuel said.

Zina said, "The Beside-Helper upon stopping a person approaching the sifting bridge asked him if he wished to be represented in the testing which was to come."

"By the Beside-Helper?"

The Beside-Helper, she explained, assumed his role of Advocate; he offered to speak on the person's behalf. But the Beside-Helper offered something more. He offered to present his own bill of particulars to the retribution mechanism in place of the bill of particulars of the person. If the person were innocent this would make no difference, but, for the guilty, it would yield up a sentence of exculpation rather than guilt.

"That's not fair," Emmanuel said. "The guilty should be punished."

"Why?" Zina said.

"Because it is the law," Emmanuel said.

"Then there is no hope for the guilty."

Emmanuel said, "They deserve no hope."

"What if everyone is guilty?"

He had not thought of that. "What does the Beside-Helper's bill of particulars list?" he asked.

"It is blank," Zina said. "A perfectly white piece of paper. A document on which nothing is inscribed."

"The retributive machinery could not process that."

Zina said, "It would process it. It would imagine that it had received a compilation of a totally spotless person."

"But it couldn't act. It would have no input data."

"That's the whole point."

"Then the machinery of justice has been bilked."

"Bilked out of a victim," Zina said. "Is that not to be desired? Should there be victims? What is gained if there is an unending procession of victims? Does that right the wrongs they have committed?"

"No," he said.

"The idea," Zina said, "is to feed mercy into the circuit. The Beside-Helper is an amicus curiae, a friend of the court. He advises the court, by its permission, that the case before it constitutes an exception. The general rule of punishment does not apply."

"And he does this for everyone? Every guilty person?"

"For every guilty person who accepts his offer of advocacy and help."

"But then you'd have an endless procession of exceptions. Because no guilty person in his right mind would reject such an offer; every single guilty person would wish to be judged as an exception, as a case involving mitigating circumstances."

Zina said, "But the person would have to accept the fact that he was, on his own, guilty. He could of course wager that he was innocent, in which case he would not need the advocacy of the Beside-Helper."

After a moment of pondering, Emmanuel said, "That would

be a foolish choice. He might be wrong. And he loses nothing by accepting the assistance of the Beside-Helper."

"In practice, however," Zina said, "most souls about to be judged reject the offer of advocacy by the Beside-Helper."

"On what basis?" He could not fathom their reasoning.

Zina said, "On the basis that they are sure they are innocent. To receive this help the person must go with the pessimistic assumption that he is guilty, even though his own assessment of himself is one of innocence. The truly innocent need no Beside-Helper, just as the physically healthy need no physician. In a situation of this kind the optimistic assumption is perilous. It's the bail-out theorem that little creatures employ when they construct a burrow. If they are wise they build a second exit to their burrow, operating on the pessimistic assumption that the first one will be found by a predator. All creatures who did not use their theorem are no longer with us."

Emmanuel said, "It is degrading to a man that he must consider himself sinful."

"It's degrading to a gopher to have to admit that his burrow may not be perfectly built, that a predator may find it."

"You are talking about an adversary situation. Is divine justice an adversary situation? Is there a prosecutor?"

"Yes, there is a prosecutor of man in the divine court; it is Satan. There is the Advocate who defends the accused human, and Satan who impugns and indicts him. The Advocate, standing beside the man, defends him and speaks for him; Satan, confronting the man, accuses him. Would you wish man to have an accuser and not a defender? Would that seem just?"

"But innocence must be presumed."

The girl's eyes gleamed. "Precisely the point made by the Advocate in each trial that takes place. Hence he substitutes his own blameless record for that of his client, and justifies the man by surrogation."

"Are you this Beside-Helper?" Emmanuel asked.

"No," she said. "He is a far more puzzling figure than I. If you are having difficulty with me, in determining—"

"I am," Emmanuel said.

"He is a latecomer into this world," Zina said. "Not found in earlier aeons. He represents an evolution in the divine strategy. One by which the primordial damage is repaired. One of many, but a main one."

"Will I ever encounter him?"

"You will not be judged," Zina said. "So perhaps not. But all humans will see him standing by the busy road, offering his help. Offering it in time—before the person starts across the sifting bridge and is judged. The Beside-Helper's intervention always comes in time. It is part of his nature to be there soon enough."

Emmanuel said, "I would like to meet him."

"Follow the travel pattern of any human," Zina said, "and you will arrive at the point where that human encounters him. That is how I know about him. I, too, am not judged." She pointed to the slate that she had given him. "Ask it for more information about the Beside-Helper."

The slate read:

TO CALL

"Is that all you can tell me?" Emmanuel asked it.

A new word formed, a Greek word:

PARAKALEIN

He wondered about this, wondered greatly, at this new entity who had come into the world . . . who could be called on by those in need, those who stood in danger of negative judgment. It was one more of the mysteries presented to him by Zina. There had been so many, now. He enjoyed them. But he was puzzled.

To call to aid: parakalein. Strange, he thought. The world evolves even as it falls more and more. There are two distinct movements: the falling, and then, at the same time, the upward-rising work of repair. Antithetical movements, in the form of a dialectic of all creation and the powers contending behind it.

Suppose Zina beckoned to the parts that fell? Beckoned them, seductively, to fall farther. About this he could not yet tell.

11

Reaching out, Herb Asher took the boy in his arms. He hugged him tight.

"And this is Zina," Elias Tate said. "Emmanuel's friend." He took the girl by the hand and led her to Herb Asher. "She's a little older than Manny.'"

"Hello," Herb Asher said. But he did not care about her; he wanted to look at Rybys's son.

Ten years, he thought. This child has grown while I dreamed and dreamed, thinking I was alive when in fact I was not.

Elias said, "She helps him. She teaches him. More than the school does. More than I do."

Looking toward the girl Herb Asher saw a beautiful pale heart-shaped face with eyes that danced with light. What a pretty child, he thought, and turned back to Rybys's son. But then, struck by something, he looked once more at the girl.

Mischief showed on her face. Especially in her eyes. Yes, he thought; there is something in her eyes. A kind of knowledge.

"They've been together four years now," Elias said. "She gave him a high-technology slate. It's some kind of advanced computer terminal. It asks him questions—poses questions to him and gives him hints. Right, Manny?"

Emmanuel said, "Hello, Herb Asher." He seemed solemn and subdued, in contrast to the girl.

"Hello," he said to Emmanuel. "How much you look like your mother."

"In that crucible we grow," Emmanuel said, cryptically. He did not amplify.

"Are—" Herb did not know what to say. "Is everything all right?"

"Yes." The boy nodded.

"You have a heavy burden on you," Herb said.

"The slate plays tricks," Emmanuel said.

There was silence.

"What's wrong?" Herb said to Elias.

To the boy, Elias said, "Something is wrong, isn't it?"

"While my mother died," Emmanuel said, gazing fixedly at Herb Asher, "you listened to an illusion. She does not exist, that image. Your Fox is a phantasm, nothing else."

"That was a long time ago," Herb said.

"The phantasm is with us in the world," Emmanuel said.

"That's not my problem," Herb said.

Emmanuel said, "But it is mine. I mean to solve it. Not now but at the proper time. You fell asleep, Herb Asher, because a voice told you to fall asleep. This world here, this planet, all of it, all its people—everything here sleeps. I have watched it for ten years and there is nothing good I can say about it. What you did it does; what you were it is. Maybe you still sleep. Do you sleep, Herb Asher? You dreamed about my mother while you lay in cryonic suspension. I tapped your dreams. From them I learned a lot about her. I am as much her as I am myself. As I told her, she lives on in me and *as* me; I have made her deathless—your wife is here, not back in that littered dome. Do you realize that? Look at me and you see Rybys whom you ignored."

Herb Asher said, "I—"

"There is nothing for you to tell me," Emmanuel said. "I read your heart, not your words. I knew you then and I know you now. 'Herbert, Herbert,' I called to you. I summoned you back to life, for your sake and for hers, and, because it was for her sake, it was for my sake. When you helped her you helped me. And when you ignored her you ignored me. Thus says your God."

Reaching out, Elias put his arm around Herb Asher, to reassure him.

"I will always speak the truth to you, Herb Asher," the boy continued. "There is no deceit in God. *I want you to live.* I made you live once before, when you lay in psychological death. God does not desire any living thing's death; God takes no delight in nonexistence. Do you know what God is, Herb Asher? God is He Who causes to be. Put another way, if you seek the basis of being that underlies everything you will surely find God. You can work back to God from the phenomenal universe, or you can move from the Creator to the phenomenal universe. Each implies the other. The Creator would not be the Creator if there were no universe, and the universe would cease to be if the Creator did not sustain it. The Creator does not exist prior to the universe in time; he does not exist in time at all. God creates the universe constantly; he is *with* it, not above or behind it. This is impossible to understand for you because you are a created thing and exist in time. But eventually you will return to your Creator and then you will again no longer exist in time. You are the breath of your Creator, and as he breathes in and out, you live. Remember that, for that sums up everything that you need to know about your God. There is first an exhalation from God, on the part of all creation; and then, at a certain point, it starts its journey back, its inhalation. This cycle never ceases. You leave me; you are away from me; you start back; you rejoin me. You and everything else. It is a process, an event. It is an activity—*my* activity. It is the rhythm of my own being, and it sustains you all."

Amazing, Herb Asher thought. A ten-year-old boy. Her son speaking this.

"Emmanuel," the girl Zina said, "you are ponderous."

Smiling at her the boy said, "Games, then? Would that be better? There are events ahead that I must shape. I must arouse fire that burns, that sears. Scripture says:

For He is like a refiner's fire.

And Scripture also says:

And who can abide the day of His coming?

I say, however, that it will be more than this; I say:

The day comes, glowing like a furnace; all the arrogant and the evil-doers shall be chaff, and that day when it comes shall set them ablaze; it shall leave them neither root nor branch.

What do you say to that, Herb Asher?'' Emmanuel gazed at him intently, awaiting his response.

Zina said:

But for you who fear my name, the sun of righteousness shall rise with healing in his wings.

''That is true,'' Emmanuel said.

In a low voice Elias said:

And you shall break loose like calves released from the stall.

''Yes,'' Emmanuel said. He nodded.

Herb Asher, returning the boy's gaze, said, ''I am afraid. I really am.'' He was glad of the arm around him, the reassuring arm of Elias.

In a reasonable tone of voice, a mild tone, Zina said, ''He won't do all those terrible things. That's to scare people.''

''Zina!'' Elias said.

Laughing, she said, ''It's true. Ask him.''

''You will not put the Lord your God to the test,'' Emmanuel said.

''I'm not afraid,'' Zina said quietly.

Emmanuel, to her, said:

I will break you, like a rod of iron.
I shall dash you, in pieces,
Like a potter's vessel.

''No,'' Zina said. To Herb Asher she said, ''There is nothing to fear. It's a manner of talking, no more. Come to me if you get scared and I will converse with you.''

''That is true,'' Emmanuel said. ''If you are seized and taken down into the prison she will go with you. She will never leave you.'' An unhappy expression crossed his face; suddenly he was, again, a ten-year-old boy. ''But—''

''What is it?'' Elias said.

''I will not say now,'' Emmanuel said, speaking with difficulty. Herb Asher, to his disbelief, saw tears in the boy's eyes. ''Perhaps I will never say it. She knows what I mean.''

''Yes,'' Zina said, and she smiled. Mischief lay in her smile, or so it seemed to Herb Asher. It puzzled him. He did not understand the invisible transaction taking place between Rybys's son and the girl. It troubled him, and his fear became greater. His sense of deep unease.

The four of them had dinner together that night.

''Where do you live?'' Herb Asher asked the girl. ''Do you have a family? Parents?''

''Technically I'm a ward of the government school we go to,'' Zina said. ''But for all intents and purposes I'm in Elias's custody now. He's in the process of becoming my guardian.''

Elias, eating, paying attention to his plate of food, said, ''We are a family, the three of us. And now you also, Herb.''

''I may go back to my dome,'' Herb said. ''In the CY30-CY30B system.''

Staring at him, Elias halted in his eating, forkful of food raised. ''Why?''

''I'm uncomfortable here,'' Herb said. He had not worked it out; his feelings remained vague. But they were intense feelings. ''It's oppressive here. There's more of a sense of freedom out there.''

''Freedom to lie in your bunk listening to Linda Fox?'' Elias said.

''No.'' He shook his head.

Zina said, "Emmanuel, you scare nim with your talk about afflicting the Earth with fire. He remembers the plagues in the Bible. What happened with Egypt."

"I want to go home," Herb said, simply.

Emmanuel said, "You miss Rybys."

"Yes." That was true.

"She isn't there," Emmanuel reminded him. He ate slowly, somberly, bite after bite. As if, Herb thought, eating was for him a solemn ritual. A matter of consuming something sanctified.

"Can't you bring her back?" he said to Emmanuel.

The boy did not respond. He continued to eat.

"No answer?" Herb said, with bitterness.

"I am not here for that," Emmanuel said. "She understood. It is not important that you understand, but it was important that she know. And I caused her to know. You remember; you were there on that day, the day I told her what lay ahead."

"Okay," Herb said.

"She lives elsewhere now," Emmanuel said. "You—"

"Okay," he repeated, with anger, enormous anger.

To him, Emmanuel said, speaking slowly and quietly, his face calm, "You do not grasp the situation, Herbert. It is not a good universe that I strive for, nor a just one, nor a pretty one; the existence of the universe itself is at stake. Final victory for Belial does not mean imprisonment for the human race, continued slavery, but nonexistence; without me, there is nothing, not even Belial, whom I created."

"Eat your dinner," Zina said in a gentle voice.

"The power of evil," Emmanuel continued, "is the ceasing of reality, the ceasing of existence itself. It is the slow slipping away of everything that is, until it becomes, like Linda Fox, a phantasm. That process has begun. It began with the primal fall. Part of the cosmos fell away. The Godhead itself suffered a crisis; can you fathom that, Herb Asher? A crisis in the Ground of Being? What does that convey to you? The possibility of the Godhead ceasing—does it convey that to you? Because the Godhead is all that stands between—" He broke off. "You can't even imagine it. No creature can imagine nonbeing, especially its own nonbeing. I must guarantee being, all being. Including yours."

Herb Asher said nothing.

"A war is coming," Emmanuel said. "We will choose our ground. It will be for us, the two of us, Belial and me, a table, on which we play. Over which we wager the universe, the being of being as such. I initiate this final part of the ages of war; I have advanced into Belial's territory, his home. I have moved forward to meet *him,* not the other way around. Time will tell if it was a wise idea."

"Can't you foresee the results?" Herb said.

Emmanuel regarded him. Silently.

"You can," Herb said. You know what the outcome will be, he realized. You know now; you knew when you entered Rybys's womb. You knew from the beginning of creation—before creation, in fact; before a universe existed.

"They will play by rules," Zina said. "Rules agreed on."

"Then," Herb said, "that's why Belial has not attacked you. That's why you've been able to live here and grow up—for ten years. He knows you're here—"

"Does he know?" Emmanuel said.

Silence.

"I haven't told him," Emmanuel said. "It is not my burden. He must find out for himself. I do not mean the government. I mean the power that truly rules, in comparison to which the government, all governments, are shadows."

"He'll tell him when he's ready," Zina said. "Good and ready."

Herb said, "Are you good and ready, Emmanuel?"

The boy smiled. A child's smile, a shift away from the stern countenance of a moment before. He said nothing. A game, Herb Asher realized. A child's game!

Seeing this he trembled.

Zina said:

> Time is a child at play, playing draughts; a child's is the kingdom.

"What is that?" Elias said.

"It is not from Judaism," Zina said obscurely. She did not amplify.

The part of him that derives from his mother, Herb Asher realized, is ten years old. And the part of him that is Yah has no age; it is infinity itself. A compound of the very young and the timeless: precisely what Zina in her arcane quote had stated.

Perhaps this was not unique, this mixture. Someone had noted it before; noted it and declared it in words.

"You venture into Belial's realm," Zina said to Emmanuel as she ate, "but would you have the courage to venture into *my* realm?"

"What realm is that?" Emmanuel said. Elias Tate stared at the girl, and, equally puzzled, Herb Asher regarded her. But Emmanuel seemed to understand her; he showed no surprise. Despite his question, Herb Asher thought, he knows—knows already.

Zina said, "Where I am not as you see me now."

An interval of silence passed, as Emmanuel pondered. He did not answer; he sat as if withdrawn, as if his mind had moved far away. Skimming countless worlds, Herb Asher thought. How strange this is. What are they talking about?

Emmanuel said slowly and carefully, "I have a dreadful land to deal with, Zina. I have no time."

"I think you are apprehensive," Zina said. She turned to her slice of apple pie and mound of ice cream.

"No," Emmanuel said.

"Come, then," she said, and, all at once, the color and fire, the mischief and delight, showed in her dark eyes. "I challenge you," she said. "Here." She reached out her hand to the boy.

"My psychopomp," Emmanuel said somberly.

"Yes; I'll be your guide."

"You would lead the Lord your God?"

"I would like to show you where the bells come from. The land out of which their sounds come. What do you say?"

He said, "I will go."

"What are you two talking about?" Elias said, with apprehension. "Manny, what is this? What does she mean? She's not taking you anywhere that I don't know about."

Emmanuel glanced at him.

"You have much to do," Elias said.

"There is no realm," Emmanuel said, "where I am not. If it is a genuine place and not fancy. Is your realm fancy, Zina?"

"No," she said. "It is real."

"Where is it?" Elias said.

Zina said, "It is here."

" 'Here'?" Elias said. "What do you mean? I see what's here; here is here."

"She is right," Emmanuel said. "The soul of God," he said to Zina, "follows you."

"And trusts me?"

"This is a game," Emmanuel said. "Everything is a game for you. I will play the game. I can do that. I will play and come back. Back to this realm."

Zina said, "Do you find this realm so valuable to you?"

"It is a dreadful place," Emmanuel said. "But it is here that I must act on that great and terrible day."

"Postpone that day," Zina said. "*I* will postpone it; I will show you the bells that you hear, and as a result that day will—" She broke off.

"It will still come," Emmanuel said. "It is foreordained."

"Then we shall play now," Zina said cryptically. Both Herb and Elias remained puzzled; Herb Asher thought, Each of them knows what the other means, but I don't. Where is she taking him if it is here? *We are here now.*

Emmanuel said, "The Secret Commonwealth."

"Damn it, no!" Elias exclaimed, and hurled his cup across the room; it shattered against the far wall, in many little pieces. "Manny—I have heard of that place!"

"What is it?" Herb Asher said, astonished at the old man's fury.

Zina said calmly, "That's the correct term. 'Of a middle nature betwixt man and angel,' " she quoted.

"You are being piped away!" Elias said furiously; leaning forward he seized hold of the boy with his great hands.

"That is so," Emmanuel said.

"You know where she is taking you?" Elias said. "You do know. You have no fear, Manny; that is a mistake. You should be afraid." To Zina he said, "Get out of here! I did not know what you are." With violence and dismay he regarded her, his lips working. "I did not know you; I didn't understand."

"He did," Zina said. "Emmanuel knew. The slate told him."

"Let us finish our meal," Emmanuel said, "and then, Zina, I will go with you." He resumed eating in his methodical way, his face impassive. "I have a surprise for you, Zina," he said.

"What?" she said. "What is it?"

"Something that you do not know." Emmanuel paused in his eating. "This was foreordained, from the start. I saw it before the universe was. My journey into your land."

"Then you know how it will end," Zina said. For the first time she seemed hesitant; she faltered. "I forget sometimes that you know everything."

"Not everything. Because of my brain damage, the accident. It has become a random variable, introducing chance."

"God plays at dice?" Zina said; she raised an eyebrow.

"If necessary," Emmanuel said. "If there is no other way."

"You planned this," Zina said. "Or did you? I can't make it out. You are impaired; you may not have known . . . You are using a tactic on me, Emmanuel." She laughed. "Very good. I can't be sure. Extremely good; I congratulate you."

Emmanuel said, "You must go through with it not knowing if I planned it out or not. So I have the advantage."

She shrugged. But it seemed to Herb Asher that she had not regained her poise. Emmanuel had shaken her. He thought, And that is good.

"Don't abandon me, Lord," Elias said in a trembling voice. "Take me with you."

"Okay." The boy nodded.

"What am I supposed to do?" Herb Asher said.

"Come," Zina said.

" 'The Secret Commonwealth,' " Elias said. "I never believed it existed." He glowered at the girl, baffled. "It doesn't exist; that's the whole point!"

"It exists," she said. "And here. Come with us, Mr. Asher. You are welcome. But there I am not as I am now. None of us is. Except you, Emmanuel."

To the boy, Elias said, "Lord—"

"There is a doorway," Emmanuel said, "to her land. It can be found anywhere that the Golden Proportion exists. Is that not true, Zina?"

"True," she said.

"Based on the Fibonacci Constant," Emmanuel said. "A ratio," he explained to Herb Asher. "1:.618034. The ancient Greeks knew it as the Golden Section and as the Golden Rectangle. Their architecture utilized it . . . for instance, the Parthenon. For them it was a geometric model, but Fibonacci of Pisa, in the Middle Ages, developed it in terms of pure number."

"In this room alone," Zina said, "I count several doors. The ratio," she said to Herb Asher, "is that used in playing cards: three to five. It is found in snail shells and extragalactic nebulae, from the pattern formation of the hair on your head to—"

"It pervades the universe," Emmanuel said, "from the microcosms to the macrocosm. It has been called one of the names of God."

In a small spare room of Elias's house Herb Asher prepared to bed down for the night.

Standing at the doorway in a heavy, somewhat rumpled robe, with great slippers on his feet, Elias said, "May I talk with you?"

Herb nodded.

"She is taking him away," Elias said. He came into the room and seated himself. "You realize that? It did not come from the direction we expected. *I* expected," he corrected himself. His face dark he sat clasping and unclasping his hands. "The enemy has taken a strange form."

Chilled, Herb said, "Belial?"

"I don't know, Herb. I've known the girl four years. I think a great deal of her. In some ways I love her. Even as much as I do Manny. She's been a good friend to him. Apparently he knew, maybe not right off . . . but somewhere along the line he figured it out. I checked; I used my computer terminal to research the word *zina*. It's Roumanian for fairy. Another world has found out Emmanuel. She approached him the first day at school. I see why, now. She was waiting. Expecting him. You see?"

"Hence the mischief I see in her," Herb Asher said. He felt weary. It had been a long day.

Elias said, "She will lead and lead, and he will follow. Follow knowingly, I think. He does foresee. It's what's called a priori knowledge about the universe. Once, he foresaw everything. Not anymore. It's strange, when you think about it, that he could foresee his own inability to foresee, his forgetfulness. I'll have to trust in him, Herb; there is no way—" He gestured. "You understand."

"No one can tell him what to do."

"Herb, I don't want to lose him."

"How can he be lost?"

"There was a rupturing of the Godhead. A primordial schism. That's the basis of it all, the trouble, these conditions here, Belial and the rest of it. A crisis that caused part of the Godhead to fall; the Godhead split and some remained transcendent and some . . . became abased. Fell with creation, fell along with the world. *The Godhead has lost touch with a part of itself.*"

"And it could fragment further?"

"Yes," Elias said. "There could be another crisis. This may be that crisis. I don't know. I don't even know if *he* knows. The human part of him, the part derived from Rybys, knows fear, but the other half—that half knows no fear. For obvious reasons. Maybe that's not good."

That night as he slept, Herb Asher dreamed that a woman was singing to him. She seemed to be Linda Fox and yet she was not; he could see her, and he saw terrible beauty, a wildness and light, and a sweet glowing face with eyes that shone at him lovingly. He and the woman were in a car and the woman drove; he simply watched her, marveling at her beauty. She sang:

You have to put your slippers on
To walk toward the dawn.

But he did not have to walk, because the lovely woman was taking him there. She wore a white gown and in her tumbled hair he saw a crown. She was a very young woman, but a woman nonetheless—not, like Zina, a child.

When he awoke the next morning the beauty of the woman and her singing haunted him; he could not forget it. He thought, She is more attractive than the Fox. I wouldn't have believed it. I would prefer her. Who is she?

"Good morning," Zina said, on her way to the bathroom to brush her teeth. He noticed that she wore slippers. But so, too, did Elias when he appeared. What does it mean? Herb asked himself.

He did not know the answer.

12

"You dance and sing all night," Emmanuel said. He thought, And it is beautiful. "Show me," he said.

"Then we shall begin," Zina said.

He sat under palm trees and knew that he had entered the Garden, but it was the garden he himself had fashioned at the beginning of creation; she had not brought him to her realm. This was his own realm restored.

Buildings and vehicles, but the people did not hurry. They sat here and there enjoying the sun. One young woman had unbuttoned her blouse, and her breasts shone with perspiration; the sun radiated down hot and bright.

"No," he said, "this is not the Commonwealth."

"I took you the wrong way," Zina said. "But it doesn't matter. There is nothing wrong with this place, is there? Does it lack? You know it doesn't lack; it is Paradise."

"I made it so," he said.

"All right," Zina said. "This is the Paradise that you created and I will show you something better. Come." She reached out and took him by the hand. "That savings and loan building has the Golden Rectangle doorway. We can enter there; it is as good as any." Holding him by the hand she led him to the corner, waited for the light to change, and then, together, they made their way down the sidewalk, past the resting people, to the savings and loan office.

Pausing on the steps Emmanuel said, "I—"

"This is the doorway," she said, and led him up the steps. "Your realm ends here and mine begins. From now on the laws are mine." Her grip on his hand tightened.

"So be it," he said, and continued on.

The robot teller said, "Do you have your passbook, Ms. Pallas?"

"In my purse." Beside Emmanuel the young woman opened her mail-pouch leather purse, fumbled among keys, cosmetics, letters, assorted valuables, until her quick fingers found the passbook. "I want to draw out—well, how much do I have?"

"Your balance appears in your passbook," the robot teller said in its dispassionate voice.

"Yes," she agreed. Opening the passbook she scrutinized the figures, then took a withdrawal slip and filled it out.

"You are closing your account?" the robot teller said, as she presented it with the passbook and slip.

"That's right."

"Has our service not been—"

"It's none of your damn business why I'm closing my account," she said. Resting her sharp elbows on the counter she rocked back and forth. Emmanuel saw that she wore high heels. Now she had become older. She wore a cotton print top and jeans, and her hair pulled back with a comb. Also, he saw, she wore sunglasses. She smiled at him.

He said to himself, She has already changed.

Presently they stood on the roof parking lot of the savings and loan building; Zina fumbled in her purse for her flycar keys.

"It's a nice day," she said. "Get in; I'll unlock the door for you." She slipped in behind the wheel of the flycar and reached for the far door's handle.

"This is a nice car," he said, and he thought, She reveals her domain by degrees. As she took me to my own garden-world first she now takes me stage by stage through the levels, the ascending levels, of her own realm. She will strip the accretions away one by one as we penetrate deeper. This, now, is the surface only.

This, he thought, is enchantment. *Beware!*

"You like my car? It gets me to work—"

He said, breaking in harshly, "You lie, Zina!"

"What do you mean?" The flycar rose up into the warm midday sky, joining the normal traffic. But her smile gave her away. "It's a beginning," she said. "I don't want to startle you."

"Here," he said, "in this world you are not a child. That was a form you took, a pose."

"This is my real shape. Honest."

"Zina; you have no real shape. I know you. For you any shape is possible. Whichever shape appeals to you at the moment. You go from moment to moment, like a soap bubble."

Turning toward him, but still watching where she drove, Zina said, "You are in my world now, Yah. Take care."

"I can burst your world."

"It will simply return. It is everywhere always. We have not gone away from where we were—back there a few miles is the school that you and I attend; back there in the house Elias and Herb Asher are discussing what to do. Spacially this is not another place and you know that."

"But," he said, "you make the laws here."

"Belial is not here," she said.

That surprised him. He had not foreseen that, and, realizing that he had not foreseen it he knew that he had not truly foreseen the total situation. To miss a single part was to miss it all.

"He never penetrated my realm," Zina said as she negotiated her way through the sky traffic over Washington, D.C. "He does not even know about it. Let's go over to the Tidal Basin and look at the Japanese cherry trees; they're in bloom."

"Are they?" he said; it seemed to him too early in the year.

"They are blooming now," Zina said, and steered her flycar toward the downtown center of the city.

"In your world," he said. He understood. "This is the spring," he said. He could see the leaves and blossoms on the trees below them. The expanses of bright green.

"Roll your window down," she said. "It's not cold."

He said, "The warmth in the Palm Tree Garden—"

"Blasting, withering dry heat," she said. "Scorching the world and turning it into a desert. You were always partial to arid land. Listen to me, Yahweh. *I will show you things you know nothing about.* You have gone from the wastelands to a frozen landscape—methane crystals, with little domes here and there, and stupid natives. You know nothing!" Her eyes blazed. "You skulk in the badlands and promise your people a refuge they never found. All your promises have failed—which is good, because what you have promised them most is that you will curse them and afflict them and destroy them. Now shut up. My time and my realm have come; this is my world and it is springtime and the air does not wither the plants, nor do you. You will hurt no one here in my realm. Do you understand?"

He said, "Who are you?"

Laughing, she said, "My name is Zina. Fairy."

"I think—" Confused, he said, "You—"

"Yahweh," the woman said, "you do not know who I am and you do not know where you are. Is this the Secret Commonwealth? Or have you been tricked?"

"You have tricked me," he said.

"I am your guide," she said. "As the *Sepher Yezirah* says:

> Comprehend this great wisdom, understand this knowledge, inquire into it and ponder it, render it evident and lead the Creator back to His throne again.

"And that," she finished, "is what I will do. But it is by a route that you will not believe. It is a route that you do not know. You will have to trust me; you will trust your guide as Dante trusted his guide, through the realms, up and up."

He said, "You are the Adversary."

"Yes," Zina said. "I am."

But, he thought, that is not all. It is not that simple. You are complex, he realized, you who drive this car. Paradox and contradictions, and, most of all, your love of games. Your desire to play. I must think of it that way, he realized, as play.

"I'll play," he agreed. "I am willing."

"Good." She nodded. "Could you get my cigarettes for me out of my purse? The traffic's getting heavy; I'm going to have trouble finding a parking spot."

He rummaged in her purse. Futilely.

"Can't you find them? Keep looking; they're there."

"You keep so many things in your purse." He found the pack of Salems and held it toward her.

"God doesn't light a woman's cigarette?" She took the cigarette and pressed in the dashboard lighter.

"What does a ten-year-old boy know about that?" he said.

"Strange," she said. "I'm old enough to be your mother. And yet you are older than I am. There is a paradox; you knew you would find paradoxes here. My realm abounds with them, as you were just thinking. Do you want to go back, Yahweh? To the Palm Tree Garden? It is irreal and you know it. Until you inflict decisive defeat on your Adversary it will remain irreal. That world is gone, and is now a memory."

"You are the Adversary," he said, puzzled, "but you are not Belial."

"Belial is in a cage at the Washington, D.C. zoo," Zina said. "In my realm. As an example of extraterrestrial life—a deplorable example. A thing from Sirius, from the fourth planet in the Sirius System. People stand around gaping at him in wonder."

He laughed.

"You think I'm joking. I'll take you to the zoo. I'll show you."

"I think you're serious." Again he laughed; it delighted him. "The Evil One in a cage at the zoo—what, with his own temperature and gravity and atmosphere, and imported food? An exotic life form?"

"He's angry as hell about it," Zina said.

"I'm sure he is. What do you have planned for me, Zina?"

She said, soberly, "The truth, Yahweh. I will show you the truth before you leave here. I would not cage the Lord our God. You are free to roam my land; you are free here, Yahweh, entirely. I give you my word."

"Vapors," he said. "The bond of a *zina*."

After some difficulty she found a slot in which to park her flycar. "Okay," she said. "Let's stroll around looking at the cherry blossoms. Yahweh; their color is mine, their pink. That is my hallmark. When that pink light is seen, I am near."

"I know that pink," he said. "It is the human phosphene response to full-spectrum white, to pure sunlight."

As she locked up the flycar she said, "See the people."

He looked about him. And saw no one. The trees, heavy with blossoms, lined the Tidal Basin in a great semicircle. But, despite the parked cars, no persons walked anywhere.

"Then this is a fraud," he said.

Zina said, "You are here, Yahweh, so that I can postpone your great and terrible day. I do not want to see the world scourged. I want you to see what you do not see. Only the two of us are here; we are alone. Gradually I will unfold my realm to you, and, when I am done, you will withdraw your curse on the world. I have watched you for years, now. I have seen your dislike of the human race and your sense of its worthlessness. I say to you, It is not worthless; it is not worthy to die—as you phrase it in your pompous fashion. The world is beautiful and I am beautiful and the cherry blossoms are beautiful. The robot teller at the savings and loan—even it is beautiful. The power of Belial is mere occlusion, hiding the real world, and if you attack the real world, as you have come to Earth to do, then you will destroy beauty and kindness and charm. Remember the crushed dog dying in the ditch at the side of the road? Remember what you felt about him; remember what you knew him to be. Remember the inscription that Elias composed for that dog and that dog's death. Remember the dignity of that dog, and at the same time remember that the dog was innocent. His death was mandated by cruel necessity. A wrong and cruel necessity. The dog—"

"I know," he said.

"You know what? That the dog was wrongly treated? That he was born to suffer unjust pain? It is not Belial that slew the dog, it is you, Yahweh, the Lord of Hosts. Belial did not bring death into the world because there has always been death; death goes back a billion years on this planet, and what became of that dog—that is the fate of every creature you have made. You cried over that dog, did you not? I think at that point you understood, but now you have forgotten. If I were to remind you of anything I would remind you of that dog and of how you felt; I would want you to remember how that dog showed you the Way. It is the way of compassion, the most noble way of all, and I do not think you genuinely have that compassion, I really don't. You are here to destroy Belial, your adversary, not to emancipate mankind; *you are here to wage war.* Is that a fit thing for you to do? I wonder. Where is the peace that you promised man? You have come with a sword and millions will die; it will be the dying dog multiplied millions of times. You cried for the dog, you cried for your mother and even Belial, but I say, If you want to wipe away all the tears, as it says in Scripture, go away and leave this world because the evil of this world, what you call 'Belial' and your 'Adversary' is a form of illusion. These are not bad people. This is not a bad world. Do not make war on it but bring it flowers." Reaching, she broke off a sprig of cherry blossoms; she extended it to him, and, reflexively, he accepted it.

"You are very persuasive," he said.

"It is my job," she said. "I say these things because I know these things. There is no deceit in you and there is no deceit in me, but just as you curse, I play. Which of us has found the Way? For two thousand years you have bided your time until you could slip back into Belial's fortress to overthrow him. I suggest that you find something else to do. Walk with me and we will see flowers. It is better. And the world will prosper as it always has. This is the springtime. It is now that flowers grow, and with me there is dancing also, and the sound of bells. You heard the bells and you know that their beauty is greater than the power of evil. In some ways their beauty is greater than your own power, Yahweh, Lord of Hosts. Do you not agree?"

"Magic," he said. "A spell."

"Beauty is a spell," she said, "and war is reality. Do you want the sobriety of war or the intoxication of what you see now, here in my world? We are alone now, but later on people will appear; I will repopulate my realm. But I want this moment to speak to you plainly. Do you know who I am? You do not know who I am, but finally I will lead you step by step back to your throne, you the Creator, and then you will know who I am. You have guessed but you have not guessed right. There are many guesses left for you—you who know everything. I am not Holy Wisdom and I am not Diana; I am not a *zina;* I am not Pallas Athena. I am something else. I am the spring queen and yet I am not that either; these are, as you put it, vapors. What I am, what I truly am, you will have to ferret out on your own. Now let's walk."

They walked along the path, by the water and the trees.

"We are friends, you and I," Emmanuel said. "I tend to listen to you."

"Then postpone your great and terrible day. There is nothing good in death by fire; it is the worst death of all. You are the solar heat that destroys the crops. For four years we have been together, you and I. I have watched as your memory returned and I have regretted its return. You afflicted that miserable woman who was your mother; you sickened your own mother whom you say you love, whom you cried over. Instead of making war against evil, cure the dying dog in the ditch and wipe away thereby your own tears. I hated to see you cry. You cried because you regained your own nature and comprehended that nature. You cried because you realized what you are."

He said nothing.

"The air smells good," Zina said.

"Yes," he said.

"I will bring the people back," she said. "One by one, until they are all around us. Look at them and when you see one whom you would slay, tell me and I will banish that person once more. But you must look at the person whom you would slay—you must see in that person the crushed and dying dog. Only then do you have the right to slay that person; only when you cry are you entitled to destroy. You understand?''

''Enough,'' he said.

''Why didn't you cry over the dog before the car crushed him? Why did you wait until it was too late? The dog accepted his situation but I do not. I advise you; I am your guide. I say, It is wrong what you do. Listen to me. Stop it!''

He said, ''I have come to lift their oppression.''

''You are impaired. I know that; I know what happened in the Godhead, the original crisis. It is no secret to me. In this condition you seek to lift their oppression through a great and terrible day. Is that reasonable? Is that how you free the prisoners?''

''I must break the power of—''

''Where is that power? The government? Bulkowsky and Harms? They are idiots; they are a joke. Would you kill them? The talion law that you laid down; I say:

> You have learnt how it was said: *Eye for eye and tooth for tooth.* But I say this to you: offer the wicked man no resistance.

''You must live by your own words; you must offer your Adversary Belial no resistance. In my realm his power is not here; *he* is not here. What is here is a sport in a cage at a public zoo. We feed it and give it water and atmosphere and the right temperature; we try to make the thing as comfortable as possible. In my realm we do not kill. There is, here, no great and terrible day, nor will there ever be. Stay in my realm or make my realm your realm, but spare Belial; spare everyone. And then you will not have to cry, and the tears will, as you promised, be wiped away.''

Emmanuel said, ''You are Christ.''

Laughing, Zina said, ''No, I am not.''

''You quote him.''

'' 'Even the devil can cite Scripture.' ''

Around them groups of people appeared, in light, summery clothing. Men in their shirtsleeves, women in frocks. And, he saw, all the children.

"The fairy queen," he said. "You beguile me. You lead me from the path with sparks of light, dancing, singing, and the sound of bells; always the sound of bells."

"The bells are blown by the wind," Zina said. "And the wind speaks the truth. Always. The desert wind. You know that; I have watched you listen to the wind. The bells are the music of the wind; listen to them."

He heard, then, the fairy bells. They echoed distantly; many bells, small ones, not church bells but the bells of magic.

It was the most beautiful sound he had ever heard.

"I cannot, myself, produce that sound," he said to Zina. "How is it done?"

"By wakefulness," Zina said. "The bell-sounds wake you up. They rouse you from sleep. You roused Herb Asher from his sleep by a crude introjection; I awaken by means of beauty."

Gentle spring wind blew about them, the vapors of her realm.

13

To himself Emmanuel said, I am being poisoned. The vapors of her realm poison me and vitiate my will.

"You are wrong," Zina said.

"I feel less strong."

"You feel less indignation. Let's go and get Herb Asher. I want him with us. I will narrow down the area of our game; I will arrange it especially for him."

"In what way?"

"We will contest for him," Zina said. "Come." She beckoned to the boy to follow her.

In the cocktail lounge Herb Asher sat with a glass of Scotch and water in front of him. He had been waiting an hour but the evening entertainment had not begun. The cocktail lounge was filled with people. Constant noise assailed his ears. But, for him, this was worth it, despite the rather large cover charge.

Rybys, across from him, said, "I just don't understand what you see in her."

"She's going to go a long way," Herb said, "if she gets any kind of a break at all." He wondered if record company scouts came here to the Golden Hind. I hope so, he said to himself.

"I'd like to leave. I don't feel well. Could we go?"

"I'd prefer not to."

Rybys sipped at her tall mixed drink fitfully. "So much noise," she said, her voice virtually inaudible.

He looked at his watch. "It's almost nine. Her first set is at nine."

"Who is she?" Rybys said.

"She's a new young singer," Herb Asher said. "She's adapted the lute books of John Dowland for—"

"Who's John Dowland? I never heard of him."

"Late-sixteenth-century England. Linda Fox has modernized his lute songs; he was the first composer to write for solo voice; before that four or more people sang . . . the old madrigal form. I can't explain it; you have to hear her."

"If she's so good, why isn't she on TV?" Rybys said.

Herb said, "She will be."

Lights on the stage began to glow. Three musicians leaped up onto it and began fussing with the audio system. Each had in his possession a vibrolute.

A hand touched Herb Asher on the shoulder. "Hi."

Glancing up he saw a young woman whom he did not know. But, he thought, she seems to know me. "I'm sorry—" he began.

"May we sit down?" The woman, pretty, wearing a floral print top and jeans, a mail-pouch purse over her shoulder, drew a chair back and seated herself beside Herb Asher. "Sit down, Manny," she said to a small boy who stood awkwardly near the table. What a beautiful child, Herb Asher thought. How did he get in here? There aren't supposed to be any minors in here.

"Are these friends of yours?" Rybys said.

The pretty, dark-haired young woman said, "Herb hasn't seen me since college. How are you, Herb? Don't you recognize me?" She held out her hand to him, and, reflexively, he took it. And then, as he shook her hand, he remembered her. They had been in school together, in a poly-sci course.

"Zina," he said, delighted. "Zina Pallas."

"This is my little brother," Zina said, motioning the boy to sit down. "Manny. Manny Pallas." To Rybys she said. "Herb hasn't changed a bit. I knew it was him when I saw him. You're here to see Linda Fox? I've never heard her; they say she's real good."

"Very good," Herb said, pleased at her support.

"Hello, Mr. Asher," the boy said.

"Glad to meet you, Manny." He shook hands with the boy. "This is my wife, Rybys."

"So you two are married," Zina said. "Mind if I smoke?" She lit a cigarette. "I keep trying to quit but when I quit I start eating a lot and get as fat as a pig."

"Is your purse genuine leather?" Rybys said, interested.

"Yes." Zina passed it over to her.

"I've never seen a leather purse before," Rybys said.

"There she is," Herb Asher said. Linda Fox had appeared on the stage; the audience clapped.

"She looks like a pizza waitress," Rybys said.

Zina, taking her purse back, said, "If she's going to make it big she's going to have to lose some weight. I mean, she looks all right, but—"

"What is this thing you have about weight?" Herb Asher said, irritated.

The boy, Manny, spoke up. "Herbert, Herbert."

"Yes?" He bent to hear.

"Remember," the boy said.

Puzzled, he started to say Remember what? but then Linda Fox took hold of the microphone, half shut her eyes, and began to sing. She had a round face, and almost a double chin, but her skin was fair, and, most important to him of all, she had long eyelashes that flickered as she sang—they fascinated him and he sat spellbound. Linda wore an extremely low-cut gown and even from where he sat he could see the outline of her nipples; she had on no bra.

Shall I sue? shall I seek for grace?
Shall I pray? shall I prove?
Shall I strive to a heavenly joy
With an earthly love?

Audibly, Rybys said, "I hate that song. I have heard her before."

Several people hissed at her to be quiet.

"Not by her, though," Rybys said. "She isn't even original. That song—" She piped down, but she was not happy.

When the song ended, and the audience had begun to clap, Herb Asher said to his wife, "You never heard 'Shall I Sue' before. Nobody else sings it but Linda Fox."

"You just like to gape at her nipples," Rybys said.

To Herb Asher the little boy said, "Would you take me to the men's room, Mr. Asher?"

"Now?" he said, dismayed. "Can't you wait until she's through singing?"

The boy said, "Now, Mr. Asher."

With reluctance he led Manny through the maze of tables to the doors at the rear of the lounge. But before they had entered the men's room Manny stopped him.

"You can see her better from here," Manny said.

It was true. He was now much closer to the stage. He and the boy stood together in silence as Linda Fox sang "Weep You No More Sad Fountains."

When the song ended, Manny said, "You don't remember, do you? She has enchanted you. Wake up, Herbert Asher. You know me well, and I know you. Linda Fox does not sing her songs at an obscure cocktail lounge in Hollywood; she is famous throughout the galaxy. She is the most important entertainer of this decade. The chief prelate and the procurator maximus invite her to—"

"She's going to sing again," Herb Asher interrupted. He barely heard the boy's words and they made no sense to him. A babbling boy, he thought, making it hard for me to hear Linda Fox. Just what I need.

After the song had ended, Manny said, "Herbert, Herbert; do you want to meet her? Is that what you want?"

"What?" he murmured, his eyes—his attention—fixed on Linda Fox. God, he thought; what a figure she has. She's practically falling out of her dress. He thought, I wish my wife was built like that.

"She will come this way," Manny said, "when she finishes. Stand here, Herb Asher, and she will pass directly by you."

"You're joking," he said.

"No," Manny said. "You will have what you want most in the world . . . that which you dreamed of as you lay on your bunk in your dome."

"What dome?" he said.

Manny said, " 'How you have fallen from heaven, bright morning star, felled—' "

"You mean one of those colony-planet domes?" Herb Asher said.

"I can't make you listen, can I?" Manny said. "If I could say to you—"

"She is coming this way," Herb Asher said. "How did you know?" He moved a few steps toward her. Linda Fox walked rapidly, with small steps, a gentle expression on her face.

"Thank you," she was saying to people who spoke to her. For a moment she stopped to give her autograph to a black youth nattily dressed.

Tapping Herb Asher on the shoulder a waitress said, "You're going to have to take that boy out of here, sir; we can't have minors in here."

"Sorry," Herb Asher said.

"Right now," the waitress said.

"Okay," he said; he took Manny by the shoulder and, with unhappy reluctance, led him back toward their table. And, as he turned away, he saw out of the corner of his eye the Fox pass by the spot at which he and the boy had stood. Manny had been right. A few more seconds and he would have been able to speak a few words to her. And, perhaps, she would have answered.

Manny said, "It is her desire to trick you, Herb Asher. She offered it to you and took it away again. If you want to meet Linda Fox I will see that you do; I promise you. Remember this, because it will come to pass. I will not see you cheated."

"I don't know what you're talking about," Herb said, "but if I could meet her—"

"You will," Manny said.

"You're a strange kid," Herb Asher said. As they passed below a light fixture he noticed something that startled him; he halted and, taking hold of Manny, he moved him directly under the light. *You look like Rybys,* he thought. For an instant a flash of memory jarred him; his mind seemed to open up, as if vast spaces, open spaces, a universe of stars, had flooded into it.

"Herbert," the boy said, "she is not real. Linda Fox—she is a phantasm of yours. But I can make her real; I confer being—it is I who makes the irreal into the real, and I can do it for you, with her."

"What happened?" Rybys said, when they reached the table.

"Manny has to leave," Herb said to Zina Pallas. "The waitress said so. I guess you'll have to go. Sorry."

Taking her purse and cigarettes, Zina rose. "I'm sorry; I guess I kept you from seeing the Fox."

"Let's go with them," Rybys said, also rising. "My head hurts, Herb; I'd like to get out of here."

Resigned, he said, "All right." Cheated, he thought. That was what Manny had said. *I will not see you cheated.* That is exactly what happened, he realized; I have been cheated this evening. Well, some other time. It would be interesting to talk to her, maybe get her autograph. He thought, Close up I could see that her eyelashes are fake. Christ, he thought; how depressing. Maybe her breasts are fake, too. There're those pads they slip in. He felt disappointed and unhappy and now he, too, wanted to leave.

This evening didn't work out, he thought as he escorted Rybys, Zina and Manny from the club onto the dark Hollywood street. I expected so much . . . and then he remembered what the boy had said, the strange things, and the nanosecond of jarred memory: scenes that appeared in his mind so briefly and yet so convincingly. This is not an ordinary child, he realized. And his resemblance to my wife—I can see it now, as they stand together. He could be her son. Eerie. He shivered, even though the air was warm.

Zina said, "I fulfilled his wishes; I gave him what he dreamed of. All those months as he lay on his bunk. With his 3-D posters of her, his tapes."

"You gave him nothing," Emmanuel said. "You robbed him, in fact. You took something away."

"She is a media product," Zina said. The two of them walked slowly along the nocturnal Hollywood sidewalk, back to her fly-car. "That is no fault of mine. I can't be blamed if Linda Fox is not real."

"Here in your realm that distinction means nothing."

"What can you give him?" Zina said. "Only illness—his wife's illness. And her death in your service. Is your gift better than mine?"

Emmanuel said, "I made him a promise and I do not lie." I shall fulfill that promise, he said to himself. In this realm or in my own realm; it doesn't matter because in either case I will make Linda Fox real. That is the power I have, and it is not the power of enchantment; it is the most precious gift of all: reality.

"What are you thinking?" Zina said.

" 'Better a live dog than a dead prince,' " Manny said.

"Who said that?"

"It is simply common sense."

Zina said, "What is your meaning?"

"I mean that your enchantment gave him nothing and the real world—"

"The real world," Zina said, "put him in cryonic suspension for ten years. Isn't a beautiful dream better than a cruel reality? Would you rather suffer in actuality than enjoy yourself in the domain of—" She paused.

"Intoxication," he said. "That is what your domain consists of; it is a drunken world. Drunken with dancing and with joy. I say that the quality of realness is more important than any other quality, because once realness departs, there is nothing. A dream is nothing. I disagree with you; I say you cheated Herbert Asher. I say you did a cruel thing to him. I saw his reaction; I measured his dejection. And I will make it up to him."

"You will make the Fox real."

"Is it your wager that I can't?"

"My wager," Zina said, "is that it doesn't matter. Real or not she is worthless; you will have achieved nothing."

"I accept the wager," he said.

"Shake my hand on it." She extended her hand.

They shook, standing there on the Hollywood sidewalk under the glaring artificial light.

As they flew back to Washington, D.C. Zina said, "In my realm many things are different. Perhaps you would like to meet Party Chairman Nicholas Bulkowsky."

Emmanuel said, "Is he not the procurator?"

"The Communist Party has not the world power that you are accustomed to. The term 'Scientific Legate' is not known. Nor is Fulton Statler Harms the chief prelate of the C.I.C., inasmuch as no Christian-Islamic Church exists. He is a cardinal of the Roman Catholic Church; he does not control the lives of millions."

"That is good," Emmanuel said.

"Then I have done well in my domain," Zina said. "Do you agree? Because if you agree—"

"These are good things," Emmanuel said.

"Tell me your objection."

"It is an illusion. In the real world both men hold world power; they jointly control the planet."

Zina said, "I will tell you something you do not understand. We have made changes in the past. We saw to it that the C.I.C. and the S.L. did not come into existence. The world you see here, my world, is an alternate world to your own, and equally real."

"I don't believe you," Emmanuel said.

"There are many worlds."

He said, "I am the generator of world, I and I alone. No one else can create world. I am He Who causes to be. You are not."

"Nonetheless—"

"You do not understand," Emmanuel said. "There are many

potentialities that do not become actualized. I select from among the potentialities the ones I prefer and I bestow actuality onto them."

"Then you have made poor choices. It would have been far better if the C.I.C. and the S.L. never came into being."

"You admit, then, that your world is not real? That it is a forgery?"

Zina hesitated. "It branched off at crucial points, due to our interference with the past. Call it magic if you want or call it technology; in any case we can enter retrotime and overrule mistakes in history. We have done that. In this alternate world Bulkowsky and Harms are minor figures—they exist, but not as they do in your world. It is a choice of worlds, equally real."

"And Belial," he said. "Belial sits in a cage in a zoo and throngs of people, vast hordes of them, gape at him."

"Correct."

"Lies," he said. "It is wish fulfillment. You cannot build a world on wishes. The basis of reality is bleak because you cannot serve up obliging mock vistas; you must adhere to what is possible: *the law of necessity*. That is the underpinning of reality: necessity. Whatever is, is because it must be; because it can be no other way. It is not what it is because someone wishes it but because it has to be—that and specifically that, down to the most meager detail. I know this because I do this. You have your job and I have mine, and I understand mine; I understand the law of necessity."

Zina, after a moment, said:

The woods of Arcady are dead,
And over is their antique joy;
Of old the world on dreaming fed;
Grey Truth is now her painted toy;
Yet still she turns her restless head.

That is the first poem by Yeats," she finished.

"I know that poem," Emmanuel said. "It ends:

But ah! she dreams not now; dream thou!
For fair are poppies on the brow:
Dream, dream, for this is also sooth.

" 'Sooth' meaning 'truth,' " he explained.

"You don't have to explain," Zina said. "And you disagree with the poem."

"Gray truth is better than the dream," he said. "That, too, is sooth. It is the final truth of all, that truth is better than any lie however blissful. I distrust this world because it is too sweet. Your world is too nice to be real. Your world is a whim. When Herb Asher saw the Fox he saw deception, and that deception lies at the heart of your world." And that deception, he said to himself, is what I shall undo.

I shall replace it, he said to himself, with the veridical. Which you do not understand.

The Fox as reality will be more acceptable to Herb Asher than any dream of the Fox. I know it; I stake everything on this proposition. Here I stand or fall.

"That is correct," Zina said.

"Any seeming reality that is obliging," Emmanuel said, "is something to suspect. The hallmark of the fraudulent is that it becomes what you would like it to be. I see that here. You would like Nicholas Bulkowsky not to be a vastly influential man; you would like Fulton Harms to be a minor figure, not part of history. Your world obliges you, and that gives it away for what it is. My world is stubborn. It will not yield. A recalcitrant and implacable world is a real world."

"A world that murders those forced to live in it."

"That is not the whole of it. My world is not that bad; there is much besides death and pain in it. On Earth, the real Earth, there is beauty and joy and—" He broke off. He had been tricked. She had won again.

"Then Earth is not so bad," she said. "It should not be scourged by fire. There is beauty and joy and love and good people. Despite Belial's rule. I told you that and you disputed it, as we walked among the Japanese cherry trees. What do you say now, Lord of Hosts, God of Abraham? Have you not proved me right?"

He admitted, "You are clever, Zina."

Her eyes sparkled and she smiled. "Then hold back the great and terrible day that you speak of in Scripture. As I begged you to."

For the first time he sensed defeat. Enticed into speaking foolishly, he realized. How clever she is; how shrewd.

"As it says in Scripture," Zina said.

I am Wisdom, I bestow shrewdness
and show the way to knowledge and prudence.

"But," he said, "you told me you are not Holy Wisdom. That you only pretended to be."

"It is up to you to discern who I am. You yourself must decipher my identity; I will not do it for you."

"And in the meantime—tricks."

"Yes," Zina said, "because it is through tricks that you will learn."

Staring at her he said, "You are tricking me so that I wake! As I woke Herb Asher!"

"Perhaps."

"Are you my disinhibiting stimulus?" Staring fixedly at her he said in a low stern voice, "I think I created you to bring back my memory, to restore me to myself."

"To lead you back to your throne," Zina said.

"*Did* I?"

Zina, steering the flycar, said nothing.

"Answer me," he said.

"Perhaps," Zina said.

"If I created you I can—"

"You created all things," Zina said.

"I do not understand you. I cannot follow you. You dance toward me and then away."

"But as I do so, you awaken," Zina said.

"Yes," he said. "And I reason back from that that you are the disinhibiting stimulus which I set up long ago, knowing as I did that my brain would be damaged and I would forget. You are systematically giving me back my identity, Zina. Then— I think I know who you are."

Turning her head she said, "Who?"

"I will not say. And you can't read it in my mind because I have suppressed it. I did so as soon as I thought it." Because, he realized, it is too much for me; even me. I can't believe it.

They drove on, toward the Atlantic and Washington, D.C.

14

Herb Asher felt himself engulfed by the profound impression that he had known the boy Manny Pallas at some other time, perhaps in another life. How many lives do we lead? he asked himself. Are we on tape? Is this some kind of a replay?

To Rybys he said, "The kid looked like you."

"Did he? I didn't notice." Rybys, as usual, was attempting to make a dress from a pattern, and screwing it up; pieces of fabric lay everywhere in the living room, along with dirty dishes, overfilled ashtrays and crumpled, stained magazines.

Herb decided to consult with his business partner, a middle-aged black named Elias Tate. Together he and Tate had operated a retail audio sales store for several years. Tate, however, viewed their store, Electronic Audio, as a sideline: his central interest in life was his missionary work. Tate preached at a small, out-of-the-way church, engaging a mostly black audience. His message, always, consisted of:

REPENT! THE KINGDOM OF GOD IS AT HAND!

It seemed to Herb Asher a strange preoccupation for a man so intelligent, but, in the final analysis, it was Tate's problem. They rarely discussed it.

Seated in the listening room of the store, Herb said to his

partner, "I met a striking and very peculiar little boy last night, at a cocktail lounge in Hollywood."

Involved in assembling a new laser-tracking phono component, Tate murmured, "What were you doing in Hollywood? Trying to get into pictures?"

"Listening to a new singer named Linda Fox."

"Never heard of her."

Herb said, "She's sexy as hell and very good. She—"

"You're married."

"I can dream," Herb said.

"Maybe you'd like to invite her to an autograph party at the store."

"We're the wrong kind of store."

"It's an audio store; she sings. That's audio. Or isn't she audible?"

"As far as I know she hasn't made any tapes or cut any records or been on TV. I happened to hear her last month when I was at the Anaheim Trade Center audio exhibit. I told you you should have come along."

"Sexuality is the malady of this world," Tate said. "This is a lustful and demented planet."

"And we're all going to hell."

Tate said, "I certainly hope so."

"You know you're out of step? You really are. You have an ethical code that dates back to the Dark Ages."

"Oh, long before that," Tate said. He placed a disc on the turntable and started up the component. On his 'scope the pattern appeared to be adequate but not perfect; Tate frowned.

"I almost met her. I was so close; a matter of seconds. She's better looking up close than anyone else I ever saw. You should see her. I know—I've got this intuition—that she's going to soar all the way to the top."

"Okay," Tate said, reasonably. "That's fine with me. Write her a fan letter. Tell her."

"Elias," Herb said, "the boy I met last night—he looked like Rybys."

The black man glanced up at him. "Really?"

"If Rybys could collect her goddam scattered wits for one second she could have noticed. She just can't goddam concentrate. She never looked at the boy. He could have been her son."

"Maybe there's something you don't know."

"Lay off," Herb said.

Elias said, "I'd like to see the boy."

"I felt I'd known him before, in some other life. For a second it started to come back to me and then—" He gestured. "I lost it. I couldn't pin it down. And there was more . . . as if I was remembering a whole other world. Another life entirely."

Elias ceased working. "Describe it."

"You were older. And not black. You were a very old man in a robe. I wasn't on Earth; I glimpsed a frozen landscape and it wasn't Terra. Elias—could I be from another planet, and some powerful agency laid down false memories in my mind, over the real ones? And the boy—seeing the boy—caused the real memories to begin to return? And I had the idea that Rybys was very ill. In fact, about to die. And something about Immigration officials with guns."

"Immigration officers don't carry guns."

"And a ship. A long trip at very high speed. Urgency. And most of all—a presence. An uncanny presence. Not human. Maybe it was an extraterrestrial, the race I'm really a part of. From my home planet."

"Herb," Elias said, "you are full of shit."

"I know. But just for a second I experienced all that. And—listen to this." He gestured excitedly. "An accident. Our ship crashing into another ship. My *body* remembered; it remembered the concussion, the trauma."

"Go to a hypnotherapist," Elias said, "get him to put you under, and remember. You're obviously a weird alien programmed to blow up the world. You probably have a bomb inside you."

Herb said, "That's not funny."

"Okay; you're from some wise, super-advanced noble spiritual race and you were sent here to enlighten mankind. To save us."

Instantly, in Herb Asher's mind, memories flicked on, and then flicked off again. Almost at once.

"What is it?" Elias asked, regarding him acutely.

"More memories. When you said that."

After an interval of silence Elias said, "I wish you would read the Bible sometime."

"It had something to do with the Bible," Herb said. "My mission."

"Maybe you're a messenger," Elias said. "Maybe you have a message to deliver to the world. From God."

"Stop kidding me."

Elias said, "I'm not kidding. Not now." And apparently that was so; his dark face had turned grim.

"What's wrong?" Herb said.

"Sometimes I think this planet is under a spell," Elias said. "We are asleep or in a trance, and something causes us to see what it wants us to see and remember and think what it wants us to remember and think. Which means we're whatever it wants us to be. Which in turn means that we have no genuine existence. We're at the mercy of some kind of whim."

"Strange," Herb Asher said.

His business partner said, "Yes. Very strange."

At the end of the work day, as Herb Asher and his partner were preparing to close up the store a young woman wearing a suede leather jacket, jeans, moccasins and a red silk scarf tied over her hair came in. "Hi," she said to Herb, her hands thrust into the pockets of her jacket. "How are you?"

"Zina," he said, pleased. And a voice inside his head said, How did she find you? This is three thousand miles away from Hollywood. Through an index of locations computer, probably. Still . . . he sensed something not right. But it did not pertain to his nature to turn down a visit by a pretty girl.

"Do you have time for a cup of coffee?" she asked.

"Sure," he said.

Shortly, they sat facing each other across a table in a nearby restaurant.

Zina, stirring cream and sugar into her coffee, said, "I want to talk to you about Manny."

"Why does he resemble my wife?" he said.

"Does he? I didn't notice. Manny feels very badly that he prevented you from meeting Linda Fox."

"I'm not sure he did."

"She was coming right at you."

"She was walking our way, but that doesn't prove I would have met her."

"He wants you to meet her. Herb, he feels terrible guilt; he couldn't sleep all night."

Puzzled, he said, "What does he propose?"

"That you write her a fan letter. Explaining the situation. He's convinced she'd answer."

"It's not likely."

Zina said quietly, "You'd be doing Manny a favor. Even if she doesn't answer."

"I'd just as soon meet you," he said. And his words were weighed out carefully; weighed out and measured.

"Oh?" She glanced up. What black eyes she had!

"Both of you," he said. "You and your little brother."

"Manny has suffered brain damage. His mother was injured in a sky accident while she was pregnant with him. He spent several months in a synthowomb, but they didn't get him in the synthowomb in time. So . . ." She tapped her fingers against the table. "He is impaired. He's been attending a special school. Because of the neurological damage he comes up with really nuts ideas. As an example—" She hesitated. "Well, what the hell. He says he's God."

"My partner should meet him, then," Herb Asher said.

"Oh no," she said, vigorously shaking her head. "I don't want him to meet Elias."

"How did you know about Elias?" he said, and again the peculiar warning sensation drifted through him.

"I stopped at your apartment first and talked to Rybys. We

spent several hours together; she mentioned the store and Elias. How else could I have found your store? It's not listed under your name."

"Elias is into religion," he said.

"That's what she told me; that's why I don't want Manny to meet him. They'd just jack each other up higher and higher into theological moonshine."

He answered, "I find Elias very levelheaded."

"Yes, and in many ways Manny is levelheaded. But you get two religious people together and they just sort of— You know. Endless talk about Jesus and the world coming to an end. The Battle of Armageddon. The conflagration." She shivered. "It gives me the creeps. Hellfire and damnation."

"Elias is into that, all right," Herb said. It almost seemed to him that she knew. Probably Rybys had told her; that was it.

"Herb," Zina said, "will you do Manny the favor he wants? Will you write the Fox—" Her expression changed.

" 'The Fox,' " he said. "I wonder if that'll catch on. It's a natural."

Continuing, Zina said, "Will you write Linda Fox and say you'd like to meet her? Ask her where she'll be appearing; they set up those club dates well in advance. Tell her you own an audio store. She's not well known; it isn't like some nationally famous star who gets bales of fan mail. Manny is sure she'll answer."

"Of course I will," he said.

She smiled. And her dark eyes danced.

"No problem," he said. "I'll go back to the store and type it there. We can mail it off together."

From her mail-pouch purse, Zina brought out an envelope. "Manny wrote out the letter for you. This is what he wants you to say. Change it if you want, but—don't change it too much. Manny worked real hard on it."

"Okay." He accepted the envelope from her. Rising, he said, "Let's go back to the shop."

As he sat at his office typewriter transcribing Manny's letter to the Fox—as Zina had called her—Zina paced about the closed-up shop, smoking vigorously.

"Is there something I don't know?" he said. He sensed more to this; she seemed unusually tense.

"Manny and I have a bet going," Zina said. "It has to do with —well, basically, it has to do with whether Linda Fox will answer or not. The bet is a little more complicated, but that's the thrust of it. Does that bother you?"

"No," he said. "Which of you put down your money which way?"

She did not answer.

"Let it go," he said. He wondered why she had not responded, and why she was so tense about it. What do they think will come of this? he asked himself. "Don't say anything to my wife," he said, then, thinking some thoughts of his own.

He had, then, an intense intuition: that something rested on this, something important, with dimensions that he could not fathom.

"Am I being set up?" he said.

"In what way?"

"I don't know." He had finished typing; he pressed the key for *print* and the machine—a smart typewriter—instantly printed out his letter and dropped it in the receiving bin.

"My signature goes on it," he said.

"Yes. It's from you."

He signed the letter, typed out an envelope, from the address on Manny's copy . . . and wondered, abruptly, how Zina and Manny had gotten hold of Linda Fox's home address. There it was, on the boy's carefully written holographic letter. Not the Golden Hind but a residence. In Sherman Oaks.

Odd, he thought. Wouldn't her address be unlisted?

Maybe not. She wasn't well known, as had been repeatedly pointed out to him.

"I don't think she'll answer," he said.

"Well, then some silver pennies will change hands."

Instantly he said, "Fairy land."

"What?" she said, startled.

"A children's book. *Silver Pennies.* An old classic. In it there's the statement, 'You need a silver penny to get into fairy land.' " He had owned the book as a child.

She laughed. Nervously, or so it seemed to him.

"Zina," he said, "I feel that something is wrong."

"Nothing is wrong as far as I know." She deftly took the envelope from him. "I'll mail it," she said.

"Thank you," he said. "Will I see you again?"

"Of course you will." Leaning toward him she pursed her lips and kissed him on the mouth.

He looked around him and saw bamboo. But color moved through it, like St. Elmo's fire. The color, a shiny, glistening red, seemed alive. It collected here and there, and where it gathered it formed words, or rather something like words. As if the world had become language.

What am I doing here? he wondered wildly. What happened? A minute ago I wasn't here!

The red, glistening fire, like visible electricity, spelled out a message to him, distributed through the bamboo and children's swings and dry, stubby grass.

YOU SHALL LOVE THE LORD YOUR GOD WITH ALL YOUR HEART, WITH ALL YOUR MIGHT, AND WITH ALL YOUR SOUL

"Yes," he said. He felt fright, but, because the liquid tongues of fire were so beautiful he felt awed more than afraid; spellbound, he gazed about him. The fire moved; it came and it passed on; it flowed this way and that; pools of it formed, and he knew he was seeing a living creature. Or rather the *blood* of a living creature. The fire was living blood, but a magical blood, not physical blood but blood transformed.

Reaching down, trembling, he touched the blood and felt a shock pass through him; and he knew that the living blood had entered him. Immediately words formed in his mind.

BEWARE!

"Help me," he said feebly.

Lifting his head he saw into infinite space; he saw reaches so vast that he could not comprehend them—space stretching out forever, and himself expanding with that space.

Oh my God, he said to himself; he shook violently. Blood and living words, and something intelligent close by, simulating the world, or the world simulating it; something camouflaged, an entity that was aware of him.

A beam of pink light blinded him; he felt dreadful pain in his head, and clapped his hands to his eyes. I am blind! he realized. With the pain and the pink light came understanding, an acute knowledge; he knew that Zina was not a human woman, and he knew, further, that the boy Manny was not a human boy. This was not a real world he was in; he understood that because the beam of pink light had told him that. This world was a simulation, and something living and intelligent and sympathetic wanted him to know. Something cares about me and it has penetrated this world to warn me, he realized, and it is camouflaged as this world so that the master of this world, the lord of this unreal realm, will not know; not know it is here and not know it has told me. This is a terrible secret to know, he thought. I could be killed for knowing this. I am in a—

FEAR NOT

"Okay," he said, and still trembled. Words inside his head, knowledge inside his head. But he remained blind, and the pain also remained. "Who are you?" he said. "Tell me your name."

VALIS

"Who is 'Valis'?" he said.

THE LORD YOUR GOD

He said, "Don't hurt me."

BE NOT AFRAID, MAN

His sight began to clear. He removed his hands from before his eyes. Zina stood there, in her suede leather jacket and jeans; only a second had passed. She was moving back, after having kissed him. Did she know? How could she know? Only he and Valis knew.

He said, "You are a fairy."

"A *what?*" She began to laugh.

"That information was transferred to me. I know. I know everything. I remember CY30-CY30B; I remember my dome. I remember Rybys's illness and the trip to Earth. The accident. I remember that whole other world, the real world. It penetrated into this world and woke me up." He stared at her, and, in return, Zina stared, fixedly, back.

"My name means fairy," Zina said, "but that doesn't make me a fairy. Emmanuel means 'God with us' but that doesn't make him God."

Herb Asher said, "I remember Yah."

"Oh," she said. "Well. Goodness."

"Emmanuel is Yah," Herb Asher said.

"I'm leaving," Zina said. Hands in her jacket pockets she walked rapidly to the front door of the store, turned the key in the lock and disappeared outside; in an instant she was gone.

She has the letter, he realized. My letter to the Fox.

Hurriedly he followed after her.

No sign of her. He peered in all directions. Cars and people, but not Zina. She had gotten away.

She will mail it, he said to himself. The bet between her and Emmanuel; it involves me. They are wagering over me, and the universe itself is at stake. Impossible. But the beam of pink light had told him; it had conveyed all that, instantly, without the passage of any time at all.

Trembling, his head still aching, he returned to the store; he seated himself and rubbed his aching forehead.

She will involve me with the Fox, he realized. And out of that involvement, depending on which way it goes, the structure of reality will— He was not sure what it would do. But that was the issue: the structure of reality itself, the universe and every living creature in it.

It has to do with being, he thought to himself, knowing this because, and only because, of the beam of pink light, which was a living, electrical blood, the blood of some immense meta-entity. *Sein,* he thought. A German word; what does it mean? *Das Nichts.* The opposite of *Sein. Sein* equaled being equaled existence equaled a genuine universe. *Das Nichts* equally nothing equaled the simulation of the universe, the dream—which I am in now, he knew. The pink beam told me that.

I need a drink, he said to himself. Picking up the fone he dropped in the punchcard and was immediately connected with his home. "Rybys," he said huskily, "I'll be late."

"You're taking her out? That girl?" His wife's voice was brittle.

"No, goddam it," he said, and hung up the fone.

God is the Guarantor of the universe, he realized. That is the foundation of what I have been told. Without God there is nothing; it all flows away and is gone.

Locking up the store he got into his flycar and turned on the motor.

Standing on the sidewalk—a man. A familiar man, a black. Middle-aged, well dressed.

"Elias!" Herb called. "What are you doing? What is it?"

"I came back to see if you were all right." Elias Tate walked up to Herb's car. "You're totally pale."

"Get in the car," Herb said.

Elias got in.

15

At the bar both men sat as they often sat; Elias, as always, had a Coke with ice. He never drank.

''Okay,'' he said, nodding. ''There's nothing you can do to stop the letter. It's probably already mailed.''

''I'm a poker chip,'' Herb Asher said. ''Between Zina and Emmanuel.''

''They're not betting as to whether Linda Fox will answer,'' Elias said. ''They're betting on something else.'' He wadded up a bit of cardboard and dropped it into his Coke. ''There is no way in the world that you're going to be able to figure out what their wager is. The bamboo and the children's swings. The stubble growing . . . I have a residual memory of that myself; I dream about it. It's a school. For kids. A special school. I go there in my sleep again and again.''

''The real world,'' Herb said.

''Apparently. You've reconstructed a lot. Don't go around saying God told you this is a fake universe, Herb. Don' tell anybody else what you've told me.''

''Do you believe me?''

''I believe you've had a very unusual and inexplicable experience, but I don't believe this is an ersatz world. It seems perfectly substantial.'' He rapped on the plastic surface of the table between them. ''No, I don't believe that; I don't believe in unreal worlds. There is only one cosmos and Jehovah God created it."

"I don't think anyone creates a fake universe," Herb said, "since it isn't there."

"But you're saying someone is causing us to see a universe that doesn't exist. Who is this someone?"

He said, "Satan."

Cocking his head, Elias eyed him.

"It's a way of seeing the real world," Herb said. "An occluded way. A dreamlike way. A hypnotized, asleep way. The nature of world undergoes a perceptual change; actually it is the perceptions that change, not the world. *The change is in us.*"

" 'The Ape of God,' " Elias said. "A Medieval theory about the Devil. That he apes God's legitimate creation with spurious interpolations of his own. That's really an exceedingly sophisticated idea, epistemologically speaking. Does it mean that parts of the world are spurious? Or that sometimes the whole world is spurious? Or that there are plural worlds of which one is real and the others are not? Is there essentially one matrix world from which people derive differing perceptions? So that the world you see is not the world I see?"

"I just know," Herb said, "that I was caused to remember, made to remember, the real world. My knowledge that this world here"—he tapped the table—"is based on that memory, not on my experience of this forgery. I am comparing; I have something to compare this world with. That is it."

"Couldn't the memories be false?"

"I know they are not."

"How do you know?"

"I trust the beam of pink light."

"Why?"

"I don't know," he said.

"Because it said it was God? The agency of enchantment can say that. The demonic power."

"We'll see," Herb Asher said. He wondered once more what the wager was, what they expected him to do.

Five days later at his home he received a long-distance person-to-person fone call. On the screen a slightly chubby female face appeared, and a shy, breathless voice said, "Mr. Asher? This is Linda Fox. I'm calling you from California. I got your letter."

His heart ceased to beat; it stilled within him. "Hello, Linda," he said. "Ms. Fox. I guess." He felt numbed.

"I'll tell you why I'm calling." She had a gentle voice, a rushing, excited voice; it was as if she panted, timidly. "First I want to thank you for your letter; I'm glad you like me—I mean my singing. Do you like the Dowland? Is that a good idea?"

He said, "Very good. I especially like 'Weep You No More Sad Fountains.' That's my favorite."

"What I want to ask you—your letterhead; you're in the retail home audio system business. I'm moving to an apartment in Manhattan in a month and I must get an audio system set up right away; we have tapes we made out here on the West Coast that my producer will be sending me—I have to be able to listen to them as they really sound, on a really good system." Her long lashes fluttered apprehensively. "Could you fly to New York next week and give me an idea of what sort of sound system you could install? I don't care how much it costs; I won't be paying for it—I signed with Superba Records and they're going to pay for everything."

"Sure," he said.

"Or would it be better if I flew to Washington, D.C.?" she continued. "Whichever is better. It has to be done quickly; they told me to stress that. This is so exciting for me; I just signed, and I have a new manager. I'm going to be making video discs later on, but we're starting with audio tapes now—can you do it? I really don't know who to ask. There're a lot of retail electronics places out here on the West Coast but I don't know anyone on the East Coast. I suppose I should be going to somebody in New York, but Washington, D.C. isn't very far, is it? I mean, you could get up there, couldn't you? Superba and my producer—he's with them—will cover all your expenses."

"No problem," he said.

"Okay. Well, here's my number in Sherman Oaks and I'll

give you my Manhattan number; both fone numbers. How did you know my Sherman Oaks address? The letter came directly to me. I'm not supposed to be listed."

"A friend. Somebody in the industry. Connections; you know. I'm in the business."

"You caught me at the Hind? The acoustics are peculiar there. Could you hear me all right? You look familiar; I think I saw you in the audience. You were standing in the corner."

"I had a little boy with me."

Linda Fox said, "I did see you; you were looking at me—you had the most unusual expression. Is he your son?"

"No," he said.

"Are you ready to write down these numbers?"

She gave him her two fone numbers; he wrote them down shakily. "I'll put in a hell of an audio system for you," he managed to say. "It's been a terrific treat talking to you. I'm convinced you're going all the way, all the way to the top, to the top of the charts. You're going to be listened to and looked at all over the galaxy. I know it. Believe me."

"You are so sweet," Linda Fox said. "I have to go, now. Thank you. OK? Goodbye. I'll be expecting to hear from you. Don't forget. This is urgent; it has to be done. So many problems but—it's exciting. Goodbye." She hung up.

As he hung up the fone Herb Asher said aloud, "I'll be god damned. I don't believe it."

From behind him Rybys said, "She called you. She actually foned you. That's quite something. Are you going to put in a system for her? It means—"

"I don't mind flying to New York. I'll acquire the components up there; no need to transport them from down here."

"Do you think you should take Elias with you?"

"We'll see," he said, his mind clouded, buzzing with awe.

"Congratulations," Rybys said. "I have a hunch I should go with you, but if you promise not to—"

"It's OK," he said, barely listening to her. "The Fox," he said. "*I talked to her*. She called me. *Me*."

"Didn't you tell me something about Zina and her little

brother having some kind of bet? They bet—one of them bet—she wouldn't answer your letter, and the other bet she would?"

"Yeah," he said. "There's a bet." He did not care about the bet. I will see her, he said to himself. I will visit her new Manhattan apartment, spend an evening with her. Clothes; I need new clothes. Christ, I have to look good.

"How much gear do you think you can unload on her?" Rybys said.

Savagely, he said, "It isn't a question of that."

Shrinking back, Rybys said, "I'm sorry. I just meant—you know. How extensive a system; that's all I meant."

"She will be getting the best system money can buy," he said. "Only the finest. What I would want for myself. Better than what I'd get for myself."

"Maybe this will be good publicity for the store."

He glared at her.

"What is it?" Rybys said.

"The Fox," he said, simply. "It was the Fox calling me on the fone. I can't believe it."

"Better call Zina and Emmanuel and tell them. I have their number."

He thought, No. This is my business. Not theirs.

To Zina, Emmanuel said, "The time is here. Now we will see which way it goes. He'll be flying to New York shortly. It won't be long."

"Do you already know what will happen?" Zina asked.

"What I want to know," Emmanuel said, "is this. Will you withdraw your world of empty dreams if he finds her—"

"He will find her worthless," Zina said. "She is an empty fool, without wit, without wisdom; she has no sense, and he will walk away from her because you cannot make something like that into reality."

Emmanuel said, "We will see."

"Yes, we shall," Zina said. "A nonentity awaits Herb Asher. She looks up to *him*."

There, precisely, Emmanuel declared in the recesses of his secret mind, *you have made your mistake*. Herb Asher does not thrive on his adoration of her; it is mutuality that is needed, and you have handed me that. When you debased her here in your domain you accidentally imparted substance into her.

And this, he thought, because you do not know what substance is; it lies beyond you. But not, he thought, beyond me. It is *my* domain.

"I think," he said, "you have already lost."

With delight, Zina said, "You do not know what I play for! You know neither me nor my goals!"

That may be so, he reflected.

But I know myself; and—I know my goals.

Wearing a fashionable suit, purchased at some considerable expense, Herb Asher boarded a luxury-class commercial rocket for New York City. Briefcase in hand—it contained specs on all the latest home audio systems finding their way onto the market—he sat gazing out the window as the three-minute trip unrolled. The rocket began to descend almost at once.

This is the most wonderful moment in my life, he declared inwardly as the retrojets fired. Look at me; I am right out of the pages of *Style* magazine.

Thank God Rybys didn't come along.

"Ladies and gentlemen," the overhead speakers announced, "we have now landed at Kennedy Spaceport. Please remain in your seats until the tone sounds; then you may exit at the front end of the ship. Thank you for taking Delta Spacelines."

"Enjoy your day," the robot steward said to Herb Asher as he jauntily exited from the ship.

"You, too," Herb said. "And plenty more besides."

By Yellow cab he flew directly to the Essex House where he had his reservation—the hell with the cost—for the next two days. Very soon he unpacked, surveyed the grand appointments of his room, and then, after taking a Valzine (the best of the latest generations of cortical stimulants) picked up the fone and dialed Linda Fox's Manhattan number.

"How exciting to know you're in town," she said when he identified himself. "Can you come over now? I have some people here but they're just leaving. This decision about my equipment, this is something I want to do slowly and carefully. What time is it now? I just got here from California."

"It's 7 P.M. New York time," he said.

"Have you had dinner?"

"No," he said. It was like a fantasy; he felt as if he was in a dream world, a kingdom of the divine. He felt—like a child, he thought. Reading my *Silver Pennies* book of poems. Apparently I found a silver penny, and made my way there. Where I have always yearned to be. Home is the sailor home from the sea, he thought. And the hunter . . . He could not remember how the verse went. Well, in any case it was appropriate; he was home at last.

And there is no one here to tell me she looks like a pizza waitress, he informed himself. So I can forget that.

"I've got some food here in my apartment; I'm into health foods. If you want some . . . I have actual orange juice, soybean curd, organic foods. I don't believe in slaughtering animals."

"Fine," he said. "Sure; anything. You name it."

When he reached her apartment—in an outstandingly lovely building—he found her wearing a cap, a turtleneck sweater and white duck shorts; barefoot, she welcomed him into the living room. No furniture at all; she hadn't moved in yet. In the bedroom a sleeping bag and an open suitcase. The rooms were large and the picture window gave her a view of Central Park.

"Hello," she said. "I'm Linda." She extended her hand. "It's nice to meet you, Mr. Asher."

"Call me Herb," he said.

"On the Coast, the West Coast, everyone introduces people by their first names only; I'm trying to train myself away from that, but I can't. I was raised in Southern California, in Riverside." She shut the door after him. "It's ghastly without any furniture, isn't it? My manager is picking it out; it'll be here the day after tomorrow. Well, he's not picking it out alone; I'm helping him. Let's see your brochures." She had noticed his briefcase and her eyes sparkled with anticipation.

She does look a little like a pizza waitress, he thought. But that's okay. Her complexion, up close, in the glare of the overhead lighting, was not as clear as he had thought; in fact, he noticed, she had a little acne.

"We can sit on the floor," she said; she threw herself down, bare knees raised, her back against the wall. "Let's see. I'm relying on you entirely."

He began, "I assume you want studio quality items. What we call professional components. Not what the ordinary person has in his home."

"What's that?" She pointed to a picture of huge speakers. "They look like refrigerators."

"That's an old design," he said, turning to the next page. "Those work by means of a plasma. Derived from helium. You have to keep buying tanks of helium. They look good, though, because the helium plasma glows. It's produced by extremely high voltage. Here, let me show you something more recent; helium plasma transduction is obsolete or soon will be."

Why do I have the feeling I'm imagining all this? he asked himself. Maybe because it's so wonderful. But still . . .

For a couple of hours the two of them sat together leaning against the wall going through his literature. Her enthusiasm was enormous, but, eventually, she began to tire.

"I am hungry," she said. "I don't really have the right clothes with me to go to a restaurant; you have to dress up back here—it's not like Southern California where you can wear anything. Where are you staying?"

"The Essex House."

Standing, stretching, Linda Fox said, "Let's go back to your suite and order room service. Okay?"

"Outstanding," he said, getting up.

After they had eaten dinner together in his room at the hotel Linda Fox paced about, her arms folded. "You know something?" she said. "I keep having this recurring dream that I'm the most famous singer in the galaxy. It's exactly like what you said on the fone. My fantasy life in my subconscious, I guess. But I keep dreaming these production scenes where I'm recording tape after tape and giving concerts, and I have all this money. Do you believe in astrology?"

"I guess I do," he said.

"And places I've never been to; I dream about that. And people I've never seen before, important people. People big in the entertainment field. And we're always rushing around from place to place. Order some wine, would you? I don't know anything about French wine; you decide. But don't make it too dry."

He knew nothing about French wine either, but he got the wine list from the hotel's main restaurant and, with the help of the wine steward, ordered a bottle of expensive burgundy.

"This tastes great," Linda Fox said, curled up on the couch, her bare legs tucked under her. "Tell me about yourself. How long have you been in retail audio components?"

"A number of years," he said.

"How did you beat the draft?"

That puzzled him. He had the idea that the draft had been abolished years ago.

"It has?" Linda said when he told her. Puzzled, the trace of a frown on her face, she said, "That's funny. I was sure there was a draft, and a lot of men have migrated out to colony worlds to escape it. Have you ever been off Earth?"

"No," he said. "But I'd like to try interplanetary travel just for the experience of it." Seating himself on the couch beside her he casually put his arm behind her; she did not pull away. "And to touch down on another planet. That must be some sensation."

"I'm perfectly happy here." She leaned her head back against his arm and shut her eyes. "Rub my back," she said. "I'm stiff from leaning against the wall; it hurts here." She touched a midpoint in her spine, leaning forward. He began to massage her neck. "That feels good," she murmured.

"Lie down on the bed," he said. "So I can get more pressure; I can't do it very well this way."

"Okay." Linda Fox hopped from the couch and padded barefoot across the room. "What a nice bedroom. I've never stayed at the Essex House. Are you married?"

"No," he said. No point telling her about Rybys. "I was once but I got divorced."

"Isn't divorce awful?" She lay on the bed, prone, her arms stretched out.

Bending over her he kissed the back of her head.

"Don't," she said.

"Why not?"

"I can't."

"Can't what?" he said.

"Make love. I'm having my period."

Period? Linda Fox has periods? He was incredulous. He drew back from her, sitting bolt upright.

"I'm sorry," she said. She seemed relaxed. "Start up around my shoulders," she said. "It's stiff there. I'm sleepy. The wine, I guess. Such . . ." She yawned. "Good wine."

"Yes," he said, still sitting away from her.

All at once she burped; her hand, then, flew to her mouth. "*Pardon* me," she said.

He flew back to Washington, D.C. the next morning. She had returned to her barren apartment that night, but the matter was moot anyhow because of her period. A couple of times she mentioned—he thought unnecessarily—that she always had severe cramps during her period and had them now. On the return trip he felt weary, but he had closed a deal for a rather large sum; Linda Fox had signed the papers ordering a top-of-the-line stereo system, and, later, he would return and supervise the installation of video recording and playback components. All in all it had been a profitable trip.

And yet—his ultimate move had fallen through because Linda Fox . . . it had been the wrong time. Her menstrual cycle, he thought. Linda Fox has periods and cramps? he asked himself. I don't believe it. But I guess it's true. Could it have been a pretext? No, it was not a pretext. It was real.

When he arrived back home his wife greeted him with a single question. "Did you two fool around?"

"No," he said. Worse luck.

"You look tired," Rybys said.

"Tired but happy." It had been a satisfying and rewarding experience; he and the Fox had sat together talking for hours. An easy person to get to know, he thought. Relaxed, enthusiastic; a good person. Substantial. Not at all affected. I like her, he said to himself. It'll be good to see her again.

And, he thought, I know she'll go far.

It was odd how strong that intuition was inside him, his sense about the Fox's future success. Well, the explanation was that Linda Fox was just plain good.

"What kind of person is she?" Rybys said. "Nothing but talk about her career, probably."

"She is tender and gentle and modest," he said, "and totally informal. We talked about a lot of things."

"Could I meet her sometime?"

"I don't see why not," he said. "I'll be flying up there again. And she said something about flying down here and visiting the store. She goes all over the place; her career is taking off at this point—she's beginning to get the big breaks she needs and deserves and I'm glad for her, really glad."

If she only hadn't been having her period . . . but I guess those are the facts of life, he said to himself. That's what makes up reality. Linda is the same as any other woman in that regard; it comes with the territory.

I like her anyhow, he said to himself. Even if we didn't go to bed. The enjoyment of her company: that was enough.

To Zina Pallas, the boy said, "You have lost."

"Yes, I have lost." She nodded. "You made her real and he still cares for her. The dream for him is no longer a dream; it is true down to the level of disappointments."

"Which is the stamp of authenticity."

"Yes," she said. "Congratulations." Zina extended her hand to Emmanuel and they shook.

"And now," the boy said, "you will tell me who you are."

16

Zina said, "Yes, I will tell you who I am, Emmanuel, but I will not let your world return. Mine is better. Herb Asher leads a much happier life; Rybys is alive . . . Linda Fox is real—"

"But you did not make her real," he said. "I did."

"Do you want back again the world you gave them? With the winter, its ice and snow, over everything? It is I who burst the prison; I brought in the springtime. I deposed the procurator maximus and the chief prelate. Let it stay as it is."

"I will transmute your world into the real," he said. "I have already begun. I manifested myself to Herb Asher when you kissed him; I penetrate your world in my true form. I am making it *my* world, step by step. What the people must do, however, is remember. They may live in your world but they must know that a worse one existed and they were forced to live in it. I restored Herb Asher's memories, and the others dream dreams."

"That's fine with me."

"Tell me, now," he said, "who you are."

"Let us go," she said, "hand in hand. Like Beethoven and Goethe: two friends. Take us to Stanley Park in British Columbia and we will observe the animals there, the wolves, the great white wolves. It is a beautiful park, and Lionsgate Bridge is beautiful; Vancouver, British Columbia is the most beautiful city on Earth."

"That is true," he said. "I had forgotten."

"And after you view it I want you to ask yourself if you would destroy it or change it in any way. I want you to inquire of yourself if you would, upon seeing such earthly beauty, bring into existence your great and terrible day in which all the arrogant and evil-doers shall be chaff, set ablaze, leaving them neither root nor branch. OK?"

"OK," Emmanuel said.

Zina said:

We are spirits of the air
Who of human beings take care.

"Are you?" he said. Because, he thought, if that is so then you are an atmospheric spirit, which is to say—an angel.

Zina said:

Come, all ye songsters of the sky,
Wake and assemble in this wood;
But no ill-boding bird be nigh,
None but the harmless and the good.

"What are you saying?" Emmanuel said.

"Take us to Stanley Park first," Zina said. "Because if you take us there, we shall actually be there; it will be no dream."

He did so.

Together they walked across the verdant ground, among the vast trees. These stands, he knew, had never been logged; this was the primeval forest. "It is exceedingly beautiful," he said to her.

"It is the world," she said.

"Tell me who you are."

Zina said, "I am the Torah."

After a moment Emmanuel said, "Then I can do nothing regarding the universe without consulting you."

"And you can do nothing regarding the universe that is contrary to what I say," Zina said, "as you yourself decided, in the beginning, when you created me. You made me alive; I am a living being that thinks. I am the plan of the universe, its blueprint. That is the way you intended it and that is the way it is."

"Hence the slate you gave me," he said.

"Look at me," Zina said.

He looked at her—and saw a young woman, wearing a crown, and sitting on a throne. "Malkuth," he said. "The lowest of the ten sefiroth."

"And you are the Eternal Infinite En Sof," Malkuth said. "The first and highest of the sefiroth of the Tree of Life."

"But you said that you are the Torah."

"In the *Zohar,*" Malkuth said, "the Torah is depicted as a beautiful maiden living alone, secluded in a great castle. Her secret lover comes to the castle to see her, but all he can do is wait futilely outside hoping for a glimpse of her. Finally she appears at the window and he is able to catch sight of her, but only for an instant. Later on she lingers at the window and he is able, therefore, to speak with her; yet, still, she hides her face behind a veil . . . and her answers to his questions are evasive. Finally, after a long time, when her lover has become despairing that he will ever get to know her, she permits him to see her face at last."

Emmanuel said, "Thus revealing to her lover all the secrets which she has up to now, throughout the long courtship, kept buried in her heart. I know the *Zohar*. You are right."

"So you know me now, En Sof," Malkuth said. "Does it please you?"

"It does not," he said, "because although what you say is true, there is one more veil to be removed from your face. There is one more step."

"True." Malkuth, the lovely young woman seated on the throne, wearing a crown, said, "but you will have to find it."

"I will," he said. "I am so close now; only a step, one single step, away."

"You have guessed," she said. "But you must do better than that. Guessing is not enough; you must know."

"How beautiful you are, Malkuth," he said. "And of course

you are here in the world and love the world; you are the sefira that represents the Earth. You are the womb containing everything, all the other sefiroth that constitute the Tree itself; those other forces, nine of them, are generated by you."

"Even Kether," Malkuth said, calmly. "Who is highest."

"You are Diana, the fairy queen," he said. "You are Pallas Athena, the spirit of righteous war; you are the spring queen, you are Hagia Sophia, Holy Wisdom; you are the Torah which is the formula and blueprint of the universe; you are Malkuth of the Kabala, the lowest of the ten sefiroth of the Tree of Life; and you are my companion and friend, my guide. But what are you actually? Under all the disguises? I know what you are and—" He put his hand on hers. "I am beginning to remember. The Fall, when the Godhead was torn apart."

"Yes," she said, nodding. "You are remembering back to that, now. To the beginning."

"Give me time," he said. "Just a little more time. It is hard. It hurts."

She said, "I will wait." Seated on her throne she waited. She had waited for thousands of years, and, in her face, he could see the patient and placid willingness to wait longer, as long as was necessary. Both of them had known from the beginning that this moment would come, when they would be back together. They were together now, again, as it had been originally. All he had to do was name her. To name is to know, he thought. To know and to summon; to call.

"Shall I tell you your name?" he said to her.

She smiled, the lovely dancing smile, but no mischief shone in her eyes; instead, love glimmered at him, vast extents of love.

Nicholas Bulkowsky, wearing his red army uniform, prepared to address a crowd of the Party faithful at the main square of Bogotá, Colombia, where recruiting efforts had of late been highly successful. If the Party could swing Colombia into the antifascist camp the disastrous loss of Cuba would be somewhat offset.

However, a cardinal of the Roman Catholic Church had recently put in an appearance—not a local person, but an American, dispatched by the Vatican to interfere with CP activities. Why must they meddle? Bulkowsky asked himself. Bulkowsky. He had discarded that name; now he was known as General Gomez.

To his Colombian advisor he said, "Give me the psychological profile on this Cardinal Harms."

"Yes, Comrade General." Ms. Reiz passed him the file on the American troublemaker.

Studying the file, Bulkowsky said, "His head is up his ass. He's a spinner of theology. The Vatican picked the wrong person." We will tie Harms into knots, he said to himself, pleased.

"Sir," Ms. Reiz said, "Cardinal Harms is said to have charisma. He attracts crowds wherever he goes."

"He will attract a lead pipe to the head," Bulkowsky said, "if he shows up in Colombia."

As a distinguished guest of an afternoon TV talkshow, the Roman Catholic Cardinal Fulton Statler Harms had lapsed into his usual sententious prose. The moderator, hoping to interrupt at some point, in order to achieve a much-needed commercial information dump, looked ill at ease.

"Their policies," Harms declared, "inspire disorder, which they capitalize on. Social unrest is the cornerstone of atheistic communism. Let me give you an example."

"We'll be back in just a moment," the moderator said, as the camera panned up on his bland features. "But first these messages." Cut to a spraycan of Yardguard.

To the moderator—since for a moment they were off camera—Fulton Harms said, "What's the real estate market like, here in Detroit? I have some funds I want to invest, and office buildings, I've discovered, are about the soundest investments of all."

"You had better consult—" The moderator received a visual signal from the show's producer; immediately he composed his face into its normal look of sagacity and said, in his informal but professional tone, "We're talking today with Cardinal Fulton Harmer—"

"Harms," Harms said.

"—Harms of the Diocese of—"

"Archdiocese," Harms said, miffed.

"—of Detroit," the moderator continued. "Cardinal, isn't it a fact that in most Catholic countries, especially those in the Third World, no substantial middle class exists? That you tend to find a very wealthy elite and a poverty-stricken population with little or no education and little or no hope of bettering themselves? Is there some kind of correlation between the Church and this deplorable situation?"

"Well," Harms said, at a loss.

"Let me put it to you this way," the moderator continued; he was perfectly relaxed, perfectly in control of the situation. "Hasn't the Church held back economic and social progress for centuries upon centuries? Isn't the Church in fact a reactionary institution devoted to the betterment of a few and the exploitation of the many, trading on human credulity? Would that be a fair statement, Cardinal, sir?"

"The Church," Harms said feebly, "looks after the spiritual welfare of man; it is responsible for his soul."

"But not his body."

"The communists enslave man's body and man's soul," Harms said. "The Church—"

"I'm sorry, Cardinal Fulton Harms," the moderator broke in, "but that's all the time we have. We've been talking with—"

"Frees man from original sin," Harms said.

The moderator glanced at him.

"Man is born in sin," Harms said, totally unable to gather his train of thought together.

"Thank you Cardinal Fulton Statler Harms," the moderator said. "And now this."

More commercials. Harms, within himself, groaned. Somehow, he ruminated as he rose from the luxurious chair in which they had seated him, somehow I feel as if I've known better days.

He could not put his finger on it, but the feeling was there.

And now I have to go to that little rat's ass country Colombia, he reflected. Again; I've been there once, as briefly as possible, and now I have to fly back this afternoon. They have me on a string and they just plain jerk me around this way and that. Off to Colombia, back home to Detroit, over to Baltimore, then back to Colombia; I'm a cardinal and I have to put up with this? I feel like stepping down.

This is not the best of all possible worlds, he said to himself as he made his way to the elevator. And TV hosts of daytime talk shows abuse me.

Libera me Domine, he declared to himself, and it was a mute appeal; save me, God. Why doesn't he listen to me? Harms wondered as he stood waiting for the elevator. Maybe there is no God; maybe the communists are right. If there is a God he certainly doesn't do anything for *me*.

Before I leave Detroit, he decided, I'll check with my investment broker about office buildings. If I have the time.

Rybys Rommey-Asher, plodding listlessly into the living room of their apartment, said, "I'm back." She shut the front door and took off her coat. "The doctor says it's an ulcer. A pyloric ulcer, it's called. I have to take phenobarb for it and drink Maalox."

"Does it still hurt?" Herb Asher said; he had been going through his tape collection, searching for the Mahler Second Symphony.

"Could you pour me some milk?" Rybys threw herself down on the couch. "I'm exhausted." Her face, puffy and dark, seemed to him to be swollen. "And don't play any loud music. I can't take any noise right now. Why aren't you at the shop?"

"It's my day off." He found the tape of the Mahler Second. "I'll put on the earspeakers," he said. "So it won't bother you."

Rybys said, "I want to tell you about my ulcer. I learned some interesting facts about ulcers—I stopped off at the library. Here." She held out a manila folder. "I got a printout of a recent article. There's this theory that—"

"I'm going to listen to the Mahler Second," he said.

"Fine." Her tone was bitter and sardonic. "You go ahead."

"There's nothing I can do about your ulcer," he said.

"You can listen to me."

Herb Asher said, "I'll bring you the milk." He walked into the kitchen and he thought, Must it be like this?

If I could hear the Second, he thought, I'd feel okay. The only symphony scored for many pieces of rattan, he mused. A Ruthe, which looks like a small broom; they use it to play the bass drum. Too bad Mahler never saw a Morley wah-wah pedal, he thought, or he would have scored it into one of his longer works.

Returning to the living room he handed his wife her glass of milk.

"What have you been doing?" she said. "I notice you haven't picked up or cleaned up or anything."

"I've been on the fone to New York," he said.

"Linda Fox," Rybys said.

"Yes. Ordering her audio components."

"When are you going back to see her?"

"I'll be supervising the installation. I want to check the system over when it's all set up."

"You really like her," Rybys said.

"It's a good sale."

"No, I mean personally. You like *her.*" She paused and then said, "I think, Herb, I'm going to divorce you."

He said, "Are you serious?"

"Very."

"Because of Linda Fox?"

"Because I'm sick and tired of this place being a sty. I'm sick and tired of doing dishes for you and your friends. I'm especially sick and tired of Elias; he's always showing up unexpectedly; he never fones before he comes over. He acts like he lives here. Half the money we spend on food goes for him and his needs. He's like some kind of beggar. He *looks* like a beggar. And that nutty religious crap of his, that 'The world is coming to an end' stuff . . . I can't take any more of it." She fell silent and then, in pain, she grimaced.

"Your ulcer?" he asked.

"My ulcer, yes. The ulcer I got worrying about—"

"I'm going to the shop," he said; he made his way to the door. "Good-bye."

"Good-bye, Herb Asher," Rybys said. "Leave me here and go stand around talking to pretty lady customers and listening to high-performance new audio components that'll knock your socks off, for half a million dollars."

He shut the door after him, and, a moment later, rose up into the sky in his flycar.

Later in the day, when no customers wandered around the store checking out the new equipment, he seated himself in the listening room with his business partner. "Elias," he said, "I think Rybys and I have come to the end."

Elias said, "What are you going to do instead? You're used to living with her; it's a basic part of you, taking care of her. Satisfying her wants."

"Psychologically," Herb said, "she is very sick."

"You knew that when you married her."

"She can't focus her attention. She's scattered. That's the technical term for it. That's what the tests showed. That's why she's so messy; she can't think and she can't act and she can't concentrate." The Spirit of Futile Effort, he said to himself.

"What you need," Elias said, "is a son. I saw how much affection you have for Manny, that woman's little brother. Why don't you—" He broke off. "It's none of my business."

"If I got mixed up with anybody else," Herb said, "I know who it would be. But she'd never give me a tumble."

"That singer?"

"Yes," he said.

"Try," Elias said.

"It's beyond my reach."

"Nobody knows what's beyond his reach. God decides what's beyond a person's reach."

"She's going to be galaxy-famous."

Elias said, "But she isn't yet. If you're going to make a move toward her, do it now."

"The Fox," Herb Asher said. "That's how I think of her." A phrase popped into his mind:

You are with the Fox, and the Fox
is with *you!*

Not Linda Fox singing but Linda Fox speaking. He wondered where the notion came from, that she would be saying that. Again vague memories, compounded of—he did not know what. A more aggressive Linda Fox; more professional and dynamic. And yet remote. As if from millions of miles off. A signal from a star. In both senses of the word.

From the distant stars, he thought. Music and the sound of bells.

"Maybe," he said, "I'll emigrate to a colony world."

"Rybys is too ill for that."

"I'll go alone," Herb said.

Elias said, "You'd be better off dating Linda Fox. If you can swing it. You'll be seeing her again. Don't give up yet. Make a try. The basis of life is trying."

"OK," Herb Asher said. "I will try."

17

Hand in hand, Emmanuel walked with Zina through the dark woods of Stanley Park. "You are myself," he said. "You are the *Shekhina,* the immanent Presence who never left the world." He thought, The female side of God. Known to the Jews and only to the Jews. When the primordial fall took place, the Godhead split into a transcendent part separated from the world; that was En Sof. But the other part, the female immanent part, remained with the fallen world, remained with Israel.

These two portions of the Godhead, he thought, have been detached from each other for millennia. But now we have come together again, the male half of the Godhead and the female half. While I was away the *Shekhina* intervened in the lives of human beings, to assist them. Here and there, sporadically, the *Shekhina* remained. So God never truly left mankind.

"We are each other," Zina said, "and we have found each other again, and again are one. The split is healed."

"Through all your veils," Emmanuel said, "beneath all your forms, there lay this . . . my own self. And I did not recognize you, until you reminded me."

"How did I accomplish that?" Zina said, and then she said, "But I know. My love of games. That is your love, your secret joy: to play like a child. To be not serious. I appealed to that; I woke you up and you remembered: you recognized me."

"Such a difficult process," he said. "For me to remember. I thank you." She had abased herself in the fallen world all this time, while he had left; the greater heroism was hers. Staying with man in all man's inglorious conditions . . . down into the prison with him, Emmanuel thought. Man's beautiful companion. At his side as she is now at mine.

"But you are back," Zina said. "You have returned."

"That is so," he said. "Returned to you. I had forgotten that you existed. I only recalled the world." You the kind side, he thought; the compassionate side. And I the terrible side that arouses fear and trembling. Together we form a unity. Separated, we are not whole; we are not, individually, enough.

"Clues," Zina said. "I kept giving you clues. But it was up to you to recognize me."

Emmanuel said, "I did not know who I was for a time, and I did not know who you were. Two mysteries confronted me, and they had a single answer."

"Let's go look at the wolves," Zina said. "They are such beautiful animals. And we can ride the little train. We can visit all the animals."

"And let them free," Emmanuel said.

"Yes," she said. "And let them, all of them, free."

"Will Egypt always exist?" he said. "Will slavery always exist?"

"Yes," Zina said. "And so will we."

As they approached the Stanley Park Zoo, Emmanuel said, "The animals will be surprised by their freedom. At first they won't know what to do."

"Then we will teach them," Zina said. "As we always have. What they know they have learned from us; we are their guide."

"So be it," he said, and placed his hand on the first metal cage. Within it a small animal peered at him hesitantly. Emmanuel said, "Come out of your cage."

The animal, trembling, came to him, and he took it in his arms.

From his audio store Herb Asher called Linda at her Sherman Oaks home. It took a little while—two robot secretaries held him up temporarily—but at last he got through.

"Hello," he said when he had her on the line.

"How's my sound system coming?" She blinked rapidly and put her finger to her eye. "My contact lens is slipping; just a second." Her face disappeared from the screen. "I'm back," she said. "I owe you a dinner. Right? Do you want to fly out to California? I'm still at the Golden Hind; I will be for another week. We're getting good audiences; I'm trying out a whole lot of new material. I want your reaction to it."

"Fine," he said, enormously pleased.

"So can we get together, then?" Linda said. "Out here?"

"Sure," he said. "You name a time."

"What about tomorrow night? It'll have to be before I go to work, if we're going to have dinner."

"Fine," he said. "Around 6 P.M. California time?"

She nodded. "Herb," she said, "you can stay at my place if you want; I've got a big house. Plenty of room."

"I'd love to," he said.

"I'll serve you some very good California wine. A Mondavi red. I want you to like California wines; that French burgundy we had in New York was very nice, but—we have excellent wines out here."

"Is there a particular place you want to have dinner?"

"Sachiko's," Linda said. "Japanese food."

"You've got yourself a deal," he said.

"Is my sound system coming along okay?" she asked.

"Doing fine," he said.

"I don't want you to work too hard," Linda Fox said. "I have a feeling you work too hard. I want you to relax and enjoy life. There's so much to enjoy: good wine, friends."

Herb said, "Laphroaig Scotch."

In amazement, Linda Fox exclaimed, "Don't tell me you know about Laphroaig Scotch? I thought I was the only person in the world who drinks Laphroaig!"

"It's been made in the traditional copper stills for over two hundred and fifty years," Herb Asher said. "It requires two distillations and the skill of an expert stillman."

"Yes; that's what it says on the package." She began to laugh. "You got that off the package, Herb."

"Yeah," he said.

"Isn't my Manhattan apartment going to be great?" she said enthusiastically. "That sound system you're putting in is what will make it. Herb—" She scrutinized him. "Do you honestly believe my music is good?"

"Yes," he said. "I know. What I say is true."

"You are so sweet," she said. "You see so much ahead for me. It's like you're my good luck person. You know, Herb, no one has ever really had confidence in me. I never did well in school . . . my family didn't think I could make it as a singer. I had skin trouble, too; really bad. Of course I actually haven't made it yet—I'm just beginning. And yet to you I'm—" She gestured.

"Someone important," he said.

"And that means so much to me. I need it so bad. Herb, I have such a low opinion of myself; I'm so sure I'm going to fail. Or I used to be so sure," she corrected herself. "But you give me— Well, when I see myself through your eyes I don't see a struggling new artist; I see something that . . ." She tried to go on; her lashes fluttered and she smiled at him apprehensively but hopefully, wanting him to finish for her.

"I know about you," he said, "as no one else does." And, indeed, that was true; because he remembered her, and no one else did. The world, collectively, had forgotten; it had fallen asleep. It would have to be reminded. And it would be.

"Come on out to the West Coast, Herb," Linda said. "Please. We'll have a lot of fun. Do you know California very well? You don't, do you?"

"I don't," he admitted. "I flew out to catch you at the Golden Hind. And I always dreamed of living in California. But I never did."

"I'll take you all around. It'll be terrific. And you can cheer me up when I'm depressed and reassure me when I'm scared. OK?"

"OK," he said, and felt, for her, great love.

"When you get out here, tell me what I do right in my music and what I'm doing wrong. But tell me most of all that I'm going to make it. Tell me I'm not going to fail, like I think I am. Tell me that the Dowland is a good idea. Dowland's lute music is so beautiful, the most beautiful music ever written. You really believe, then, you're sure that my music, the kind of things I sing will take me to the top?"

"I'm positive," he said.

"How do you know these things? It's as if you have a gift. A gift that you in turn give to me."

"It is from God," Herb Asher said. "My present to you. My confidence in you. Accept what I say; it is true."

Gravely, she said, "I sense magic around us, Herb. A magic spell. I know that sounds silly, but I do. A beauty to everything."

"A beauty," he said, "that I find in you."

"In my music?"

"In you both."

"You're not making this up?"

"No," he said. "I swear by God's own name. By the Father that created us."

"From God," she echoed. "Herb, it scares me. You scare me. There is something about you."

Herb Asher said, "Your music will take you all the way." He knew because he remembered. He knew because, for him, it had already happened.

"Really?" Linda said.

"Yes," he said. "It will carry you to the stars."

18

The small animal, released from its cage, crept into Emmanuel's arms. He and Zina held it and it thanked them. Both of them felt its gratitude.

"It's a little goat," Zina said, examining its hooves. "A kid."

"How kind of you," the kid said to them. "I have waited a long time to be released from my cage, the cage you put me in, Zina Pallas."

"You know me?" she said, surprised.

"Yes, I know you," the kid said, as it pressed itself against her. "I know both of you, although you two are really one. You have reunited your sundered selves, but the battle is not over; the battle begins now."

Emmanuel said, "I know this creature."

The little goat, in Zina's arms, said, "I am Belial. Whom you imprisoned. And whom you now release."

"Belial," Emmanuel said, "My adversary."

"Welcome to my world," Belial said.

"It is *my* world," Zina said.

"Not anymore." The goat's voice gained strength and authority. "In your rush to free the prisoners you have freed the greatest prisoner of all. I will contend against you, deity of light. I will take you down into the caves where there is no light. Nothing of your radiance will shine, now; the light has gone out, or soon will. Your game up to now has been a mock game in which you played against your own self. How could the deity of light lose when both sides were portions of him? Now you face a true adversary, you who drew order out of chaos and now draw me out of that order. I will test the powers that you have. Already you have made a mistake; you freed me without knowing who I am. I had to tell you. Your knowledge is not perfect; you can be surprised. Have I not surprised you?"

Zina and Emmanuel were silent.

"You made me helpless," Belial said, "placed in a cage, and then you felt sorry for me. You are sentimental, deity of light. It will be your downfall. I accuse you of weakness, the inability to be strong. I am he who accuses and I accuse my own creator. To rule you must be strong. It is the strong who rule; they rule the weak. You have, instead, protected the weak; you have offered help to me, your enemy. Let us see if that was wise."

"The strong should protect the weak," Zina said. "The Torah says so. It is a basic idea of the Torah; it is basic to God's law. As God protects man, so man should protect the disadvantaged, even down to animals and the nobler trees."

Belial said, "This runs contrary to the nature of life, the nature you implanted in it. This is how life evolves. I accuse you of violating your own biological foundations, the order of the world. Yes, by all means, free every prisoner; loose a tide of murderers on the world. You have begun with me. Again I thank you. But now I leave you; I have as much to do as you have—perhaps more. Let me down." The goat leaped from their arms and ran off; Zina and Emmanuel watched it go. And as it ran it grew.

"It will undo our world," Zina said.

Emmanuel said, "We will kill it first." He raised his hand; the goat vanished.

"It is not gone," Zina said. "It has concealed itself in the world. Camouflaged itself. We cannot now even find it. You know that it won't die. Like us it is eternal."

In the other cages the remaining imprisoned animals clamored to be released. Zina and Emmanuel ignored them; instead, they looked this way and that for the goat whom they had let out—let out to do as it wished.

"I sense its presence," Zina said.

"I, too," Emmanuel said somberly. "Our work is undone already."

"But the battle is not over," Zina said. "As it said itself, 'The battle now begins.' "

"So be it," Emmanuel said. "We will fight it together, the two of us. As we did in the beginning, before the fall."

Leaning toward him, Zina kissed him.

He felt her fear. Her intense dread. And that dread lay within him, too.

What will become of them now? he asked himself. The people whom he wished to free. What kind of prison will Belial contrive for them with his endless ability to contrive prisons? Subtle ones and gross ones, prisons within prisons; prisons for the body, and, worse by far, prisons for the mind.

The Cave of Treasures under the Garden: dark and small, without air and without light, without real time and real space—walls that shrink and, caught tight, minds that shrink. And we have allowed this, Zina and I; we have colluded with the goat-thing to bring this about.

Its release is their constraint, he realized. A paradox; we have given freedom to the builder of dungeons. In our desire to emancipate we have crushed the souls of all the living.

It will affect every one of them in this world, from the highest to the lowest. Until we can return the goat-thing to its box; until we can place it back within its container.

And now it is everywhere; it is not contained. The atoms of the air are now its abode; it is inhaled like vapor. And each creature, breathing it in, will die. Not completely and not physically, but nonetheless death will come. We have released death, the death of the spirit. For all that now lives and wishes to live. This is our gift to them, done out of kindness.

"Motive does not count," Zina said, aware of his thoughts.

Emmanuel said, "The road to hell." Literally, he thought, in this case. That is the only door we have opened: the door to the tomb.

I pity the small creatures the most, he thought. Those who have done the least harm. They above all do not deserve this. The goat-thing will single them out for the greatest suffering; it will afflict them in proportion to their innocence . . . this is its method by which the great balance is tilted from rectitude, and the Plan undone. It will accuse the weak and destroy the helpless; it will use its power against those least able to defend themselves. And, most of all, it will devour the little hopes, the meager dreams of the small.

Here we must intervene, he said to himself. To protect the small. This is our first task and the first line of our defense.

Lifting off from his abode in Washington, D.C., Herb Asher joyfully began the flight to California and Linda Fox. This is going to be the happiest period of my life, he said to himself. He had his suitcases in the back seat and they were filled with everything that he might need; he would not be returning to Washington, D.C. and Rybys for some time—if ever. A new life, he thought as he guided his car through the vividly marked transcontinental traffic lanes. It's like a dream, he thought. A dream fulfilled.

He realized, suddenly, that soupy string music filled his car. Shocked, he ceased thinking and listened. *South Pacific*, he realized. The song "I'm Gonna Wash That Man Right Out of My Hair." Eight hundred and nine strings, and not even divided strings. Was his car stereo on? He glanced at its indicator light and dial. No, it was not.

I am in cryonic suspension! he thought. It's that huge FM transmitter next door. Fifty thousand watts of audio drizzle messing up everyone at Cry-Labs, Incorporated. Son of a bitch!

He slowed his car, stunned and afraid. I don't get it, he thought in panic. I remember being released from suspension; I was ten years frozen and then they found the organs for me and brought me back to life. Didn't they? Or was that a cryonic fantasy of my dead mind? Which this is, too . . . oh, my God. No wonder it has seemed like a dream; it is a dream.

The Fox, he thought, is a dream. *My* dream. I invented her as I lay in suspension; I am inventing her now. And my only clue is this dull music seeping in everywhere. Without the music I would never have known.

It is diabolic, he thought, to play such games with a human being, with his hopes. With his expectations.

A red light on his dashboard lit up, and simultaneously a bleep-bleep-bleep sounded. He had, in addition to everything else, become the target of a cop car.

The cop car came up beside him and grappled onto his car. Their mutual doors slid back and the cop confronted him. "Hand me your license," the cop said. His face, behind its plastic mask, could not be seen; he looked like some kind of World War I fortification, something that had been built at Verdun.

"Here it is." Herb Asher passed his license to the cop as their two cars, now joined, moved slowly forward as one.

"Are there any warrants out on you, Mr. Asher?" the cop said as he punched information into his console.

"No," Herb Asher said.

"You're mistaken." Lines of illuminated letters appeared on the cop's display. "According to our records, you're here on Earth illegally. Did you know that?"

"It's not true," he said.

"This is an old warrant. They've been trying to find you for some time. I am going to take you into custody."

Herb Asher said, "You can't. I'm in cryonic suspension. Watch and I'll put my hand through you." He reached out and touched the cop. His hand met solid armored flesh. "That's strange," Herb Asher said. He pressed harder, and then realized, all at once, that the cop held a gun pointed at him.

"You want to bet?" the cop said. "About the cryonic suspension?"

"No," Herb Asher said.

"Because if you fool around anymore I will kill you. You are a wanted felon. I can kill you any time I wish. Take your hand off me. Get it away."

Herb Asher withdrew his hand. And yet he could still hear *South Pacific*. The soupy sound still oozed at him from every side.

"If you could put your hand through me," the cop said, "you'd fall through the floor of your car. Think the logic through. It isn't a question of my being real; it's a question of everything being real. For you, I mean. It's your problem. Or you think it's your problem. Were you in cryonic suspension at one time?"

"Yes."

"You're having a flashback. It's common. Under pressure your brain abreacts. Cryonic suspension provides a womblike sense of security that your brain tapes and later on retrieves. Is this the first time it's happened to you, this flashback? I've come across people who've been in cryonic suspension who never could be convinced by any evidence, by what anyone said or whatsoever happened, that they were finally out of it."

"You're talking to one of them now," Herb Asher said.

"Why do you think you're in cryonic suspension?"

"The soupy music."

"I don't—"

"Of course you don't. That's the point."

"You're hallucinating."

"Right." Herb Asher nodded. "That's my point." He reached out for the cop's gun. "Go ahead and shoot," he said. "It won't hurt me. The beam will go right through me."

"I think you belong in a mental hospital, not a jail."

"Maybe so."

The cop said, "Where were you going?"

"To California. To visit the Fox."

"As in the Fox and the Cat?"

"The greatest living singer."

"I never heard of him."

"Her," Herb Asher said. "She's not well known in this world. In this world she's just beginning her career. I'm going to help make her famous throughout the galaxy. I promised her."

"What's the other world compared to this?"

"The real world," Herb Asher said. "God caused me to remember it. I'm one of the few people who remembers it. He appeared to me in the bamboo bushes and there were words in red fire telling me the truth and restoring my memories."

"You are a very sick man. You think you're in cryonic suspension and you remember another universe. I wonder what would have happened to you if I hadn't grappled onto you."

"I'd have had a good time," Herb Asher said, "out on the West Coast. A hell of a lot better time than I'm having now."

"What else did God tell you?"

"Different things."

"God talks to you frequently?"

"Rarely. I'm his legal father."

The cop stared at him. "What?"

"I'm God's legal father. Not his actual father; just his legal father. My wife is his mother."

The cop continued to stare at him. The laser pistol wavered.

"God caused me to marry his mother so that—"

"Hold out both your hands."

Herb Asher held out both his hands. Immediately cuffs closed around his wrists.

"Continue," the cop said. "But I should tell you that anything you say may be held against you in a court of law."

"The plan was to smuggle God back to Earth," Herb Asher said. "In my wife's womb. It succeeded. That's why there's a warrant out for me. The crime I committed was smuggling God back to Earth, where the Evil One rules. The Evil One secretly controls everyone and everything here. For example, you are working for the Evil One."

"I'm—"

"But you don't realize it. You have never heard of Belial."

"True," the cop said.

"That proves my point," Herb Asher said.

"Everything you have said since I grappled onto you has been recorded," the cop said. "It will be analyzed. So you're God's father."

"Legal father."

"And that's why you're wanted. I wonder what the statute violation is, technically. I've never seen it listed. Posing as God's father."

"Legal father."

"Who's his real father?"

"He is," Herb Asher said. "He impregnated his mother."

"This is disgusting."

"It's the truth. He impregnated her with himself, and thereby replicated himself in microform by which method he was able to—"

"Should you be telling me this?"

"The battle is over. God has won. The power of Belial has been destroyed."

"Then why are you sitting here with the cuffs on and why am I pointing a laser gun at you?"

"I'm not sure. I'm having trouble figuring that out. That and *South Pacific*. There are a few bits and pieces I can't seem to get to go in place. But I'm working on it. What I am positive about is Yah's victory."

" 'Yah.' I guess that's God."

"Yes; his actual name. His original name. When he was living on the top of the mountain."

The cop said, "I don't mean to compound your troubles, but you are the most fucked-up human being I have ever met. And I see a lot of different kinds of people. They must have slushed your brain when they put you in cryonic suspension. They must not have gotten to you in time. I'd say that about a sixth of your brain is working and that sixth isn't working right, not at all. I'm taking you to a far, far better place than you have ever been, and they will do far, far better things to you than you can possibly imagine. In my opinion—"

"I'll tell you something else," Herb Asher said. "You know who my business partner is? The prophet Elijah."

Into his microphone the cop said, "This is 356 Kansas. I am bringing an individual in for psychiatric evaluation, a white male about—" To Herb Asher he said, "Did I give you your license back?" The cop put his gun back in its holster and rummaged beside him for Herb Asher's license.

Herb Asher lifted the gun from the cop's holster and pointed it at him; he had to hold both hands together because of the cuffs, but nonetheless he was able to do it.

"He has my gun," the cop said.

The intercom speaker sputtered, "You let a slusher get your gun?"

"Well, he was running off at the mouth about God; I thought he was . . ." The cop's voice trailed off lamely.

"What is the individual's name?" the speaker sputtered.

"Asher. Herbert Asher."

"Mr. Asher," the speaker sputtered, "please return the officer's gun."

"I can't," Herb Asher said. "I'm frozen in cryonic suspension. And there's a fifty-thousand-watt FM transmitter next door playing *South Pacific*. It's driving me crazy."

The speaker sputtered, "Suppose we instruct the station to shut down its transmitter. Then will you return the officer's gun?"

"I'm paralyzed," Herb Asher said. "I'm dead."

"If you're dead," the speaker sputtered, "you have no need of a gun. In fact, if you're dead, how are you going to fire the gun? You said yourself that you're frozen. People in cryonic suspension can't move; they're like Lincoln Logs."

"Then tell the officer to take the gun away from me," Herb Asher said.

The speaker sputtered, "Take the—"

"The gun is real," the cop said, "and Asher is real. He's crazy. He's not frozen. Would I arrest a dead man? Would a dead man be flying to California? There's a warrant out on this man; he is a wanted felon."

"What are you wanted for?" the speaker sputtered. "I'm talking to you, Mr. Asher. I'm talking to a dead man who's frozen stiff at zero degrees."

"Much colder than that," Herb Asher said. "Ask them to play the Mahler Second Symphony. And play it the way it was originally written; not an all-string verson. I can't stand any more of this all-string music, this easy-listening music. It's not easy for me. At one time I had to listen to *Fiddler on the Roof* for months. 'Matchmaker, Matchmaker' lasted for days. And it was at a very critical time in my cycle; I was—"

"All right," the speaker sputtered reasonably. "What do you say to this? We'll have the FM station play the Mahler Second Symphony and in exchange you'll return the officer's gun. What is the— Wait a minute." Silence.

"There's a lapse of logic here," the cop beside Herb Asher said. "You're falling into his *idée fixe*. You know what I'm hearing? I'm hearing *folie à deux*. This has got to stop. There is no FM transmitter broadcasting *South Pacific*. If there were, I would hear it. You can't call the station—any station—and have them play the Mahler Second; it won't work."

The speaker sputtered, "But he'll *think* so, you stupid son of a bitch."

"Oh," the cop said.

"Give me a few minutes, Mr. Asher," the speaker sputtered, "to get hold—"

"No," Herb Asher said. "It's a trick. I won't give up the gun." To the cop beside him he said, "Release my car."

"Better release his car," the speaker sputtered.

"And take off the cuffs," Herb Asher said.

"You'll really like the Mahler Second Symphony," the cop said. "It's got a choir in it."

"Do you know what the Mahler Second has in it?" Herb Asher said. "Do you know what it's scored for? I'll tell you what it's scored for. Four flutes, all alternating with piccolos, four oboes, the third and fourth alternating with English horns, an E-flat clarinet, four clarinets, the third alternating with bass clarinet, the fourth with second E-flat clarinet, four bassoons, the third and fourth alternating with contrabassoon, ten horns, ten trumpets, four trombones—"

"Four trombones?" the cop said.

"Jesus Christ," the speaker sputtered.

"—a tuba," Herb Asher continued. "Organ, two sets of timpani, plus an additional single drum off-stage, two bass drums, one off-stage, two pairs of cymbals, one off-stage, two gongs, one of relatively high pitch, the other low, two triangles, one off-stage, a snare drum, preferably more than one, glockenspiel, bells, a Ruthe—"

"What is a 'Ruthe'?" the cop beside Herb Asher asked.

" 'Ruthe' literally means 'rod,' " Herb Asher said. "It's made of a lot of pieces of rattan; it looks like a large clothes-brush or a small broom. It's used to play the bass drum. Mozart wrote for the Ruthe. Two harps, with two or more players to each part if possible—" He pondered. "Plus the regular orchestra, naturally, including a full string section. Have them use their mixing board to downplay the strings; I've heard enough strings. And be sure the two soloists, the soprano and alto, are good."

"That's it?" the radio sputtered.

"You've fallen back into his delusion," the cop beside Herb Asher said.

"You know," the radio said, "he sounds rational enough. Are you sure he's got your gun? Mr. Asher, how does it happen that you know so much about music? You seem to be quite an authority."

"There are two reasons," Herb Asher said. "One is due to my living on a planet in the star system CY30-CY30B; I operate a sophisticated bank of electronic equipment, both video and audio; I receive transmissions from the mother ship and record them and then beam them to the other domes both on my planet and on nearby planets, and I handle traffic from Fomalhaut, as well as domestic emergency traffic. And the other reason is that the prophet Elijah and I own a retail audio components store in Washington, D.C."

"Plus the fact," the cop beside Herb Asher said, "that you're in cryonic suspension."

"All three," Herb Asher said. "Yes."

"And God tells you things," the cop said.

"Not about music," Herb Asher said. "He doesn't have to. He did erase all my Linda Fox tapes, however. And he cooked my Linda Fox incoming—"

"There is another universe," the cop seated beside Herb Asher explained, "where this Linda Fox is incredibly famous. Mr. Asher is flying out to California to be with her. How he can manage to do that while frozen in cryonic suspension beats the hell out of me, but those are his plans, or were his plans until I grappled him."

"I am still going there," Herb Asher said, and then realized that he had made a mistake to tell them this; now they could track him down, even if he escaped. He had done a foolish thing; he had said too much.

Regarding him intently, the cop said, "I do believe that his self-monitoring circuit has notified him that he has spoken injudiciously."

"I wondered when it would cut in," the speaker sputtered.

"Now I can't go to the Fox," Herb Asher said. "I'm not going there. I'm going back to my dome in the CY30-CY30B System. You lack jurisdiction there. Also, Belial does not rule there. Yah rules there."

The cop said, "I thought you said Yah came back here and, I would presume, if he did come back here, he now rules."

"It has become obvious to me during the course of this conversation," Herb Asher said, "that he does not rule here, at least not completely. *Something is wrong.* I knew it when I started hearing the sappy, soupy string music. I especially knew it when you grappled me and when you told me there's a warrant out for me. Maybe Belial has won; maybe that's it. You are all servants of Belial. Take the cuffs off me or I'll kill you."

The cop, reluctantly, removed the cuffs.

"It would seem to me, Mr. Asher," the speaker sputtered, "that there are internal contradictions in what you say. If you will concentrate on them you will see why you give the impression of being brain-slushed. First you say one thing and then you say another. The only lucid interval in your discourse came when you discussed the Mahler Second Symphony, and that is probably due, as you say, to the fact that you're in the retail audio components business. It is a last remnant of a once intact psyche. Understand that if you go in with the officer you will not be punished; you will be treated as the lunatic that you obviously are. No judge would convict a man who says what you say."

"That's true," the cop beside Herb Asher agreed. "All you have to do is tell the judge about God speaking to you from the bamboo bushes and you're home free. And especially when you tell him that you're God's father—"

"Legal father," Herb Asher corrected.

"That will make a big impression on the court," the cop said.

Herb Asher said, "There is a great war being fought at this moment between God and Belial. The fate of the universe is at stake, its actual physical existence. When I took off for the West Coast I assumed—I had reason to assume—that everything was okay. Now I am not sure; now I think that something dark and awful has gone wrong. You police are the paradigm of it, the epitome. I would not have been grappled if Yah had in fact won. I will not go on to California because that would jeopardize Linda Fox. You'll find her, of course, but she doesn't know anything; she is—in this world, anyhow—a struggling new talent whom I was trying to help. Leave her alone. Leave me alone, too; leave us all alone. You do not know whom you serve. Do you understand what I'm saying? You are in the service of evil, whatever else you may think. You are machines processing an old warrant. You do not know what I've done, or been accused of doing . . . you can make no sense of what I say because you do not understand the situation. You are going by rules that don't apply. This is a unique time. Unique events are taking place; unique forces are squared off against one another. I will not go to Linda Fox but on the other hand I do not know where I will go instead. Maybe Elias will know; maybe he can tell me what to do. My dream was shot down when you grappled me, and maybe her dream, too; Linda Fox's dream. Maybe I can't now help her become a star, as I promised. Time will tell. The outcome will determine it, the outcome of the great battle. I pity you because whatever the outcome you are destroyed; your souls are gone now."

Silence.

"You are an unusual man, Mr. Asher," the cop beside him said. "Crazy or not, whatever it is that has gone wrong with you, you are one of a kind." He nodded slowly, as if deep in thought. "This is not an ordinary kind of insanity. This is not like anything I have ever seen or heard before. You talk about the whole universe—*more* than the universe, if that is possible. You impress me and in a way you frighten me. I am sorry I grappled you, now that I have listened to you. Don't shoot me. I'll release your vehicle and you can fly off; I won't pursue you. I'd like to forget what I've heard in the last few minutes. You talk about God and a counter-God and a terrible battle that seems to be lost, lost to the power of the counter-God, I mean. This does not fit with anything I know of or understand. Go away. I'll forget you and you can forget about me.'' Wearily, the cop plucked at his metal mask.

''You can't let him go,'' the speaker sputtered.

''Oh, yes I can,'' the cop said. ''I can let him go and I can forget everything he's said, everything I've heard.''

''Except that it's recorded,'' the speaker sputtered.

The cop reached down and pressed a button. ''I just erased it,'' he said.

''I thought the battle was over,'' Herb Asher said. ''I thought God had won. God has not won. I know that even though you are letting me go. But maybe it is a sign, your releasing me. I see some response in you, some amount of human warmth.'''

''I am not a machine,'' the cop said.

''But will that continue to be true?'' Herb Asher said. ''I wonder. What will you be a week from now? A month? What will we all become? And what power do we have to affect it?''

The cop said, ''I just want to get away from you, a long distance away.''

''Good,'' Herb Asher said. ''It can be arranged. Someone must tell the world the truth,'' he added. ''The truth you know, that I told you: that God is in combat and losing. Who can do it?''

''You can,'' the cop said.

''No,'' Herb Asher said. But he knew who could. ''Elijah can,'' he said. ''It is his task; this is what he has come for, that the world will know.''

''Then get him to do it,'' the cop said.

''I will,'' Herb Asher said. ''That's where I will go; back to my partner, back to Washington, D.C.''

I will forego the Fox, he said to himself; that is the loss I must accept. Bitter sorrow filled him as he realized this. But it was a fact; he could not be with her now, not until later.

Not until the battle had been won.

As the cop ungrappled his vehicle from Herb Asher's he said a strange thing. ''Pray for me, Mr. Asher,'' he said.

''I will,'' Herb Asher said.

His vehicle released, he swung it in a great looping arc, and headed back toward Washington, D.C. The police car did not follow. The cop had kept his word.

19

From their audio shop he called Elias Tate, waking him up from deepest sleep. "Elijah," he said. "The time has come."

"What?" Elias muttered. "Is the store on fire? What are you talking about? Was there a break-in? What did we lose?"

"Unreality is coming back," Herb Asher said. "The universe has begun to dissolve. It is not the store; it is everything."

"You're hearing the music again," Elias said.

"Yes."

"That is the sign. You are right. Something has happened, something he—they—did not expect. Herb, there has been another fall. And I slept. Thank God you woke me. Probably it is not in time. The accident—they allowed an accident to occur, as in the beginning. Well, thus the cycles fulfill themselves and the prophecies are complete. My own time to act has now come. Because of you I have emerged from my own forgetfulness. Our store must become a center of holiness, the temple of the world. We must patch into that FM station whose sound you hear; we must use it as it has in its own time made use of you. It will be our voice."

"What will it say?"

Elias said, "It will say, sleepers awake. That is our message to the listening world. Wake up! Yahweh is here and the battle has begun, and all your lives are in the balance; all of you now are weighed, this way or that, for better, for worse. No one escapes, even God himself, in all his manifestations. Beyond this there is no more. So rise up from the dust, you creatures, and begin; begin to live. You will live only insofar as you will fight; what you will have, if anything, you must earn, each for himself, and each now, not later. Come! This will be the tune that we will play over and over. And the world will hear, for we shall reach it all, first a little part, then the rest. For this my voice was fashioned at the beginning; for this I have come back to the world again and again. My voice will sound now, at this final time. Let us go. Let us begin. And hope it is not too late, that I did not sleep too long. We must be the world's information source, speaking in all the tongues. We will be the tower that originally failed. And if we fail now, then it ends here, and sleep returns. The insipid noise that assails your ears will follow a whole world to its grave, and rust will rule and dust will rule—not for a little time but for all time and all men, even their machines; for all that lies ahead."

"Gosh," Herb Asher said.

"Observe our pitiful condition at this moment. We, you and I, know the truth but have no way to bring it to the world. With the station we will have a way; we will have *the* way. What are the call letters of that station? I will fone them and offer to buy them."

"It's WORP FM," Herb Asher said.

"Hang up, then," Elias said. "So that I can call."

"Where will we get the money?"

"I have the money," Elias said. "Hang up. Time is of the essence."

Herb Asher hung up.

Maybe if Linda Fox will make a tape for us, he thought, we can play it on our station. I mean, it shouldn't all be limited to warning the world. There are other things than Belial.

His fone rang; it was Elias. "We can buy the station for thirty million dollars," Elias said.

"Do you have that much?"

"Not immediately," Elias said. "But I can raise it. We will sell the store and our inventory for openers."

"Jesus Christ," Herb Asher protested weakly. "That's how we make our living."

Elias glared at him.

"Okay," Herb said.

"We will have a baptismal sale," Elias said, "to liquidate our inventory. I will baptize everyone who buys something from us. I will call on them to repent at the same time."

"Then you fully remember your identity," Herb Asher said.

"I do now," Elias said. "But for a time I had forgotten."

"If Linda Fox will let you interview her—"

"Only religious music will be played on the station," Elias said.

"That's as bad as the soupy strings. Worse. I'll say to you what I said to the cop; play the Mahler Second—play something interesting, something that stimulates the mind."

"We'll see," Elias said.

"I know what that means," Herb Asher said. "I had a wife who used to say 'We'll see.' Every child knows that means—"

"Perhaps she could sing spirituals," Elias said.

Herb Asher said, "This whole business is beginning to get me down. We have to sell the store; we have to raise thirty million dollars. I can't cope with *South Pacific* and I don't expect to be able to cope any better with 'Amazing Grace.' Amazing Grace always sounded to me like some bimbo at a massage parlor. If I'm offending you I'm sorry, but that cop almost hauled me off to jail. He said I'm here illegally; I'm a wanted man. That means you're probably wanted, too. What if Belial kills Emmanuel? What happens to us? There's no way we can survive without him. I mean, Belial pushed him off Earth; he defeated him before. I think he's going to defeat him this time. Buying one FM station in Washington, D.C. isn't going to change the tide of battle."

"I'm a very persuasive talker," Elias said.

"Yeah, well Belial isn't going to be listening to you and neither will be the ones he controls. You're a voice—" He paused. "I was going to say, 'A voice crying in the wilderness.' I guess you've heard that before."

Elias said, "We could very well both wind up with our heads on silver platters. As happened to me once before. What has happened is that Belial is out of his cage, the cage Zina put him in; he is unchained. He is released onto this world. But what I say to you is, 'Oh ye of little faith!' But everything that can be said has been said centuries ago. I will concede Linda Fox a small amount of air time on our station. You can tell her that. She may sing whatever she wishes."

"I'm hanging up," Herb Asher said. "I have to call her and tell her I'm not coming out to the West Coast for a while. I don't want her involved in my troubles. I—"

"I'll talk to you later," Elias said. "But I suggest you call Rybys; when I last saw her she was crying. She thinks she may have a pyloric ulcer. And it may be malignant."

"Pyloric ulcers aren't malignant," Herb Asher said. "This is where I came in, hearing that Rybys Rommey is sitting around crying over her illness; this is what got me involved. She is ill for illness's sake, for its own sake. I thought I was going to escape from this, finally. I'll call Linda Fox first." He hung up the fone.

Christ, he thought. All I want to do is fly to California and begin my happy life. But the macrocosm has swallowed me and my happy life up. Where is Elias going to get thirty million dollars? Not by selling our store and inventory. God probably gave him a bar of gold or will rain down bits of gold, flakes of gold, on him like that manna in the wilderness that kept the ancient Jews alive. As Elias says, everything was said centuries ago and everything happened centuries ago. My life with the Fox would have been new. And here I am once more subjected to sappy, soupy string music which will soon give way to gospel songs.

He dialed Linda Fox's private number, that of her home in Sherman Oaks. And got a recording. Her face appeared on the little fone screen, but it was a mechanical and distorted face; and, he saw, her skin was broken out and her features seemed pudgy, almost fat. Shocked, he said, "No, I don't want to leave a message. I'll call back." He hung up without identifying himself. Probably she'll call me in a while, he decided. When I don't show up. After all, she is expecting me. But how strange she looked. Maybe it's an old recording. I hope so.

To calm himself he turned on one of the audio systems there

at the store; he used a reliable preamp component that involved an audio hologram. The station he selected was a classical music station, one he enjoyed. But—

Only a voice issued from the transducers of the system. No music. A whispering voice almost inaudible; he could barely understand the words. What the hell is this? he asked himself. What is it saying?

". . . weary," the voice whispered in its dry, slithery tone. ". . . and afraid. There is no possibility . . . weighed down. Born to lose; you are born to lose. You are no good."

And then the sound of an ancient classic: Linda Ronstadt's "You're No Good." Over and over again Ronstadt repeated the words; they seemed to go on forever. Monotonous, hypnotic; fascinated, he stood listening. The hell with this, he decided finally. He shut down the system. But the words continued to circulate and recirculate in his brain. You are worthless, his thoughts came. You are a worthless person. Jesus! he thought. This is far worse than the sappy, soupy all-strings easy-listening garbage; this is lethal.

He foned his home. After a long pause Rybys answered. "I thought you were in California," she murmured. "You woke me up. Do you realize what time it is?"

"I had to turn back," he said. "I'm wanted by the police."

Rybys said, "I'm going back to sleep." The screen darkened; its light went out and he found himself facing nothing, confronted by nothingness.

They are all asleep or on tape, he thought. And when you manage to get them to say something they tell you you're no good. The domain of Belial insinuates the paucity of value in everything. Great. Just what we need. The only bright spot was the cop asking me to pray for him. Even Elias is acting erratically, suggesting that we buy an FM radio station for thirty million dollars so that we can tell people—well, whatever he's going to tell people. On a par with selling them a home audio system and baptizing them as a bonus. Like giving them a free stuffed animal.

Animal, he thought. Belial is an animal; it was an animal voice that I heard on the radio just now. Lower than human, not greater. Animal is the worst sense: subhuman and gross. He shivered. And meanwhile Rybys sleeps, dreaming of malignancy. Her perpetual cloud of illness, whether she is conscious or not; it is always with her, always there. She is her own pathogen, infecting herself.

He shut off the lights, left the store, locked up the front door and made his way to his parked car, wondering to himself where to go. Back to his ailing, complaining wife? To California and the mechanical, pudgy image he had seen on the fone screen?

On the sidewalk, near his parked car, something small moved. Something that hesitantly retreated from him, as if in fear. An animal, larger than a cat. Yet it didn't seem to be a dog.

Herb Asher halted, bent down, holding out his hand. The animal came uncertainly toward him, and then all at once he heard its thoughts in his mind. It was communicating with him telepathically. I am from the planet in the CY30-CY30B star system, it thought to him. I am one of the autochthonic goats that in former times was sacrificed to Yah.

Staggered, he said, "What are you doing here?" Something was wrong; this was impossible.

Help me, the goat-creature thought. I followed you here; I traveled after you to Earth.

"You're lying," he said, but he opened his car and got out his flashlight; bending down he turned the yellow light on the animal.

Indeed he had a goat before him, and not a very large one; and yet it could not be an ordinary Terran goat—he could discern the difference.

Please take me in and care for me, the goat-creature thought to him. I am lost. I have strayed away from my mother.

"Sure," Herb Asher said. He reached out and the goat came hesitantly toward him. What a strange little wizened face, and such sharp little hooves. Just a baby, he thought; see how it trembles. It must be starving. Out here it'll get run over.

Thank you, the goat-creature thought to him.

"I'll take care of you," Herb Asher said.

The goat-creature thought, I am afraid of Yah. Yah is terrible in his wrath.

Thoughts of fire, and the cutting of the goat's throat. Herb Asher shivered. The primal sacrifice, that of an innocent animal. To quell the anger of the deity.

"You're safe with me," he said, and picked up the goat-creature. Its view of Yah shocked him; he envisioned Yah, now, as the goat-creature did, and it was a dreadful entity, this vast and angry mountain deity who demanded the sacrifice of tiny lives.

Will you save me from Yah? the goat-creature quavered; its thoughts were limpid with apprehension.

"Of course I will," Herb Asher said. And he tenderly placed the goat-creature in the back of his car.

You won't tell Yah where I am, will you? the goat-creature begged.

"I swear," Herb Asher said.

Thank you, the goat-creature thought, and Herb Asher felt its joy. And, strangely, its sense of triumph. He wondered about that as he got in behind the wheel and started up the engine. Is this some kind of a victory for it? he asked himself.

I am merely glad to be safe, the goat-creature explained. And to have found a protector. Here on this planet where there is so much death.

Death, Herb Asher thought. It fears death as I fear death; it is a living organism like me. Even though in many ways it is quite different from me.

The goat-creature thought to him, I have been abused by children. Two children, a boy and a girl.

Picture, then, in Herb Asher's mind: a cruel pair of children, with savage faces and hostile, blazing eyes. This boy and girl had tormented the goat-creature and it was terrified of falling back into their hands once more.

"That will never happen," Herb Asher said. "I promise. Children can be dreadfully cruel to animals."

In its mind the goat-creature laughed; Herb Asher experienced its glee. Puzzled, he turned to look at the goat-creature, but in the darkness behind him it seemed invisible; he sensed it, there in the back of his car, but he could not make it out.

"I'm not sure where to go," Herb Asher said.

Where you originally were going, the goat-creature thought. To California, to Linda.

"Okay," he said, "but I don't—"

The police won't stop you this time, the goat-creature thought to him. I will see to that.

"But you are just a little animal," Herb Asher said.

The goat-creature laughed. You can give me to Linda as a present, it thought.

Uneasily, he turned his car in the direction of California, and rose up into the sky.

The children are here in Washington, D.C., now, the goat-creature thought to him. They were in Canada, in British Columbia, but now they have come here. I want to be far away from them.

"I don't blame you," Herb Asher said.

As he drove he noticed a smell in his car, the smell of the goat. The goat stank, and this made him uneasy. What a stench, he thought, considering how small it is. I guess it's normal for the species. But still . . . the odor was beginning to make him sick. Do I really want to give this smelly thing to Linda Fox? he asked himself.

Of course you do, the goat-creature thought to him, aware of what was going on in his mind. She will be pleased.

And then Herb Asher caught a really dreadful mental impression from the goat-creature's mind, one that horrified him and made him drive erratically for a moment. A sexual lust on the part of the creature for Linda Fox.

I must be imagining it! Herb Asher thought.

The goat-creature thought, I want her. It was contemplating her breasts and her loins, her whole body, made naked and available. Jesus, Herb Asher thought. This is dreadful. What have I gotten myself into? He started to steer his car back toward Washington, D.C.

And he found that he could not control the steering wheel. The goat-creature had taken over; it was in power within Herb Asher, at the center of his mind.

She will love me, the goat-creature thought, and I will love her. And, then, its thoughts passed beyond the limits of Herb Asher's comprehension. Something to do with making Linda Fox into a thing like the goat-creature, dragging her down into its domain.

She will be a sacrifice in my place, the goat-creature thought. Her throat—I will see it cut as mine has been.

"No," Herb Asher said.

Yes, the goat-creature thought.

And it compelled him to drive on, toward California and Linda Fox. And, as it compelled and controlled him, it exulted in its glee; within the darkness of his car it danced its own kind of dance, a drumming sound that its hooves made: made in triumph. And anticipation. And intoxicated joy.

It was thinking of death, and the thought of death made it celebrate with rapture and an awful song.

He drove as erratically as possible, hoping that once again a police car would grapple him. But as the goat-creature had promised none did.

The image of Linda Fox in Herb Asher's mind continued to undergo a dismal transformation; he envisioned her as gross and bad-complexioned, a flabby thing that ate too much and wandered about aimlessly, and he realized, then, that this was the view of the accuser; the goat-creature was Linda Fox's accuser who showed her—who showed everything in creation—under the worst light possible, under the aspect of the ugly.

This thing in my back seat is doing it, he said to himself. This is how the goat-creature sees God's total artifact, the world that God pronounced as good. It is the pessimism of evil itself. The nature of evil is to see in this fashion, to pronounce this verdict of negation. Thus, he thought, it unmakes creation; it undoes what the Creator has brought into being. This also is a form of unreality, this verdict, this dreary aspect. Creation is not like this and Linda Fox is not like this. But the goat-creature would tell me that—

I am only showing you the truth, the goat-creature thought to him. About your pizza waitress.

"You are out of the cage that Zina put you in," Herb Asher said. "Elias was right."

Nothing should be caged, the goat-creature thought to him. Especially me. I will roam the world, expanding into it until I fill it; that is my right.

"Belial," Herb Asher said.

I hear you, the goat-creature thought back.

"And I'm taking you to Linda Fox," Herb Asher said. "Whom I love most in all the world." Again he tried to take his hands from the steering wheel and again they remained locked in place.

Let us reason, the goat-creature thought to him. This is my view of the world and I will make it your view and the view of everyone. It is the truth. The light that shone originally was a spurious light. That light is going out and the true nature of reality is disclosed in its absence. That light blinded men to the real state of things. It is my job to reveal that real state.

Gray truth, the goat-creature continued, is better than what you have imagined. You wanted to wake up. Now you are awake; I show you things as they are, pitilessly; but that is how it should be. How do you suppose I defeated Yahweh in times past? By revealing his creation for what it is, a wretched thing to be despised. This is his defeat, what you see—see through my mind and eyes, my vision of the world: my correct vision. Recall Rybys Rommey's dome, the way it was when you first saw it; remember what she was like; consider what she is like now. Do you suppose that Linda Fox is any different? Or that you are any different? You are all the same, and when you saw the debris and spoiled food and rotting matter of Rybys's dome you saw how reality really is. You saw life. You saw the truth.

I will soon show you that truth about the Fox, the goat-creature continued. That is what you will find at the end of this trip: exactly what you found in Rybys Rommey's deteriorated dome that day, years ago. Nothing has changed and nothing is different. You could not escape it then and you cannot escape it now.

What do you say to that? the goat-creature asked him.

"The future need not resemble the past," Herb Asher said.

Nothing changes, the goat-creature answered. Scripture itself tells us that.

"Even a goat can cite Scripture," Herb Asher said.

They entered the heavy stream of air traffic routed toward the Los Angeles area; cars and commercial vehicles moved on all sides of them, above them, below them. Herb Asher could discern police cars but none paid him any attention.

I will guide you to her house, the goat-creature informed him.

"Creature of dirt," Herb Asher said, with fury.

A floating signal pointed the way ahead. They had almost reached California.

"I will wager with you that—" Herb Asher began, but the goat-creature cut him off.

I do not wager, it thought to him. I do not play. I am the strong and I prey on the weak. You are the weak, and Linda Fox is weaker yet. Forget the idea of games; that is for children.

"You must be like a little child," Herb Asher said, "to enter the Kingdom of God."

I have no interest in that kingdom, the goat-thing thought to him. This is my kingdom here. Lock the auto-pilot computer of your car into the coordinates for her house.

His hands did so, without his volition. There was no way he could hold back; the goat-creature had control of his motor centers.

Call her on your car fone, the goat-creature told him. Inform her that you are arriving.

"No," he said. But his fingers placed the card with her fone number into the slot.

"Hello." Linda Fox's voice came from the little speaker.

"This is Herb," he said. "I'm sorry I'm late. I got stopped by a cop. Is it too late?"

"No," she said. "I was out anyhow for a while. It'll be nice to see you again. You're going to stay, aren't you? I mean, you're not going back tonight."

"I'll stay," he said.

Tell her, the goat-creature thought to him, that you have me with you. A pet for her, a little kid.

"I have a pet for you," Herb Asher said. "A baby goat."

"Oh, really? Are you going to leave it?"

"Yes," he said, without volition; the goat-creature controlled his words, even the intonation.

"Well, that is so thoughtful of you. I have a whole bunch of animals already, but I don't have a goat. I guess I'll put it in with my sheep, Herman W. Mudgett."

"What a strange name for a sheep," Herb Asher said.

"Herman W. Mudgett was the greatest mass-murderer in English history," Linda Fox said.

"Well," he said, "I guess it's okay."

"I'll see you in a minute. Land carefully. You don't want to hurt the goat." She broke the connection.

A few minutes later his car settled gently down on the roof of her house. He shut the engine off.

Open the door, the goat-creature thought to him.

He opened the car door.

Coming toward the car, lit by pale lights, Linda Fox smiled at him, her eyes sparkling; she waved in greeting. She wore a tank top and cutoffs, and, as before, her feet were bare. Her hair bounced as she hurried and her breasts rose and fell.

Within the car the stench of the goat-creature grew.

"Hi," she said breathlessly. "Where's the little goat?" She looked into the car. "Oh," she said. "I see. Get out of the car, little goat. Come here."

The goat-creature leaped out, into the pale light of the California evening.

"Belial," Linda Fox said. She bent to touch the goat; hastily, the goat scrambled back but her fingers grazed its flanks.

The goat-creature died.

20

"There are more of them," she said to Herb Asher, who stood gazing numbly at the corpse of the goat. "Come inside. I knew by the scent. Belial stinks to high heaven. Please come in." She took him by the arm and led him to the doorway. "You're shaking. You knew what it was, didn't you?"

"Yes," he said. "But who are you?"

"Sometimes I am called Advocate," Linda Fox said. "When I defend I am the Advocate. Sometimes Comfort; that is when I console. I am the Beside-Helper. Belial is the Accuser. We are the two adversaries of the Court. Please come inside where you can sit down; this has been awful for you, I know. Okay?"

"Okay." He let her lead him to the roof elevator.

"Haven't I consoled you?" Linda Fox asked. "In the past? As you lay alone in your dome on an alien world, with no one to talk to or be with? That is my job. One of my jobs." She put her hand on his chest. "Your heart is pounding away. You must have been terrified; it told you what it was going to do with me. But you see, it didn't know where you were taking it. Where or to whom."

"You destroyed it," he said. "And—"

"But it has proliferated throughout the universe," Linda said. "This is only an instance, what you saw on the roof. Every man has an Advocate and an Accuser. In Hebrew, for the Israelites of antiquity, *yetzer ha-tov* was the Advocate and *yetzer ha-ra* was the Accuser. I'll fix you a drink. A good California zinfandel; a Buena Vista zinfandel. It's a Hungarian grape. Most people don't know that."

In her living room he sank down in a floating chair, gratefully. He could still smell the goat. "Will I ever—" he began.

"The smell will go away." She glided over to him with a glass of red wine. "I already opened it and let it breathe. You'll like it."

He found the wine delicious. And his heartbeat had begun to return to normal.

Seated across from him, Linda Fox held her own wine glass and gazed at him attentively. "It didn't harm your wife, did it? Or Elias?"

"No," he said. "I was alone when it came up to me. It pretended to be a lost animal."

Linda Fox said, "Each person on Earth will have to choose between his *yetzer ha-tov* and his *yetzer ha-ra*. You choose me and so I saved you . . . you choose the goat-thing and I cannot save you. In your case I was the one you chose. The battle is waged for each soul individually. That is what the rabbis teach. They have no doctrine of fallen man as a whole. Salvation is on a one by one basis. Do you like the zinfandel?"

"Yes," he said.

"I will use your FM station," she said. "It will be a good place to air new material."

"You know about that?" he said.

"Elijah is too stern. My songs will be appropriate. My songs gladden the human heart and that is what matters. Well, Herb Asher; here you are in California with me, as you imagined in the beginning. As you imagined in another star system, in your dome, with your holographic posters of me that moved and talked, the synthetic versions of me, the imitations. Now you have the real me with you, seated across from you. How does it feel?"

He said, "Is it real?"

"Do you hear two hundred sugary strings?"

"No."

Linda Fox said, "It's real." She set her wine glass down, rose to her feet, came toward him and bent to put her arms around him.

He woke up in the morning with the Fox against him, her hair brushing his face, and he said to himself, This is actually so; it is not a dream, and the evil goat-creature lies dead on the roof, my particular goat-thing that came to degrade my life.

This is the woman I love, he thought as he touched the dark hair and the pale cheek. It is beautiful hair and her lashes are long and lovely, even as she sleeps. It is impossible but it is true. That can happen. What had Elias told him about religious faith? "*Certum est quia impossibile est.*" "This is therefore credible, just because it is absurd." The great statement by the early Church father Tertullian, regarding the resurrection of Jesus Christ. "*Et sepultus resurrexit; certum est quia impossibile est.*" And that is the case here.

What a long way I have gone, he thought, stroking the woman's bare arm. Once I imagined this and now I experience this. I am back where I began and yet I am totally elsewhere from where I began! It is a paradox and a miracle at the same time. And this, even, is California, where I imagined it to be. It is as if in dreaming I presaw my future reality; I experienced it beforehand.

And the dead thing on the roof is proof that this is real. Because my imagination could not give rise to that stinking beast whose mind glued itself to my mind and told me lies, told me ugly stories about a fat, short woman with bad skin. An object as ugly as itself—a projection of itself.

Has anyone loved another human as much as I love her? he asked himself, and then he thought, She is my Advocate and my Beside-Helper. She told me Hebrew words that I have forgotten that describe her. She is my tutelary spirit, and the goat-thing came all the way here, three thousand miles, to perish when she put her fingers against its flank. It died without even a sound, so easily did she kill it. She was waiting for it. That is—as she said

—her job, one of her jobs. She has others; she consoled me, she consoles millions; she defends; she gives solace. And she is there in time; she does not arrive too late.

Leaning, he kissed Linda on the cheek. In her sleep she sighed. Weak and in the power of the goat-creature, he thought; that is what I was when I came here. She protected me because I was weak. She does not love me as I love her, because she must love all humans. But I love her alone. With everything that I am. I, the weak, love her who is strong. My loyalty is to her, and her protection is for me. It is the Covenant that God made with the Israelites: that the strong protect the weak and the weak give their devotion and loyalty to the strong in return; it is a mutuality. I have a covenant with Linda Fox, and it will not be broken ever, by either one of us.

I'll fix breakfast for her, he decided. Stealthily, he got up from the waterbed and made his way into the kitchen.

A figure stood there waiting for him. A familiar figure.

"Emmanuel," Herb Asher said.

The boy shone in a ghostly way, and Herb Asher realized that he could see the wall and the counter and cabinets behind the boy. This was an epiphany of the divine; Emmanuel was in fact somewhere else. And yet he was here; here and aware of Herb Asher.

"You found her," Emmanuel said.

"Yes," Herb Asher said.

"She will keep you safe."

"I know," he said. "For the first time in my life."

"Now you need not ever withdraw again," Emmanuel said, "as you did in your dome. You withdrew because you were afraid. Now you have nothing to fear . . . because of her presence. She as she is now, Herbert—real and alive, not an image."

"I understand," he said.

"There is a difference. Put her on your radio station; help her, help your protectress."

"A paradox," Herb Asher said.

"But true. You can do a lot for her. You were right when you thought of the word *mutuality*. She saved your life last night." Emmanuel lifted his hand. "She was given to you by me."

"I see," he said. He had assumed that was the case.

Emmanuel said, "Sometimes in the equation that the strong protect the weak there is the difficulty in determining who is strong and who is weak. In most ways she is stronger than you, but you can protect her in certain specific ways; you can shelter her back. That is the real law of life: mutual protection. In the final analysis everything is both strong and weak, even the *yetzer ha-tov*—your *yetzer ha-tov*. She is a power and she is a person; it is a mystery. You will have time, in the life ahead for you, to fathom that mystery, a little. You will know her better and better. But she knows you now completely; just as Zina has absolute knowledge of me, Linda Fox has absolute knowledge of you. Did you realize that? That the Fox has known you totally, for a very long time?"

"The goat-creature didn't surprise her," he said.

"Nothing surprises the *yetzer ha-tov* of a human being," Emmanuel said.

"Will I ever see you again?" Herb Asher asked.

"Not as you see me now. Not as a human figure such as yourself. I am not as you see me; I now shed my human side, that derived from my mother, Rybys. Zina and I will unite in a syzygy which is macrocosmic; we will not have a soma, which is to say, a physical body distinct from the world. The world will be our body, and our mind the world's mind. It will also be your mind, Herbert. And the mind of every other creature that has chosen its *yetzer ha-tov,* its good spirit. This is what the rabbis have taught, that each human—but I see you know this; Linda has told you. What she has not told you is a later gift that she holds in store for you: the gift of ultimate exculpation for your life in its entirety. She will be there when you are judged, and the judgment will be of her rather than you. She is spotless, and she will bestow this perfection on you when final scrutiny comes. So fear not; your ultimate salvation is assured. She would give her life for you, her friend. As Jesus said, 'Greater love has no man than that he give up his life for his friends.' When she touched the goat-creature she—well, I had better not say."

"She herself died for an instant," Herb Asher said.

"For an instant so brief that it scarcely existed."

"But it did occur. She died and returned. Even though I saw nothing."

"That is so. How did you know?"

Herb Asher said, "I could feel it this morning when I looked at her sleeping; I could feel her love."

Wearing a flowered silk robe, Linda Fox came sleepily into the kitchen; she stopped short when she saw Emmanuel.

"Kyrios," she said quietly.

"Du hast den Mensch gerettet," Emmanuel said to her. *"Die giftige Schlange bekämpfte . . . es freut mich sehr. Danke."*

Linda Fox said, *"Die Absicht ist nur allzuklar. Lass mich fragen: wann also wird das Dunkel schwinden?"*

"Sobald dich führt der Freundschaft Hand ins Heiligtum zum ew'gen Band."

"O wie?" Linda Fox said.

"Du—" Emmanuel gazed at her. *"Wie stark ist nicht dein Zauberton, deine Musik. Sing immer für alle Menschen, durch Ewigkeit. Dabei ist das Dunkel zerstören."*

"Ja," Linda Fox said, and nodded.

"What I told her," Emmanuel said to Herb Asher, "is that she has saved you. The poisonous snake is overcome and I am pleased. And I thanked her. She said that its intentions were clear to her. And then she asked when the darkness would disappear."

"What did you answer?"

"That is between her and me," Emmanuel said. "But I told her that her music must exist for all eternity for all humans; that is part of it. What matters is that she understands. And she will do what she has to. There is no misunderstanding between her and us. Between her and the Court."

Going to the stove—the kitchen was neat and clean, with everything in its place—Linda Fox pressed buttons, then brought out food from the refrigerator. "I'll fix breakfast," she said.

"I was going to do that," Herb Asher said, chagrined.

"You rest," she said. "You've gone through a lot in the last twenty-four hours. Being stopped by the police, having Belial take control of you . . ." She turned to smile at him. Even with her hair tousled she was—well, he could not say; what she was for him could not be put into words. At least not by him. Not at this moment. Seeing her and Emmanuel together overwhelmed him. He could not speak; he could only nod.

"He loves you very much," Emmanuel said to her.

"Yes," she said, somberly.

"*Sei fröhlich,*" Emmanuel said to her.

Linda said to Herb Asher, "He's telling me to be happy. I am happy. Are you?"

"I—" He hesitated. *She asked when the darkness would disappear,* he remembered. The darkness has not disappeared. The poisonous snake is overcome but the darkness remains.

"Always be joyful," Emmanuel said.

"OK," Herb Asher said. "I will."

At the stove Linda Fox fixed breakfast and he thought he heard her sing. It was hard for him to tell, because he carried in his mind the beauty of her tunes. It was always there.

"She is singing," Emmanuel said. "You are right."

Singing, she put on coffee. The day had begun.

"That thing on the roof," Herb Asher said. But Emmanuel had disappeared, now; only he himself and Linda Fox remained.

"I'll call the city," Linda Fox said. "They'll haul it away. They have a machine that does that. Hauls away the poisonous snake. From the lives of people and the roofs of houses. Turn on the radio and get the news. There will be wars and rumors of wars. There will be great upheavals. The world—we've seen only a little part of it. And then let's call Elijah about the radio station."

"No more string versions of *South Pacific,*" he said.

"In a little while," Linda Fox said, "things will be all right. It came out of its cage and it is going back."

He said, "What if we lose?"

"I can see ahead," Linda said. "We will win. We have already won. We have always already won, from the beginning, from before creation. What do you take in your coffee? I forget."

Later, he and Linda Fox went back up on the roof to view the remains of Belial. But to his surprise he saw not the carcass of a wizened goat-thing; instead he saw what looked like the remains of a great luminous kite that had crashed and lay in ruins all across the roof.

Somberly, he and Linda gazed at it as it lay broken everywhere, vast and lovely and destroyed. In pieces, like damaged light.

"This is how he was once," Linda said. "Originally. Before he fell. This was his original shape. We called him the Moth. The Moth that fell slowly, over thousands of years, intersecting the Earth, like a geometrical shape descending stage by stage until nothing remained of its shape."

Herb Asher said, "He was very beautiful."

"He was the morning star," Linda said. "The brightest star in the heavens. And now nothing remains of him but this."

"How he has fallen," Herb Asher said.

"And everything else with him," she said.

Together they went back downstairs to call the city. To have the machine come along to haul the remains away.

"Will he ever be again as he once was?" Herb Asher said.

"Perhaps," she said. "Perhaps we all may be." And then she sang for Herb Asher one of the Dowland songs. It was the song the Fox traditionally sang on Christmas day, for all the planets. The most tender, the most haunting song that she had adapted from John Dowland's lute books.

When the poor cripple by the pool did lie
Full many years in misery and pain,
No sooner he on Christ had set his eye,
But he was well, and comfort came again.

"Thank you," Herb Asher said.

Above them the city machine worked, gathering up the remains of Belial. Gathering together the broken fragments of what had once been light.

About the Author

Philip K. Dick came to prominence with his early short stories in the 1950s but is best known for his novels. The first, *The Solar Lottery,* gained him a strong reputation and he has continued to produce a body of important work up through the present day. He is generally regarded in England and Europe as the leading American SF writer. He is best known for his 1963 Hugo winner, *The Man in the High Castle.*

He has lived for many years in California where he briefly attended university. Before he started to write science fiction, he ran a record store dealing in classical music and worked in radio. He currently lives in Santa Ana.

He has been married five times and has three children.